About the author

The daughter of a Welsh coalminer, Elizabeth Cottrell won a scholarship to Cambridge and has a Ph.D. in History. Her first job was teaching in Staffordshire where she married a local farmer, gaining experience reflected in this book.

She then pursued a career in research, writing on industry, finance and education. A regular broadcaster, she became a panellist on Radio 4's *Any Questions*. Such expressions of personal opinion had to stop when Elizabeth became a Special Adviser in the Departments of Culture, Employment, Education and Agriculture. In this role she once took a serious risk in a meeting, saying to Mrs Thatcher, "You are wrong, Prime Minister." She got away with it!

A short story prize in the London Writers' Competition encouraged Elizabeth to write fiction. This is her first novel.

A widow, Elizabeth lives in her native Wrexham with her daughter Alexandra.

THE CEREMONIOUS HOUSE

ELIZABETH COTTRELL

THE CEREMONIOUS HOUSE

Vanguard Press

A CIP catalogue record for this title is
available from the British Library.

ISBN 978 1 80016 356 0

*Vanguard Press is an imprint of
Pegasus Elliot MacKenzie Publishers Ltd.*
www.pegasuspublishers.com

First Published in 2022

**Vanguard Press
Sheraton House Castle Park
Cambridge England**

Printed & Bound in Great Britain

Dedication

To my daughter, Alexandra

Prologue

"And may her bridegroom bring her to a house
Where all's accustomed, ceremonious;"
W.B.Yeats *A Prayer for My Daughter*

Aulis Price was seventeen when her Music mistress died. Aulis neither played nor sang, so no one, least of all the girl herself, could have known that that event was going to change her life.

Miss Millard, the Headmistress of Northam Girls' Grammar School, was quick to seize the opportunity provided by this apparently inconvenient death. For years Miss Millard had been trying to bring a fresh look to the school's Speech Day, but the majestic figure of Miss Kerfoot-Williams, wielding her conductor's baton, had always stood in her way. Now the headmistress could do what she wanted. Before the Music Department could regroup to marshal their depleted ranks, she had assigned the organisation of the Speech Day programme to the Head of English.

Mrs Willis was young, new and full of iconoclastic zeal. She decided that literature, not music, should dominate events. So out went Mona Thomas's eternal flute solo and the perennial string trio: the 'Nymphs and Shepherds' did as they were told and went away. In their place came a feast of prose and poetry. The First Form gave a selection from *Hiawatha*; the head girl read Polonius' advice to Hamlet, and there were many delights in between.

Aulis Price's contribution was to recite Yeats' *Prayer for My Daughter*. Like all Mrs Willis' pupils she had been well rehearsed and her performance was pleasing, but she made no great impression. Of course her parents were proud of her, though her award of the Latin Prize meant far more to her father. For the rest of the audience Aulis was just a pleasant girl who had done well. Recitations are ephemeral. People would soon forget Mrs Willis' day of triumph and Aulis' part in it.

Only Aulis never forgot. Yeats' poem stayed — always in the back of her mind. If she ever thought of marriage it was in terms of grace and space; of green lawns on sunny afternoons where babies full of "innocence and beauty" slept in Silver Cross prams. Deep down she despised her own background, the three-bedroom semi, her father's frustrated intellectualism, her mother's slapdash ways. She saw no escape in the lives her contemporaries were embracing — their highest ambition a smart little box with all mod cons. and the latest Ford Anglia.

No one realised how Aulis felt — perhaps she herself

did not. But when she found the 'Ceremonious House' she knew that it was her destiny, whether for bane or blessing.

Chapter One
La Belle Dame

Until I met Martin Peverell, I had never known the excitement of love. Now, as I heard his footsteps on the stairs, I felt my bones melting with desire. Two minutes later he was in my bed sitting-room and I was in his arms. Our kiss was long and deep.

Satisfied for the moment, I moved to get my coat, saying, 'We'd better get going, Martin. Isn't the table booked for 7.30?'

Martin was apologetic. 'I'm sorry, my love. I've had to cancel it. Change of plan — you're coming home with me!'

'What! Why? I was so looking forward to eating at 'The Pear Tree'. They say the food's delicious. It's a bit much to cancel without asking me. What's happened?'

Looking slightly shamefaced Martin explained, 'I've had a little set-to with Mother. Apparently, Pa has a meeting in Stafford and won't be home till late. Mother doesn't want to be alone — you know there's been a spate of burglaries recently. I explained that I'd got a date. She wanted the details and it ended up with her saying she'd like to meet you. We always try to please her if we can, so I agreed.'

I was hesitant. 'But Martin, I'm not sure if I'm ready to meet your mother.'

'Oh, come on, Aulis. After all, if you're going to marry me, you'll have to meet her sometime — you may as well get it over with.'

'Hold on Martin, that's a very big if, I haven't said yes yet.'

'But you will, won't you, Aulis? You know I can't live without you.'

I too knew that I would, but I wasn't giving in without a struggle, as I protested. 'Anyway, you don't make this meeting sound very inviting, "get it over with". Is your mother such an ogre?'

Martin didn't dismiss my query out of hand as I expected. He answered thoughtfully, not meeting my gaze and shifting uncomfortably from one foot to another: 'I don't know. To me she's just Mother, with her funny little ways. I don't analyse people the way you do, Aulis. Mother has upset some of my previous girlfriends, but they weren't strong and independent like you. I think she'll respect you, and come to like you.'

I was not reassured. 'Oh, this gets better and better. And to make things worse I missed dinner because we were going out. I'll really make a good impression if my stomach rumbles!'

Martin was pleased with himself. 'I thought of that. Mother says she'll get you something to eat.'

So off we went, covering the five miles between Manley and Martin's home, Abbotshall, far too quickly for my liking.

I had another panic on the way. 'Martin, I didn't ask you. Do I look all right? Am I suitably dressed to meet your mother?'

Martin was very comforting. 'You look absolutely right, after all you were dressed to go out to dinner. That blue dress brings out the blue of your eyes and the auburn lights in your hair beautifully.'

I cheered up a little. 'You are nice, Martin. The best compliment I ever get from my father is to be told that I look clean and tidy!'

Martin smiled. 'Well, there are outfits I prefer you in — your birthday suit, for example — but I suppose that would hardly be appropriate on this occasion.'

I blessed Martin for trying to reduce my anxiety but it was a vain attempt. As he slowed down and I realised that we had arrived at Abbotshall I felt even more anxious. Hungry as I was, I doubted if I could eat anything. Then I told myself not to be so silly. I was meeting Martin's mother — a middle-aged woman — not some monster, real or imagined.

I stood still and looked straight at Abbotshall, staring it firmly in the face.

The gaunt Georgian house, with its heavy gables and tall, slender chimneys, had long fascinated me. From the large bay windows at the front lawns and flowerbeds sloped down to the road. A wide drive separated the house from its cluster of farm buildings, so that it seemed to be distancing itself from the source of its prosperity

Now I was standing on the doorstep, shivering in the December cold with a mixture of excitement and apprehension. Martin's arm around my shoulders steadied me. He opened the outer door and called. A warm voice answered, caressing the language with rounded lengthened vowels in bell-line tones like the Queen's but with the depth that comes with age. My spirits rose.

Clutching my hand Martin led me along a cold stone-flagged passage into a long low kitchen. The heat from a huge cream and black Aga enfolded us. The purple quarry tiles of the floor shone. The walls, the two great housekeepers' cupboards on either side of the door, every visible piece of paintwork, all were in clinically clean magnolia. The one glossy wall calendar that broke the virgin white seemed a vulgar intrusion. An old kitchen table at the far end of the room had been given a modern Formica top, cold ice-blue. Despite the dimmed lighting from two neon strips the general effect was dazzling and faintly hostile. There was nothing here of the welcoming farm kitchen — no dogs or cats — no smells of delicious baking.

Martin's mother rose from her chair and came slowly towards me, leaning forward slightly from the hips. This walk, combined with her sharp shoulders and high well-rounded breasts suggested the figurehead of a ship, ready to face any storm. Was I just a minor squall to be dealt with as easily as others her son had provoked, or was I to be the final tempest which she had always dreaded?

Her approach was mildly reassuring, her hand outstretched in welcome. I grasped it eagerly only to find it cold and lifeless, giving no answering pressure to my greeting. Had I been too enthusiastic, not English enough? Four years at an English university had taught me that we Welsh were sometimes too impulsive, 'gushing' our critics called it.

Yet surprisingly Mrs Peverell presented her cheek for a kiss. As I brushed the sallow parchment skin with my lips the Aga's warmth seemed to recede.

Nor were her first words encouraging, despite those seductive tones. 'Now that I've met you, I can't think why they call you Owlish. You don't even wear glasses. Is it because you're a schoolteacher?'

I was used to this. 'My name is Aulis.'

Martin broke in. I was to find that he often did when his mother was particularly inane. 'It's classical, Mother. Aulis is the place where Iphigenia was sacrificed in "The Iliad".

His mother made the connection. 'Oh yes, Martin tells me that you teach Latin. Of course we had to let Martin learn it at school because he was in the top form and all the boys who really mattered, the ones useful to know, learned Latin. But I must say I think it's utterly useless — unless you're a vicar or something I suppose.'

19

I smiled thinly. 'My father wouldn't agree with you. He loves Latin.'

'So he's probably responsible for your name. Is he a vicar?

'No, he's a teacher.'

'Oh, I see. Do you have another name?'

'Yes, Mary.'

'Oh, very nice dear. Perhaps we could call you Mary. Do you have any brothers or sisters?'

'Yes, two older brothers.'

I managed not to reveal that their names were Hector and Jason. 'And what do they do?'

Years later I would have made one of them a brain surgeon and the other a barrister. Now I just told the truth. 'One's a teacher and the other is a lecturer.'

'Oh, I see.' (Obviously one of her favourite phrases). 'Nothing very special. So no one in your family knows anything about business or money. Well, I'm sure that you needn't see much of them.'

Why didn't I leave then and spare myself all that lay ahead? Simply because she was smiling, showing the crinkles of laughter lines. There was a hint of warmth, even a twinkle, in the grey eyes behind their masking spectacles. Then I saw the gesture that was to become so familiar. The eyes were lowered inwards like those of a fox; simultaneously there was a supercilious flare of the nostrils, so that she was literally looking down her nose, as without doubt she was metaphorically. Her lips, curled back to smile, were thin and pale. I suddenly thought of my own mother with her silly, superstitious sayings, 'thin lips, mean nature' was a favourite one.

Why was my name to be changed and my family banned? What impression had Martin given his family? I had not yet committed myself to marrying him.

Perhaps she was just teasing me. I knew that teasing, which I had never understood or liked, was something the English enjoyed.

Like her kitchen with its gleaming paintwork and shining pots and pans, everything about this woman breathed understated quality. The grey hair might be arranged in the conventional set of her generation, but no village barber had produced that stylish cut. Her navy-blue jumper and matching skirt were undoubtedly Jaeger. (My Aunt Sarah was a regular customer of the Jaeger shop in Chester, so I was familiar with the distinctive quality and style of their clothes.)

The thought of Aunt Sarah steadied me. My father's eldest sister, she was spare and dignified, a relative to be proud of. But then I remembered that Aunt Sarah had acquired her good taste and "posh" accent in her years of good service to the gentry. Given her dismissive attitude to teachers Mrs Peverell would doubtless brush my aunt aside as a "mere servant".

Martin's mother was as polished as the tiles on which she stood; was she as diamond hard? Apart from her voice there was nothing ample about her. Her name, Mollie, had suggested someone round and cuddly. Instead, the compact wiry figure made her seem taller than her five foot four inches. She carried no excess fat; her stomach was as flat as her small neat bottom. Her breasts were taut and firm as a girl's. Her hands were long, thin and beautifully kept, very different from my pudgy, nail-bitten paws. Even her shadow, large upon the gleaming floor, was all angles, so unlike my stocky little figure. I supposed that she would see that as yet another sign of my lowly origin.

Even as I studied her, she was studying me and had no hesitation in expressing her views. 'You're very short, aren't you, Aulish? Is that because you're Welsh?'

'I don't know…'

Martin came to my defence. 'Aulis is no shorter than you, Mother. Stand together and you'll see that you're virtually the same height.'

Ridiculous as it seemed, we did so and he was proved right.

I hastened to flatter Mollie. 'You look taller, Mrs Peverell, because you have such a lovely figure.'

She was pleased. 'Thank you, dear. I've always kept myself slim, despite having children. Of course you'd look better if your skirt wasn't so tight and you didn't wear such bright colours. I could give you advice on dressing more suitably.'

'Thank you,' I murmured faintly, too shocked to quite take in how rude she had been to someone she had just met. I concentrated on sitting correctly on the hard cushion-less Windsor chair, my back straight, my knees close together like a schoolgirl in the Head's study.

Indeed, I had often felt more comfortable in the Head's study.

Martin broke the rather awkward silence by saying that he must "look up" the cows. (I later discovered that this wasn't a misnomer for "lock up" but a Midlands term for the last nightly check on the animals).

Mollie jumped up. 'Goodness how thoughtless I've been. I gather you've not had dinner, Aulish. Will bacon and eggs suit you, with toast and coffee?'

'Thank you, that will be lovely,' I spoke meekly.

Mollie bustled about, frying the eggs and bacon, making the toast and coffee When all was ready she put my meal on the kitchen table and I sat down to eat, first taking care to say thanks. 'Thank you very much. This is lovely. I'm sorry to be a nuisance.'

Standing with her back to the Aga, looking down at me, she spoke casually at first. 'It's not much trouble. An Aga makes life very easy, as you may find out.'

Then came the rapier thrust. 'Do you intend to marry Martin?'

Slightly stunned, almost choking on my bacon, I was hesitant. 'I… don't… know.'

'Has he asked you?'

Gathering my wits together, I spoke with care. 'I think that is for him to tell you.'

'That means that he has. He usually does. Well, dear, farmers aren't rich, you know. That's only what urban people think. And Peverells are particularly not rich. I'm sorry if that disappoints you.'

She finished with a deprecating, mirthless little laugh, possibly designed to take the sting out of her words.

I was goaded into more confident speech. 'I'm not interested in money. If I were to marry Martin it would be because I loved him and believed that he loved me.'

Mollie found this very amusing. 'Oh, my dear, what a little schoolgirl you are. Martin's been in love with so many girls — it never lasts though some of them have been much more suitable than you.'

'Why am I not suitable?'

Mollie spoke slowly and kindly, as to a simple child. 'Oh dear, where do I begin? Well you obviously know nothing about farming. And your background's all wrong. I'm sure that schoolteachers are very good sort of people, but they won't do here. I doubt you have any domestic skills. Martin should marry a girl who understands our life and can contribute to it, who shares our standards. Someone who comes with a little money of her own — a girl who hasn't had to go out to work.'

This last phrase conjured up a picture of me scrubbing floors, aproned and turbaned; very different from the smartly-suited, black-gowned Miss Aulis Price, B.A., reading Cicero with the sixth form.

Before I could decide whether to be furious or amused there was a rush of pure, cold air as Martin came in. His broad-shouldered figure and smiling, honest face brought warmth and reality back to the room, reminding me why I was there. I loved this man. I wanted to meld my spirit into his genial strength, to bask in the constant warmth of his nature; and my body ached for him.

Martin strolled up to the Aga to warm his hands, saying cheerfully, 'Look out, Mother, the kettle's boiling.'

Mollie responded quickly, giving me her twinkly smile. 'Goodness, I didn't notice. Aulish and I have been having such a jolly chat.'

The rest of the evening passed in fairly harmless trivial conversation then Martin drove me home. To my surprise he seemed to think that the meeting had gone well, saying in a satisfied tone, 'I'm so pleased, Aulis. You made a good impression on Mother — that's rare and very important.'

I disagreed. 'You could have fooled me. I know you didn't hear everything she said, but what about the remarks on my "unsuitable" clothes — you said I looked nice.'

'You did! But it's not so much what Mother said as the fact that she was taking an interest in you — that suggests that she might accept you. It would be great if you two got on. Mother's rather lonely, especially with my sister quite far away. Mother's never accepted a girlfriend of mine before.'

I was flattered, but unconvinced. 'Well, she has an odd way of showing acceptance. It might be a start if she said my name correctly. There's one thing, Martin — I'm not giving you up just because your mother might want me to.'

Martin shrugged this off. 'Oh, I'm sure she doesn't. Anyway, here we are. I must hurry back because Mother's alone. I'll phone you.' A quick kiss and he was gone.

Left on my front-door step I wanted to be impressed by Martin's concern for his mother. Surely a man who was so caring would show the same concern for his wife, or would Mother always come first? Annoyed as I had been by Mollie's rudeness, I was also excited by Martin's assurance that she was taking an interest in me and his picture of the future companionship which she and I might have.

A rational reaction to that evening would have been to decide that Martin's mother was devious, nasty and narrow-minded: that whatever her attractions or those of her son nothing could compensate for the misery she had the power to cause. That is the conclusion to which any reasonable person should have come.

Someone less reasonable, but perhaps more intuitive, would have fled from Mollie Peverell and that house as if from the Pestilence itself. Even I, naïve as I was, could see that this woman had humiliated me, dismissing my education, my job and my family as worthless. Yet looking and speaking as she did, her standards and ideas must be right.

I remembered similar women from my childhood and youth: our District Commissioner in Guides, the vicar's wife, old Lady Pratt who had been Chairman of Governors at school. It was true that I had never heard any of them being overtly rude like Mrs Peverell, but then, I reasoned, I had never seen them alone with their families. For me they were shining domestic goddesses, a world away from the harassed clutter of my home. My mother in the morning, hunting frantically for her stockings because she had a day's supply teaching, my father shouting for the car-keys, myself rushing to school clutching a half-eaten piece of toast.

I wanted to join the sorority of Mollie Peverell, to be the recipient of her loving warmth, not of this evening's coldness. I was foolish enough to believe that if I abandoned everything of which she disapproved, teaching, Latin, tight skirts, and, possibly, my name and my family, if I let her guide and nurture me, I would one day be admitted to membership of that select group.

Chapter Two
Sunday at Abbotshall

Far from fleeing, the following Sunday found me ensconced at Abbotshall, as a properly invited guest. Martin fetched me after church for lunch and tea. I assumed, foolishly, that this meant that I had passed his mother's initial test. In an effort to counter some of Mollie's criticisms I dug out my eight-gored, navy-blue school skirt, teaming it with a white polo-necked jumper. I must have looked like a cross between a schoolgirl and a chorister, but at least no derogatory remarks were passed about my appearance.

This time I really saw the beauty of Martin's surroundings. In the dining-room the furniture shone, the mahogany polished to a rich glowing brown. I particularly admired the sideboard. Free from Victorian curlicues it was just a smooth sheet of wood on top of three drawers and two cupboards of clean, simple design.

Martin's father, whom I now met for the first time, appreciating my gasp of admiration, was delighted to tell me about its special features. 'Lovely, isn't it? Late eighteenth century, made in the village. Let me show you the drawers; look, no nails anywhere, pure dowelling, the drawers glide sweet as a nut.' He pulled them out to demonstrate.

Mollie, all twinkles today, remonstrated with her characteristic little laugh. 'Really, darling! I don't suppose Aulish is an expert on antiques.'

I knew that I mustn't read into this harmless remark any innuendo about my background, so I smiled and said, 'No, but I do love good furniture.'

I agreed with Peter that the table and chairs, products of the same village carpenter, shared the sideboard's understated loveliness. The rest of the room was a fitting setting for them. Long blue velvet curtains hung at the large bay window, complementing the blue and grey pattern of the carpet. The alcoves on either side of the fireplace housed white built-in cupboards. Behind the leaded lights of their doors fine china gleamed.

Mollie caught my interested gaze. 'The furniture's Peter's pride, the china's mine. It's mostly Coalport and comes from my family.'

Martin broke in, speaking in the teasing tone that I was to find he often used with his mother. 'Ma loves all her old bits and pieces of china, don't you, Ma?'

Obviously hating this vulgar title, Mollie fixed Martin with an icy glare and continued her conversation with me. 'Tell me, Aulish, where did you learn about furniture?'

I made myself ignore any imagined emphasis on the "you" and was about to launch with enthusiasm into the story of my father's eldest sister, Aunt Sarah. How she had gone into service at Margrave Hall when she was fourteen, rising from the lowest rung of the maidservants to running the hall as cook/housekeeper to Lord and Lady Margrave, treated by them as a trusted friend. When Lady Margrave died she left Aunt Sarah a handsome annuity.

In our family we were terribly proud of Aunt Sarah. All set to share my pride with Martin's parents I suddenly remembered some words of my mother's during one of her quarrels with Dad. 'Oh, Sarah, this, Sarah, that; when all's said and done your precious sister was only a servant.'

I realised again, as I had done at our first meeting in the kitchen, that that was how Mollie would see Aunt Sarah. So I merely gave an accurate, if slightly misleading, reply. 'I used to visit Margrave Hall when I was a child. My Aunt Sarah, my father's eldest sister, knew Lord and Lady Margrave.'

I felt, rather than saw, Mollie's look of disbelief. However, nothing was said as we continued our delicious lunch. Mollie then proposed that we move to the lounge for coffee. Her use of this term surprised me. Lounge was one of my father's forbidden words. We had to say sitting-room, though he really preferred the old-fashioned parlour.

Whatever one called it, it was another beautiful room. Crimson velvet curtains this time, with a long window-seat cushioned in the same colour. I could imagine a child, or two, curled up there reading. No books were visible, but a charming Canterbury held stacks of *Farmers' Weekly* and *Country Life*. The carpet was moss green and the fireplace built entirely of russet bricks.

Mr Peverell was keen to point these out to me. 'My wife found all these; poked around everywhere in the buildings until she'd got enough, then told the men how to lay them in the shape she wanted.'

He smiled at her and I thought, 'If Martin's going to love me like that, it would be all I ever wanted.'

I sat beside Mollie on the chintz covered sofa, where red roses rioted over their cream background, and metaphorically pinched myself. Could this really be for me? Was I coming here, to my ceremonious house, way beyond anything I could have imagined, married to a man I was beginning to adore?

After lunch Martin took me for a walk around the farm to see his beloved cattle. I loved it all, especially the calves with their amazingly long lashes framing great brown eyes, and their little topknots like fringes.

Freed from the repressive atmosphere which his mother seemed to create, Martin was like a boy let out of school. He chatted enthusiastically about the farm and his plans for its future. Catching his mood, I asked what I hoped were intelligent questions. Clasping my hands, his eyes shining, he said, 'Oh, Aulis, we can have such a good life here together. It could be such fun — everything flourishing — crops, animals, babies.'

Dazed with happiness, all I could say was, 'Oh yes, Martin, yes, yes.'

In the food-store, just off the milking parlour, he kissed me passionately. 'Marry me, Aulis. I'm desperate for you. I could take you now if you'd let me and hang the consequences.'

'No, Martin. You know that I refuse to lose my virginity until I'm married.'

'Then say that you'll marry me. I realise that you're a bit worried about Mother; she has that effect on girls, but you can see that my parents like you, Pa's fairly smitten. Let's go in and tell them that we're engaged.'

'No, I still need time; especially, perhaps, to consider your mother. And there are my parents too; they hardly know that you exist, leave alone that it's serious.'

Bred to respect the courtesies of life Martin could see the force of this argument. 'All right, but you must tell them soon. I want you, Aulis.'

This time I responded to his embrace and our bodies moved in harmony. I wanted him too, but according to my deepest principles it had to be as a lawful wedded wife. And somewhere at the back of my mind I noted that Martin hadn't said that he loved me — only that he wanted me, physically. Was I just being silly and playing with words, and did it matter? His lust was no greater than mine. Wasn't that what grown-up married love was about, not some poetic romance?

It was time for milking, so Martin suggested that while he did that I should go back to the house. 'You can meet Aunt Emily. That'll be fun.'

I'd already been told that Mollie's sister was expected for tea. So I tripped cheerfully across the farmyard and in through the back door, which was ajar. It led into a huge utility room, where, among other things, the wellingtons were kept. I'd left my shoes by the further door, also ajar, which led into the passage. Seeing the mud on my boots I kicked them off and began to walk across the floor in my stockinged feet. No one heard me coming. Obviously, the kitchen door at the end of the passage was open and from within Mollie was pouring forth an absolute tirade, presumably to Aunt Emily. I knew that I shouldn't listen, but I couldn't help it. I was frozen, transfixed not only by what she was saying but by the venom in her voice. 'Emily, what am I going to do? You know how I've worked and contrived for this place and this family. Unaided I've transformed the Peverells from yeomen farmers into gentry; this house from a mere farmhouse into a gentleman's residence.

'I've made Peter important, a magistrate and a councillor, so that no one can see what an old funk and what a useless farmer he is. All my share of Daddy's money has gone into this farm. And yet we've got poorer and poorer.

'At least my children have been educated, with egg money. They speak properly now. Martin doesn't say 'Muther' or 'ever likely' or 'i'the'ead', or other ghastly Midland phrases. Diana's wedding was a triumph too, more egg money. Of course I can't stand Grant Llewellyn but he'll probably drink himself to death. Then Di can come back here with the darling children. She's quite capable of running the farm, with Martin to do the labouring. When dear little Charlie is older, he can take over. We might even manage to send him to Cirencester.

'Now all my plans will be spoiled by a silly little flibbertigibbet with nothing to recommend her. Her auntie at Margrave Hall indeed; yes, slaving in the kitchen, I'll be bound. I tell you this girl will be no good to Martin; she'll be a rotter like poor Alan Carter's wife. There'll be no hope that she won't have children; these people breed like rabbits. It'll be more and more mouths to feed, she'll ruin the farm, my beautiful house and Charlie's inheritance.'

'Anyway, Martin shouldn't marry. He's nearly thirty-five, yet he can't take responsibility and relies utterly on me. This overgrown schoolgirl will never stiffen his backbone.'

'Couldn't you tell her what he's like, Emily? Yet she seems so desperate for a man, or rather for Abbotshall, that she probably wouldn't listen. Opposition only seems to make her keener. I've seen that already. My only hope, and that's a very faint one, is that as she's nobody from nowhere I'll be able to break her and mould her into our ways.

'Oh, Emily, I don't deserve this. Haven't I had my great sorrow?' She finished on a sob.

I heard a quiet, soothing voice replying, presumably Aunt Emily, but I couldn't catch what she was saying. I crept out again into the yard. I don't know how long I cowered there, trembling with shock and distress, devastated by the strength of Mollie's feeling against me. Once more I had the chance to flee, and this time I should have taken it. The silliest thing kept me there. I hadn't got my own car and I couldn't face a five mile walk on a dark winter evening. That was the rational excuse I gave myself. I think that the truth was that I was like a wounded bird, not capable of much movement. So I stayed and in time took the consequences.

When I'd regained control of myself, I went in again, this time banging the back door and shouting 'hello' quite loudly enough to confirm Mollie's conviction of my vulgarity. She had quite recovered her composure. I was to find out that she could do that with remarkable speed.

I was soon being introduced to Aunt Emily, a shorter, fatter and far less polished version of Mollie. She was also rude, but in a way that I understood. After a perfunctory greeting she continued talking to Mollie about people they knew and I didn't. Discourteous as this was it wasn't as personal as Mollie's antagonism. It was also probably fortunate in the circumstances that neither of them made any attempt to include me in the conversation. Aunt Emily talked mostly of a Mr Noakes, what he liked to eat, what he said about the weather, farming, the prices of things. She was clearly concerned not to upset him. 'I won't be able to stay long, Mollie. Mr Noakes worries if I'm out too late.'

My parents' next-door neighbour always referred to her husband like this. 'Mr Smith will soon be home for his dinner. Mr Smith loves a good apple pie.' So I assumed that Aunt Emily was Mrs Noakes.

I was glad when Martin and his father came in and we were able to have tea. I was very quiet and soon made my excuses to leave, offering profuse, if not entirely truthful, thanks for a lovely day.

Martin drove me home, starting to chat cheerily about the day. 'Didn't that go well! You can't have any doubts now about Mother liking you. She was charming all day. I've rarely known her so pleasant — certainly not with a girlfriend of mine.'

I couldn't argue, because nothing had gone wrong while Martin was present. I could hardly complain about a conversation that I wasn't meant to hear. However, I did have one legitimate grouse, which I was determined to air, saying peevishly, 'I wish your mother would say my name properly. It's not difficult and we did make it clear the first time we met.'

Martin was dismissive. 'If you've nothing more than that to worry about count yourself lucky. Mother often gets names wrong — she calls Geraint Llewellyn Grant, for goodness' sake.'

I was temporarily diverted. 'Is his name Geraint? I'd never have guessed from the way she said it.' This led to another thought. 'Is it just people that she dislikes that she gets wrong — or Welsh people — or perhaps she dislikes all Welsh people.'

Martin was getting angry. 'Aulis, you're just being childish. I've told you Mother doesn't dislike you. How can you be so silly about a mere slip of the tongue?'

But I hadn't finished yet. There was just one more question I had to ask. 'Martin, what is your mother's great sorrow?'

I saw his hands stiffen on the wheel. Then he replied, with ice in his voice, 'You'll have to ask her yourself. I wouldn't dream of doing so.'

I shrank into my seat, feeling that I had committed some grave social error. We drove in cold silence for a while, until Martin took his left hand off the wheel and squeezed my right knee. I plucked up courage to ask about Mr Noakes, saying timidly, 'Aunt Emily must be very fond of her husband. She's always quoting him. And he's obviously concerned for her, worrying about her being out late. Why didn't he come with her?'

Martin looked puzzled, then started to laugh, his good humour apparently restored. 'She hasn't got a husband. Noakes is her employer. He's a grumpy old farmer and she keeps house for him. Just as well, or I suppose she'd have to live with us.'

I was curiously pleased. Aunt Emily was "slaving in a kitchen"; probably a small one, for a small farmer, whereas my Aunt Sarah had been Head Servant to the nobility. I enjoyed the irony.

Chapter Three
Doubts and Certainties

Martin didn't leave me on the doorstep this time but came up to my room, where he soon had the fire going. Once I was thoroughly warm, we were on my bed, naked in each other's arms, going as far as we dared, as they used to say. The happiness we found in physical love was a glorious revelation to me, accustomed only to the fumblings of inexperienced youths.

But tonight, in the intervals of lovemaking, we both felt the need to talk. Martin began, saying, as he stroked my hair, 'Do you have to go home tomorrow? You're going to be away for the best part of three weeks. I can't bear it. Can't you stay here?'

I laughed. 'Hardly! There'd be no food, for a start. They only provide meals in term-time. Anyway, I want to see my family. You're with yours all the time.'

'And you could be too. Shall I get Mother to invite you for Christmas? Then you could meet Di and Geraint and the children, and Aunt Emily will be over for the day. It would be such fun!'

I thought that Martin was being rather insensitive. 'No, Martin, I want my own people. And I want time to think.'

'What about?'

I bit the bullet. 'About us, you and me, whether this relationship is going anywhere, and whether I want it to.'

Martin pushed my hair back and looked at me. 'Aulis, my darling, you're crying.'

He cuddled me as if I were a little girl, kissing the tears on my cheeks. His voice was warm with love. 'You know where we're going. We're going to be married, farm at Abbotshall and have a large, cheerful family. We discussed it all this afternoon when we went round the farm. I can't wait to get started, so what's happened since then? You can't have gone off me already!'

I still couldn't bring myself to tell him of his mother's conversation with Aunt Emily. Apart from confessing to eavesdropping, to repeat Mollie's words would give them new life. So I just said, sounding, even to myself, like a whining schoolgirl, 'I don't think your mother likes me very much — at least it's not about liking — she doesn't think I'm suitable, have the right background, to be your wife. And she could be right, our families are very different.'

Martin was pleading and patient. 'Look, Aulis, I know Mother's difficult. She has her funny little ways, like the business with your name, and they can be very annoying. To put it bluntly, Mother's probably the reason that I'm still unmarried at thirty-four.'

'So he knows how she operates,' I thought.

He went on, 'But on the other hand, I've never wanted anyone as much as I want you. I think Mother knows that and therefore she'll give in gracefully. In any case, as I've already told you, she really does like you. She's never welcomed any of my previous girlfriends as warmly as she welcomed you, talking about her china and Margrave Hall!'

'God help the others,' I thought, but all I said was, 'Well, I don't know. I so want to believe you, Martin. All right, my name might be a small thing, but perhaps it's symptomatic. I still think that our families are too different, in important ways, for a union between them to work.'

Martin was less patient now. 'For God's sake, Aulis! It's not the families that are marrying each other, it's you and me.'

I was uncharacteristically firm. 'We carry their genes. Your mother said things to me, the first night in the kitchen, that suggested that she despised my family,'

'How can she, when she's never met them? Neither have I, for that matter. You've met most of my family now, and I must meet yours. Tell me something about them. I remember that you told Mother that your father's a teacher.'

'Yes, he's deputy headmaster of a church primary school. He's got about a year to go before he retires.'

'Well, I know nothing about schools but that sounds perfectly respectable to me. Does your mother go out to work?'

Once again, I had the vision of someone scrubbing floors, but I told myself that it was just a common phrase, so I bit back my instinctive sarcastic comment. 'She works part-time. She does supply teaching.'

'What's that?'

'She gets asked to go into a school when a regular teacher is ill or away for some reason. It could be for a day or several weeks.'

Martin nodded. 'A bit like contract milking. And your brothers — what do they do? I know you told Mother, but I've forgotten. All I can remember is that they have classical names, like you.'

I laughed. 'Which I was careful not to tell your mother. Hector has an Oxford M.A. and a lectureship at a prestigious Church of England Teacher Training College. He's working for his Ph.D. Jason teaches English and General Subjects at a boys' prep school in Australia. He's just married an Australian girl so he'll probably stay out there.'

Martin was reassuring. 'So what's wrong with any of that? It all sounds far too intellectual for me — except the boys' prep school — I went to one of those, though not in Australia, of course.'

That broke the tension and we were glad to have a laugh. Martin continued, 'Seriously, Aulis, a farmer feeds the body, a teacher feeds the mind. Aren't both those jobs important? It looks to me as if our children will have brains and practical ability, plus your beauty, of course.'

He made it all sound so simple, but I was determined to get my point across. 'Martin, my parents live in a semi-

41

detached house and have a Triumph Herald. You have acres and vehicles and that huge house.'

Martin smiled. 'Inconvenient and unnecessary — the house I mean. The acres and vehicles we have to have because we're farmers. What's wrong with a Triumph Herald? Far better than a Ford! Objections overruled!

'Martin, please be serious. My grandfather was a miner and my aunt a servant.'

'And what's my aunt — a servant. They should get on fine. I know nothing about mining, except that we'd all look pretty silly if there was no coal. What does it matter what someone does, as long as they do an honest day's work. You're a snob, Aulis, just like Mother — you'll soon be best friends!'

We laughed and loved again, until, all too soon, it was time for Martin to go. Wishing me a Happy Christmas, he said firmly, 'Now look, Aulis, you must arrange for me to meet your parents early in the New Year. It's important that we all get to know one another — and I have a question to ask them.

Mollie was right, I was in some ways still a schoolgirl. Preoccupied by my socio-economic concerns, I asked anxiously, 'What question?'

'Oh, my darling! For your hand in marriage, of course.'

As he took me in his arms for a last lingering embrace, I put all my worries aside and gave myself up to the joy of the moment.

Morning, and the absence of Martin, brought back all my worries and confusion. I was going home for Christmas and the two-hour drive gave me plenty of thinking time. First of all, I tried to take a rational look at Mollie's outburst to Aunt Emily.

Why were the Peverells poor, if indeed they were? I knew very little about money and had always seen it in fairly simple terms. My father had a salary, from which household bills were paid. My mother's earnings, as a supply teacher, were spasmodic, so they went into a savings account, which was used for treats, outings or extra special clothes, for example. From my earliest childhood I'd been used to going into banks with my mother. At a time when a large proportion of the population didn't even have a bank account, I'd been brought up to believe that we were quite financially literate and superior. Since I'd been teaching, I'd felt positively rich, paying my salary into my own bank account every month.

However, I had no idea how a business was run. I reasoned that a shop-keeper bought goods from a wholesaler, then sold them at a higher price to make a profit. What did a farmer do — sell milk and corn — but how and to whom? I began to understand why Mollie might think me ignorant, but I was young and intelligent. Anything could be learned.

Next question — why did Mollie have such a low opinion of her own son? I began to consider Martin as if I were writing a reference for him. He had passed his

School Certificate so he must be academically adequate. He seemed to know a lot about cattle, though I was no judge. He certainly worked long hours, though again I had no idea about the quality of his work. I had been out with him often enough to know that he wasn't an excessive drinker or a gambler. He was interesting, talked well, had read enough to be able to recognise a character from Dickens, which was more than some of the boys I'd met at university could do.

As for taking responsibility, perhaps Martin had never been given the chance. I could see that it would be easy to please Mollie by letting her run everything and then enjoy the comfortable life she would provide. Martin might prefer that to having constant battles with her. I guessed that he and his father liked peaceful lives — perhaps that was a weakness.

For me Martin was warm and loving and seemed utterly reliable, the strong rock I had always hoped to find. The ten-year age gap between us contributed to that feeling. Martin was only a year older than my brother Hector. I thought of both of them as grown-up, with far more knowledge and experience than I had.

Turning to Mollie's criticism of me, while accepting her concern about my lack of business knowledge, I was puzzled by her contemptuous attitude towards me as a person and apparently towards my family. I was well-spoken, well-educated, reasonably well-dressed for my age. Indeed, I always felt that I was one of the smartest of the younger staff at school. I realised that my life had been sheltered, but I'd found myself accepted socially in all the circles in which I'd moved. After all there had been a fair few public school people at university. And my brother had been to Oxford. Why had I created such a bad impression?

So far as my family were concerned, what right had she to judge us when she knew nothing about us? We weren't grand like the Peverells but we had done well in those "states of life into which it had pleased God to call us".

I had been driving almost automatically and suddenly realised that I was nearly home. The holiday had come at a good time. I was going to enjoy Christmas, reappraise my family and think about my relationship with Martin. As I turned into the familiar road I felt the old warm sense of homecoming, with its promise of food and fun and total abdication of responsibility. My mother would prepare my meals, my father look after my car, while I would read and lounge and sleep, the cossetted only daughter of a happy family.

Chapter Four
Christmas at Home

Even as I turned my key in the lock, I could hear my mother's excitement. 'Bill, Bill she's here — Aulis is here.'

I almost fell into the hall as she clasped me to her sequined bosom. As usual my mother was wearing a dress bought for some long-ago celebration and now demoted, most unsuitably, for everyday wear.

I struggled to release myself. 'Hold on, I'm not in your favourite infants' class.'

'Well let's get you in the warm, put the kettle on and make you a nice hot snack — bacon and tomatoes with fried bread, I thought.'

'Oh yes please!' I loved this greasy mixture.

'But where's your dad? Bill, will you come!'

'I'm here, Bronwen. I thought that at least it was an attack by the Volsci. And how are you, Aulis? You must come and see my latest acquisition.'

'Oh, you and your books, Bill! She hasn't got her coat off yet.'

But Dad was already leading me into the front room, where his Loeb editions of the Greek and Latin classics were ranged in perfect order along the shelves. I duly admired the latest, a new edition of Livy, enjoying the cerebral pleasure I always got from this room.

'Come on, you two, supper's ready.'

Sequins now splashed with fat, my mother was putting the well-filled plates on the table. I munched greedily, drinking in the familiar atmosphere of home. Of course it was mildly eccentric. Why, on top of the highly respectable oak bookcase, should there be a side plate, a rolled-up pair of socks, one of my father's stiff collars and a hairbrush?

'So let's hear all about school. Have you had any naughty girls this term?' My mother, anxious to share in a world that she at least partly understood.

'Yes — and I want to know how the Lower Sixth are enjoying Cicero.' My father, so proud that I was teaching his beloved Latin.

Oh, what the hell, I thought, this was home. So I chatted away, making them happy, and put the subject of Martin away for another day. The room was warm, even the clutter seemed cosy and homelike and that evening was almost the best part of the holiday.

Next day my mother demanded my company for the big Christmas shop. I knew that what she really wanted was to show me off in Northam, her successful, professional daughter. Amused by her harmless pride, I readily agreed to go.

Our progress down the High Street was impeded by constant meetings and greetings, inevitable in a small town. We met a couple of girls who had been at school with me, now proudly pushing their prams. I had no problems with them or their babies. the problem was, my mother's glance at me — half arch, half sorrowful.

Our first stop was "The Coffee Pot", to fortify ourselves for the job ahead. Over our coffee and cream cakes, the rapport which we had so far achieved started to splinter, as it so often did. My mother began, 'Now we can have a nice cosy chat. Have you met anyone this term?'

I deliberately misunderstood her. 'Yes, loads of people. There are several new staff and…'

She cut me short. 'Don't be silly, Aulis. Have you met a young man?' Heavy capitals were implied.

I paused for a moment. They would have to know sometime. 'Yes, I have actually. He's called Martin, and he's a local farmer.'

My mother was pleasantly amazed. 'Oh, Aulis, you've never told me so much before. A farmer! So he's well-off — that's good!'

Feeling slightly nauseated by this reaction I remembered and repeated Mollie's words. 'Farmers aren't rich, that's only what urban people think.'

Unperturbed, my mother pressed on. 'Well never mind — so long as you love him. Is it really serious? I can't wait to tell your dad and all the family!'

I was horrified. 'Mum, you are to say nothing yet. I've not known him long — there's nothing to tell — and it's not their business. Tell Dad if you must — but no one else!'

'All right, all right! You're always so touchy, Aulis, just like your dad. Most girls would want people to know they'd got a man — at last!'

Ignoring this sally I suggested that we discussed what we needed to buy. Hector and his family were coming for Christmas Day and my mother was very concerned that the food should be appropriate and traditional. She outlined her plans. 'I thought I'd get three packets of stuffing and two of bread sauce. Do you think that'll be enough? The pudding will only need unwrapping and boiling — and I've ordered the cake from Roberts's, they're Northam's best bakery. The icing's always so thick and sweet.'

I could hear Mollie outlining her Christmas preparations. 'I feed the cake with brandy every day. I've made four large puddings and several tiny ones for old people in the village. Then there'll be chopping onions and rolling breadcrumbs for the stuffing and bread sauce — not my favourite job.'

I shook myself. I'd always enjoyed Mum's Christmases — what was different now? Wasn't it more fun to have her around to play Monopoly, rather than chopping bread in the kitchen. Surely my admiration for Mollie didn't have to extend to her breadcrumbs!

So I said firmly. 'Just do your usual, Mum. Your Christmases are always lovely.'

Her beam of gratitude was my reward.

When the visitors arrived on Christmas morning it was all noise and jollity. Hector's wife, Norma, was a

49

favourite with both my parents. Clever enough to have gone to university, she had chosen instead the local training college and primary school teaching, so establishing a great bond with them.

Norma was halfway through her second pregnancy and was immediately whisked off to the kitchen by my mother. 'Come and give me a hand, Norma. Then you can tell me how everything's going.'

Then my father. 'Come into the study, Hector. I want to know how your research on the Civil War is progressing.'

This left me to entertain three-year-old Helen.

'Good practice for you; get your hand in.' My mother specialised in cheap hints.

Helen was a solid, serious child, who regarded me with critical detachment. I smiled encouragingly and was disarmed when she climbed on to my knee, only to find that her purpose was purely scientific. With a fat, sticky finger, she poked my stomach, then made her triumphant announcement. 'You haven't got a baby in your tum,

My mum's got a baby in her tum.'

Helen continued to produce this marvel of creative wit throughout the day, to almost universal approval. 'That's a bit rude, pet,' laughed my mother. 'But isn't she clever, Mum,' enthused Norma. 'Very forward for her age,' added Hector. 'A real Price,' purred my father.

No one seemed to consider that I might not find it funny. I knew it was ridiculous to be so irritated by a small child, but I found myself longing for Martin and the dignity of Abbotshall.

Lunch over, Norma sprang into action. 'Come on, Aulis. Let's do the washing-up, so that Grandma and Helen can enjoy themselves.'

Sweeping me into the kitchen and closing the door, talking as she worked, she went straight to the point. 'Your mother says you've got a boyfriend and it could be serious.'

I might have guessed that Mum would tell Norma. 'Yes.' I replied, determined not to elaborate on the subject.

Norma seemed embarrassed. 'We thought, that is, Hector thought, perhaps one of us should speak to you.'

I waited, bewildered, while Norma hurried on, anxious to cover her confusion. 'You're a clever girl, Aulis, but you live in a dream world. It's about time you knew what people think of your family. I love your mother and get on well with her. But she's a byword, everyone knows she's the reason your dad never got a headship. Then there's him, with his precise speech and his superior attitude; and all the time living like this.'

'Like what?' I was baffled by the intensity of her tone, 'Look around you, Aulis. Look at this kitchen. Food sitting here uncovered, tea towels on the floor, the cooker all splashes. I know Christmas Day is chaotic, but that dirt round the taps, for example, that's crusted in. In the bathroom there's fluff and dust under the bowl and behind the lavatory. Have you ever been in another house where they have a filthy black kettle which they boil on the fire? And your father just shuts himself up in that room and lets everyone else take the consequences.' As she finished speaking, she was practically crying.

While I might have my own reservations about my mother's housekeeping, I wasn't taking this from an in-law. I was as heated as Norma. 'All right, Mum's not the best housekeeper in the world — but she's good at more important things. My parents are professionals. We own our own house, we're educated. And I don't go looking for dust in other people's houses.'

Norma was unmoved. 'Well, perhaps you should. Aulis, I've said I love and admire your parents but their attitudes do impact on what other people may think of their children. And it'll be worse for you because you're a girl. Girls are assumed to take after their mothers.'

'What will be worse for me? I don't understand.'

Norma was impatient. 'Oh, Aulis, grow up. People will assume that you will have the same domestic habits as your mother. I gather your boyfriend's a farmer. Because my dad's a greengrocer I've been to lots of farms with him. I can imagine what your boyfriend's home is like, charming and comfortable. My advice to you is to make sure you have Martin well and truly hooked before you bring him here, and don't bring his parents here at all.'

'But you don't know them.'

'No, but I know the reaction of any moderately capable housewife, my mother, for example, to this place.

Round here people admire your dad and respect your parents for the way they've educated all of you. A stranger will know nothing of that and will just see the mess. Don't let them, Aulis, not if you want this man.'

I was shocked, yet Norma had only put flesh on the vague dissatisfaction that my home had begun to evoke. Not that I was grateful. I never quite forgave Norma for bringing to light things which I would have preferred to lie dormant.

Hector's face appeared round the door. I intercepted the knowing look he flashed at Norma, but he merely said, 'Have you finished here? Helen wants you to hear her rabbit song.'

My mother had transformed the truculent child into a pleasant, smiling little girl. Wasn't that worth more than polishing furniture all day long? As I looked round the room with my unscaled eyes, although I felt ashamed of myself, I knew that for me, it wasn't. I wanted life to be "accustomed and ceremonious". I wanted Martin and Mollie and Abbotshall and their clean peace.

As soon as Christmas was over, longing for a sympathetic ear, I was round at Marie's. We had been friends all through school and university, sweating over Latin proses together, giggling about our latest boyfriends. Marie had married soon after graduation and was now a full-time mother. Katie was three, James one and there was another baby on the way. Marie was now busy planning similar delights for me.

'If you have one straight away, they'll all be little together. It'll be such fun! But tell me more about Martin. However did you meet?'

'At a drinks party run by the Local History Society.'

'Is he keen on History then? That really would suit you.'

'Well, only in the way of churches and family stuff.'

'Oh, not highbrow enough for a Price. So what attracted you?'

'I'd gone with a History staff from school who promptly deserted me. Martin saw that I was by myself and came over and rescued me.'

'Didn't he know anyone either?'

'Oh no, he knew lots of people and introduced me. Then he was going on to a dance and asked me to go with him.'

'But Aulis, my love, you're no great dancer!'

'No, I know, but it was such fun. He makes everything jolly and happy and you don't have to perform all the time. It's like being comforted by a great cuddly bear, strong and reliable.'

'Is he very large then?'

I considered. 'He's not that tall — about five feet, nine. But he's broad, strong and sturdy. Oh, Marie, he's just like the "Yeomen of England", in that operetta thing the choir sang at school. Do you remember? He has a lovely fresh complexion, "Stained with the ruddy tan", it was in the song. He has very English bright blue eyes and

54

springy black curls on his temples like a little black lamb.'

Marie was impressed. 'I'm amazed how you remember things from school — I remember hardly anything. But gosh, Aulis, you really are smitten with Martin. So why have you got any doubts?'

'Well, there's the age difference — he's ten years older than me. I don't think it matters, but some people might.'

Marie could answer this from her own experience. 'Ken's seven years older than me and I would say that's largely a good thing; his extra experience calms and steadies me.'

I was reassured. 'Good! That's what I think Martin will do for me.'

'So what's next?' asked Marie. 'Well, there's Norma.'

'What on earth has she got to do with it — it's none of her business. She's only one of the scarlet virgins.'

Smiling at our schoolgirl name for the red-blazered girls from the local training college I told Marie, with some hesitation, what Norma had said about my mother's domestic deficiencies and how they would reflect on me.

Marie was indignant. 'What nonsense! We all loved coming to your house because your mother always had time for us. She was interesting and different. Norma's just jealous because all her mother can do is sell vegetables in the market! So that's her settled. Now, Aulis, have you any serious doubts?'

'Yes! What do we have in common, except this vague History thing? We don't seem to have any shared interests or experiences. What would we talk about if we were married — what do you and Ken talk about?'

'Oh, what colour to paint the bathroom, the iniquities of Ken's boss and, endlessly, the children, present and future. You could talk about cows calving, ewes lambing and your children. Anyway, one doesn't talk all the time. You spend a third of your life in bed. How's that side of things?'

Smiling at Marie's statistical knowledge, I could answer with confidence. 'Oh, Marie, it's wonderful. We want each other so much. Just thinking of it now makes me weak with longing. I could melt with happiness when he strokes my breasts.'

'All right, I get the picture.' Marie shot a warning glance at me, indicating Katie, now fixing me with a fascinated stare. 'Now tell me about his family, the house, the whole picture. It sounds like a book, like those Whiteoak stories we used to read.'

How could I explain to bouncing, sensible, modern Marie the mixture of fascination and dread which I felt for Abbotshall and Mrs Peverell?

'There's so much to say. Where shall I start?'

'Start here! Tell me about the kitchen. You can learn so much about people from their kitchen.' Marie looked round complacently at her own sunny kitchen, bright in pale blue and primrose yellow.

This was easy. I could always visualise the room where I had first encountered Mollie.

'Mrs Peverell's kitchen is white, like a clinic, and everything in it is brown or metallic. Her kitchen tools have dark brown handles, not jolly blue ones like yours.'

Marie laughed. 'Probably because they're real teak and more expensive.'

I went on. 'They hang down on the wall, so that the slotted spoon is a fox's triangular face, with the narrow, pointed nose and pricked up ears. When she stands beside them there are two fox faces looking at you. The warm wooden handles turn into cold metal, just as she changes from warmth to coldness in a second, in the course of a sentence.'

'Then there's the silver coffee pot, reflecting one's face like a twisted mirror at a fair. The spout curves upwards, like a swan's neck, so it looks down its nose at you, just like Mollie does. The smooth wooden handle fits snugly into one's hand, warm and comforting, but leads only to cold metal. The lid slides effortlessly on to the pot, and that's how she wears her clothes.'

'How many more anthropomorphic objects has she got?' Marie was trying not to laugh.

'Well, there's the pepper mill; that's the disapproving aunt. Brown teak again, a little, fat, short-waisted woman, with her hair piled in a bun on the top of her head. Smooth to the touch, with a deceptive appearance of good humour, while inside is the hot-tempered pepper.'

'Goodness, Aulis, and you didn't even read English.' Then she added, more gently, 'But if you don't like these people, should you get involved with them? It seems to me that, given their particular circumstances, you can't have Martin, without his family. Is he really worth this misery you seem to feel about his mother?'

I tried again to explain the compulsion that was driving me. 'Do you remember that poem by Yeats that Willis made us learn in the Sixth, *A Prayer for my Daughter*? It's like that.'

'You mean all that "ceremonious house" and "horn of plenty" stuff. H'm! Remember that I did read English and I know that poetry and real life don't always match up. Please don't make a mistake. I couldn't bear you to get hurt.'

The conversations with Marie and Norma, in their different ways, cleared my mind. Norma was right. I needed to be in the real world, using kitchen tools, not full of silly fancies about them. Most of all I wanted Marie's fruitful happiness. I had no real doubts about Martin. After all, I told myself firmly, I was not going to marry his mother. I resolved that next time Martin proposed I would say an unqualified yes.

But would there be a next time? As I drove up to the staff boarding-house the evening before term began, I saw Martin's Singer parked outside. My mouth was dry with apprehension and I could feel my heart pounding. Was Martin going to repeat his proposal, or was he going to tell me — kindly — as was his way — that he had thought better of it, that he realised that we were not suited after all? Had his mother won?

Chapter Five
Engagement

A few more minutes of suspense remained. Martin was there beside me, picking up my case. 'Let's get you indoors, Miss Price. It's cold out here.'

A well-prepared fire was burning brightly in my bed sitting-room. But even as I stretched out my hands to the warmth Martin seized them and enveloped me in one of his great bear-hugs. 'Now sit down, Aulis. I have to talk to you.'

This is it, I thought. It's been fun, but not really suitable, Mother says. Then I realized that Martin was on his knees.

'Darling Aulis, will you marry me? You know that I'm not poetic but I love you to distraction. Please say yes!'

'Oh yes, Martin, yes, yes'.

Then we were locked together on my bed, our hands frantically finding each other's secret places.

Eventually I rolled over and sat up. 'Can I tell my parents? In any case I should tell them I've arrived safely.'

'No, you don't tell them. I have to ask your father. See if they can have us next Sunday. And as the phone's on the landing I suggest you put something on before you go out there.'

My father answered the phone. 'Yes, Aulis, we'll be glad to meet your friend.'

'Oh, Dad, it's much more than that.'

I could hear my mother grabbing the receiver. 'Has he asked you? Can't wait to meet him. What does he like to eat?'

She was almost as incoherent and excited as I was.

So the following Sunday found us on our way to Northam. Martin was nervous about meeting my parents, especially my highly academic father.

I tried to reassure him. 'Don't worry — he'll approve of you. You did Latin and Greek at school.'

Martin was pondering. 'Aulis, I've been wondering — if your grandfather was a miner, how did your dad get to be a teacher?'

I was angry and determined to get my own back on Mollie. 'Miners are not necessarily stupid, you know, that's only what rural people think. My dad won a scholarship to grammar school, and then a grant from the church to go to college.'

'But if he's as clever as you say, why is he only a teacher in an ordinary school — and why didn't he go to university?'

'Not only was my grandfather a miner, he was killed down the pit when my dad was only fifteen. Dad was terribly lucky to be able to stay on at school after that, leave alone go to college. University would have been out of the question. And primary schools are not ordinary, they're very important — everyone goes to them.'

'Well, I didn't.'

'You must have gone to something similar, anyway, only a tiny percentage of children go to fee-paying schools.'

'Hey, Aulis, I don't care a rap about schools. Let's not argue — except that you look gorgeous when you're angry.'

He stopped briefly in a lay-by so that we could have a long, satisfying kiss.

The welcome was all that we could have wished. My mother, in new and clean sequins, clasped both of us in her rather short arms, while my father smiled warmly. Remembering Norma's comments, I pleaded urgency and so managed to dust the basin and lavatory before Martin saw them. When I came downstairs Martin was in the front room with my father and my mother was bursting to have a chat. 'Daddy's so impressed that Martin wants to ask him formally for your hand. You know how your dad likes the old-fashioned ways.'

A terrible thought struck me. 'Dad couldn't say no, could he?'

'Don't be daft. It's only a custom. But isn't Martin nice — and nice-looking too. What are his people like? I bet they're posh. Is the house very smart? I don't know what they'll say when they see this place.'

I made a tremendous effort. 'Well, I'll have to come and help you have a good spring-clean, won't I?'

Before my mother could reply to this unprecedented offer, my father and Martin emerged, looking very pleased with each other. My father kissed my cheek. 'I think you have chosen well, Aulis. And so have you, Martin. We hope that you will be very happy together.'

'Oh Bill — you're not making a speech in Assembly!' My mother gave us both great hugs and kisses, laughing and crying at the same time.

Drying her eyes, she began to bustle about. 'Now come on, let's all have tea. I thought you'd like a plate of boiled ham, Martin, and help yourself to salad.'

To my mother salad meant lettuce, tomato and egg. She always cooked the eggs too late and too soft, so that they sat smoking, as they melted into the tomatoes.

Martin chewed manfully as we progressed to tinned peaches.

'And look,' my mother exclaimed joyfully. 'The evaporated milk is in Aulis's Coronation mug from school — she'll have to take that with her when she gets married.'

I shuddered inwardly, as I thought of Mollie's exquisite china.

My mother's only disappointment was Martin's refusal of a foil-covered triangle of Swiss processed cheese. 'Oh, dear, and I got it specially for you. I thought being a farmer you'd like cheese.'

I thought of Abbotshall, where sliced bread and bought cakes were never seen. Well Martin didn't seem to mind so why should I?

All went well until we discussed the date of the wedding. My mother couldn't resist thinking about small children. 'Helen will be five next year — she'll be old enough to make a lovely little bridesmaid.'

Martin crushed my impatient reply. 'Oh no, Mrs Price, we're going to be married this year.'

'Of course, in the summer holidays. That'll be lovely.'

'No I'm afraid it'll have to be in the autumn, after both corn and potatoes have been harvested. We're planning on October.'

'So that'll be in half-term,' said my father.

I could keep quiet no longer. Using my new Mollietone I burst in, 'That's not an issue. I'm finishing at school at the end of the summer term. I've given in my notice.'

'You've what!' My father, normally so temperate and quiet, could have these sudden eruptions. 'But you'll only have taught for two years. What a waste! All that taxpayers' money you've taken.'

My mother was anxious to smooth things over. 'Now Bill, Aulis will have plenty to do. And if I'm not much mistaken, she'll soon be busy with other things and perhaps not feeling too well,' with a large, crude wink at me.

Martin, recovering from my father's unexpected outburst, rushed to her support. 'That's right, Mrs Price. Aulis will have lots to do at Abbotshall.'

My father seemed determined to be difficult. 'Are you going to move in with your parents then? I don't think Aulis will like that and I shan't be very happy if my daughter doesn't have her own home.'

But again, Martin could respond sweetly. 'I agree, Mr Price, that wouldn't do at all. My parents own a cottage at the bottom of the drive. They've rented it out for short-term lets but they always meant to move there when I married. Mother will have a wonderful summer doing it up and furnishing it, because of course we get all the family furniture at Abbotshall and Mother's leaving the carpets and curtains.'

My mother was overwhelmed. 'What a lucky girl you are, Aulis. All your friends are paying mortgages and buying furniture on HP and you're getting all this.'

I repeated the lesson I had learned from Mollie. 'It's nothing to do with me. Martin must have Abbotshall and all the Peverell things — it's how landed families live. Aunt Sarah could tell you that.'

My father gave me a reproving look but my mother was adamant. 'I still think you should be very grateful. And there you are, Bill, she'll be fully occupied cleaning and polishing that lovely house. I do wish I could see it.'

Martin's reply endeared him even more to my mother. 'And so you shall, Mrs Price. My mother has particularly asked me to invite you and Mr Price to come over one Sunday, sometime in the summer, perhaps.'

This was news to me but, faced with my mother's delight, I could say nothing. She was ecstatic. 'How lovely! Bill isn't that grand — I'm so excited — and Aulis will be there of course, and meeting your mother and father, won't it be lovely, Bill?'

My father smiled thinly; we all knew how he hated visiting, but he murmured polite acquiescence.

On the way back I took Martin to task. 'Why didn't you tell me your mother was inviting them? It came as quite a shock.'

'You'd have only fussed and got in a worse state than you were. You can be so odd where Mother's involved. And I must say your dad's got some funny ideas — all that stuff about taxpayers' money.'

I couldn't be bothered to argue. 'Martin let's forget about it all and just enjoy the journey and being together. We both have parents with strong views — don't let them divide us.'

For answer there was another layby, another loving session. If this was Martin's solution for everything, I thought, it was a very enjoyable one.

But that day was symptomatic of the whole course of my engagement — periods of happiness interspersed with bouts of misery.

Mollie's initial reaction had been surprisingly warm, expressed in a charming formal letter: '

'We must get to know you much better now that you are to be one of the family. We will all welcome you and try to help you in your new life. You will find Martin very easy, not demanding like some men, though of course I speak only as his mother.'

I didn't quite understand this last sentence, but was delighted by Mollie's friendly tone. Yet from day to day, she was as tetchy as ever. We had ridiculous spats about various personal articles she was proposing to leave in the house. Mollie would suddenly announce, 'I'm leaving you my little mint-chopper. I've found it so useful.'

'Thank you, but shouldn't you take it if you need it?'

'Oh well of course if you don't want it, that's that. I just thought it might be useful. Martin loves mint sauce.'

Then there would be protestations to and fro — all very wearisome.

But these were just pinpricks. More serious was the disagreement over my engagement ring. The Saturday after we had seen my parents, Martin phoned and said, in the masterful way I loved. 'Be ready at two o'clock. Sam's doing the milking so we can have the afternoon to buy our ring. Then Mother's asked you back to tea.'

I was ready and waiting and we were soon on our way to Stafford. Martin was obviously on a mission, as he asked me, 'Have you any preference about stones, Aulis?'

'No, I know very little about jewellery. I've never really had any.'

'In that case may I buy you a sapphire? The blue would match your eyes and a sapphire is such a soft, gentle stone, not cold and hard like a ruby, for example.'

I was entranced. 'Martin, you never cease to surprise me. Yes please, I'd love a sapphire.'

As if it were meant, as my mother would say, I saw the perfect ring sitting in the window of the first jeweller we visited. 'Look, Martin, a diamond shaped sapphire set in a frame of small diamonds. I think that's perfect!'

'Then you shall have it, my love.'

The ring was swiftly bought, ceremoniously placed on my finger and we were driving back to Abbotshall.

Would I never learn! I burst cheerfully into the kitchen, flashing my ring finger. 'Look what I've got!'

Mollie's smile of welcome froze. The mood change was swift, even for her. She was white with fury, her mouth set in a thin, grim line, as she threw across the table a magnificent ring.

I gasped with admiration. 'Oh Mollie, how beautiful! Look at those rubies, rocks of liquid fire, and those huge diamonds.'

Her voice was trembling with anger. 'Yes, and it should be yours, you silly little fool. Even you can appreciate it, apparently my son could not. He knows that this is the Peverell engagement ring, always given to the eldest son's fiancée. I was more than happy to give it up, but Martin seems to have rejected it. For once I don't blame you, Aulish, though I suppose that cheap little ring was your choice. I'd like both of you to leave now.'

We fled like carpeted schoolchildren.

Once in the car I turned on Martin. 'Why did you not mention your mother's ring — at least give me the option of having it? I know she's touchy, but this time she has reason.'

Martin's answer surprised me. 'I want to start clean and fresh. I want the ring to be yours, not Mother's.'

'But all those brides, Martin. You know how I love tradition.'

'Don't worry! You'll get more than enough tradition at Abbotshall, and at least some of it will be genuine. Now let's forget it and go out to dinner.'

So I shut up. But I was puzzled by Martin's words and sad about Mollie's ring, because it would have bound me closer to her. Now that opportunity was lost. Yet I stroked my little ring lest it should feel unwanted.

Once again we survived one of Mollie's storms. Determined to placate her I emphasised my gratitude when she offered to lend me her veil, a magnificent sheet of Brussels lace. Like all her gifts, it came with a sting. 'This is for you, Aulish. I shall be so glad for Martin's bride to wear it and I don't suppose your family have anything suitable.'

Dangerous as it might be, I couldn't resist a reply. 'I don't know. I expect Aunt Harriet had a veil.'

Mollie's question was sharp. 'Who's Aunt Harriet?'

'My father's married sister. It's her granddaughter, Gillian, who will be a little bridesmaid with Lucy.' Lucy was Martin's niece.

'So why wasn't she at the fitting day? I thoroughly approved of your friend Marie, lots of children and no job. But what about this Gillian? What does her father do? Does she speak nicely? Will she be a suitable companion for Lucy on the day?'

I answered wearily. 'Gillian is a perfectly nice little girl. Her father's a chemist and she didn't come to the fitting day because she had a cold.'

The fitting day had been an opportunity for Marie and Lucy to be fitted for their bridesmaids' dresses. It also marked my first meeting with Martin's only sister, Diana, and her children, Lucy, aged eight and Charlie, six.

Marie was an instant success. She brought her very new baby, Jonathan. Di and Mollie adored him and once Mollie knew that Marie was breastfeeding her acceptance was guaranteed. 'What a lovely friend for you, Aulish,' Mollie purred. And to Marie, 'You'll always be welcome at Abbotshall, dear.' Warm goodbyes were exchanged.

As Marie relaxed afterwards over a snack in my room, she was keen to review the day. 'What did you think of Diana? Didn't Martin say that she could really handle Mollie? I didn't see much sign of that, did you?'

I was anxious to be loyal. 'Martin's very fond of Di. She seems a perfectly pleasant, sensible woman.'

'Yes, but no personality. She's like a blurred image of Mollie, the fox features just make her look permanently shy. And those clothes — frump wasn't the word — that suit was mud-coloured.'

'Don't be mean!'

'I'm not, merely truthful. And don't tell me you were impressed. You looked just like your father when she said, "Did you do Froebel or Montessori?" and "It must be horrid having to go out to work"'

I laughed. My mother was always telling me to stop looking like my dad. But I still defended Diana. 'Yes, well, those are Mollie's attitudes. Di's just been brought up to be purely domestic.'

'Oh yes, when you said, "I understand you went to Domestic Science College," and she said, "Only on the 'Brides-to-Be' course", I could have died laughing.'

'Di couldn't help it. I reckon she was lucky to get away from Mollie even for that.'

Marie was unstoppable. 'I'll tell you one thing, Di may have been OK as a bride, but I don't think much of her mothering skills. That boy isn't much of an advert, is he? Lying on the floor having a tantrum at the age of six. It would have been a smacked bottom and bed for Katie if she'd behaved like that, and she's only three!'

'But Mollie told you that he mustn't be thwarted because he's so intelligent.'

'I thought you were going to explode when she said that!'

We were laughing then suddenly I was crying. 'Oh, Marie. I wouldn't care about anything if one day Mollie would look adoringly at a child of mine the way she looks at Charlie.'

Marie was all compunction. 'Don't cry, Aulis. They're not worth it. Are you sure you want to go ahead with this marriage? I know you love Martin and I like him a lot, but the heartache these people will give you! You can see after today that Di's going to be no support, and while Mollie is charming to outsiders like me, she must

71

be truly awful to live with. I don't want you to be unhappy.'

Tears dried now, I was adamant. 'No, I do love Martin and he loves me, that's what really matters. And I'm going to make Mollie like me — whatever it takes!'

Marie persisted. 'Why is that so important, Aulis? I realize that you'll have to live very near each other so life will be much easier if you get on reasonably well, but why are you so keen on this woman — needing her to like you so much — seemingly desperate for her approval?

It wasn't easy to explain, to put into words feelings of which I was somewhat ashamed. 'I think I need a role-model, Marie, and I need some mother-love.'

Marie was astounded. 'For God's sake, Aulis! You have a perfectly good mother of your own!'

'But we've never really got on. I've always had an edgy relationship with my mother. Mollie is everything that my mother is not!'

'But what's wrong with your mum? I would say she's a lot easier than Mrs Peverell. Your mother is bright, Aulis, and interesting. She loves her teaching, she reads books, she's got lots to talk about, she's fun! Mollie struck me as narrow-minded, with no interests outside her own house and family. This isn't Norma's nonsense haunting you is it?'

I was quite sure. 'No, the disquiet was there long before Norma added to it. Mollie may have a small arena but within that she seeks for perfection. Look at her clothes and her appearance, her house and garden, nothing out of place.'

Marie was roused now. 'And is that soulless tidiness all that life is about? I don't think there's much generosity of spirit there — and it flows out of your mother.'

'I don't agree, and by the way, milk is flowing out of you.'

Marie suddenly realized that she needed baby Jonathan and proceeded to deal with the problem. Mother and baby satisfied, they soon set off for home.

I was glad that our conversation had come to this abrupt end. For one thing I didn't want to hear any more criticism of Di. Not only did I feel loyalty to her as Martin's well-loved sister, I wanted to believe in her. In my new life I would need friends, and Di seemed an obvious candidate.

Perhaps more importantly, I didn't want any more probing into my feelings about Mollie. Not even to myself could I explain my adoration of Mollie and my need for a close personal relationship with her. I could acknowledge the deficiencies in my relationship with my own mother. I had the curious thought that my mother was over-familiar — that she invaded my space — poking and prying into my life with her hints and euphemisms. I felt guilty for having these feelings, but Mum need never know. Meanwhile I could work on the warm, uncluttered friendship — the meeting of kindred minds — which I planned to have with Mollie, moulding myself in her image.

I achieved a significant coup in this project by arranging not to be married at Northam. Mollie was constantly worrying about having to go there for the wedding.

'How can Peter and I, as well as Martin, be away from the farm for a whole day? It's dangerous to leave animals like that. You can't rely on the men, they're only hirelings, and they'd have no phone. What if a cow got milk fever and there was no one to get the vet? We'll just have to be as quick as we can at the reception.'

That's when I had my brilliant idea. 'You're absolutely right and you mustn't worry like this. Why don't we get married here, in Monks Leigh? It's much easier for my parents and family to travel than for you to leave the farm for all those hours.'

Mollie was taken aback, deprived of a major means of distressing me, yet touched by my suggestion. 'Oh, Aulish, how wonderful! Are you sure they wouldn't mind? How good of you to understand.'

A little squeeze of her arm around my shoulders, a grateful smile, and my day was made. Now, as Norma had advised, Mollie need never see my home. What was more it was unlikely that my less salubrious relations, like Uncle John and Aunt Nellie, would bother to travel to Monks Leigh.

The only question was, what would my parents say?

Chapter Six
Meetings

There was of course a row, but not as I'd imagined. My mother, immediately and to me surprisingly, took my side. 'I can see how important the animals are. And it will give everyone the chance to see Abbotshall. After all it's only what the Royal Family do, isn't it? I mean Princess Marina came from Greece but she was married in London, where his people were.'

My father was furious. 'But we are not the Royal Family. You're getting as bad as Aulis, with her grand ideas about landed families. I know you read Mills and Boon and Barbara Cartland, but I thought she had more sense.'

'It's about time the girl had some romance and dreams in her life. She's in love.'

'Does that mean that she shows no respect for her family? Girls, non-royal, of course, always marry from their own home.'

Norma, Hector and I watched fascinated as my parents continued to exchange insults. Hector tried to intervene to calm them down but they both waved him away imperiously. They were in full flow now.

'Her family,' sneered my mother. 'You mean your family, don't you? Well, it'll be a good thing if it keeps your John and Nellie away — and as they're too mean to leave the village I doubt if they'd travel to Monks Leigh. So far as manners are concerned John's never left the pit, and Nellie's never left the hovel she was born in. That's one embarrassment Aulis will be spared. I'm sorry, Bill, but your eldest brother is as common as muck, and his wife's worse.'

'Neither of them are as bad as your Aunt Elsie, with her cigarettes and her ill-chosen comments. She called Norma a posh cow for getting married when she wasn't pregnant.'

Although Norma and I were beginning to enjoy the sight of my parents' hurling insults at each other Norma could not hold her tongue for long. She broke in, 'Well I think it's Aulis' wedding and she should get married wherever she wants to.'

My father looked at Norma in surprise, as if the dog had spoken, but my mother quickly decided that she was grateful for the support. 'There you are, Bill, that's what young people think. And all your respectable relations will come. Your brother Jim will bring Sarah and Harriet will come with Joan and Nigel, because they've got to bring Gillian to be bridesmaid. I don't think I'll ask Aunt Elsie, she did behave disgracefully at Hector's wedding. Now let's all calm down and have a nice cup of tea.'

She gave my father a meaningful look and he subsided. My mother's unspoken message was that

Norma, who was very close to giving birth, must not be too excited or upset.

So the matter was settled. I could be married at Monks Leigh and keep Mollie happy. My father was still sulking some weeks later when my parents received Mollie's invitation to visit Abbotshall for tea on a Sunday afternoon.

'Of course you'll come, Bill. Don't be so childish! This is very important for Aulis.' My mother was adamant.

With much muttering and grumbling he came. As soon as we arrived he was carried off by Martin, who was his usual warm, cheery self, to watch the milking, so my father had no immediate opportunity to display his truculence.

An awkward trio was left, myself, my mother and Mollie. Somewhat overawed by her surroundings but determined to keep her end up, my mother was soon in excruciating full flow. 'Yes, all our children have been to college. My eldest son has a very good job, not in a school like Aulis, in a college. His wife, Norma, was a teacher too. Norma's very particular, keeps her house like a new pin. You should see their garden, lawns in front, each side of the drive, with a shady bit under a tree for the pram.'

It got worse.

'They have four bedrooms. They call one the nursery, makes me laugh a bit, but I told you, Norma's very particular. The baby's in there now of course and

77

Helen's got her own room. Of course Norma's people are quite well-off, her father's got a shop, you know.'

Mollie finally managed to get a word in. 'Mrs Price, would you like a tour of the house, to see where Aulish will be living?'

'That would be lovely, Mrs Peverell.'

Off we trailed, my mother causing me some more uncomfortable moments. When we came to the nursery suite, all brown paint and linoleum, Mollie observed. 'Martin and Aulish will have to do these rooms up, when the time comes.'

'Yes, Mrs Peverell, and if I'm not much mistaken it'll be sooner rather than later, though you never can tell with Aulis. I don't think she likes children very much and her father would like her to wait a while. But I think that the christening shouldn't be too long after the wedding. Not a honeymoon baby of course. I always think that's a bit common, and if it comes early people get the wrong idea.' She finished with a merry laugh.

Mollie's tone was icy. '"Honeymoon baby?" Not a phrase I'm familiar with, Mrs Price. Martin was born forty weeks to the day from our wedding day.'

We had been all over the ground and first floors, and were poised to go up to the second. Mollie hesitated. 'I don't know whether you want to go to the attics, Mrs Price? There's not much to see in them.'

I wonder if things would have been different if my mother had said 'yes' and we had seen much earlier what awaited us there. While she still hesitated over her reply

Martin called to say that they were in and we went down to the dining-room for tea. The chance was lost.

Tea brought no immediate relief from embarrassment. Mollie lifted the cover from a large willow-pattern platter, saying cheerfully, 'We have a rather large salmon here. We thought it would be perfect for a summer afternoon. We do love salmon.'

My mother was eager to agree. 'Oh so do we! "John West's" is my favourite, though I'm sure this one will be very nice.'

Mollie had now uncovered the dish, to reveal a large salmon, surrounded by lettuce, cucumber, watercress and cherry tomatoes. My mother stared without comprehension. To her salmon was a round cylinder, the shape of its tin.

Equally and fortunately, Mollie had never heard of John West. She answered politely, 'Is he your local fishmonger? This is one that Daddy caught. We've been keeping it in the freezer for a special occasion.'

Ignoring the implicit compliment, my mother ploughed on, determined to keep her end up. She felt it necessary to comment on every article of food. 'Lovely lettuce — nearly as good as the ones Norma's father sells. Homemade mayonnaise — I won't, thank you, we're not ones for salad cream.'

I wished for an earthquake, or at least that I might faint. I cast my silent father an agonised glance. He often appeared oblivious to my mother's social gaffes, or even to enjoy them, wearing a small, wry smile, although that wasn't visible today. I supposed that he was unlikely to help me because he was still sulking about the wedding not being at Northam. I was therefore agreeably surprised when he turned to Peter and said, 'Do you do a lot of fishing, Mr Peverell?'

Peter smiled. 'Not as much as I would like to. Do you fish at all?'

'Not these days. My brother and I used to do a little when we were boys. We had a useful stream at the bottom of our garden.'

My mother and I were astonished at these revelations, and so was Mollie. She spoke more warmly, 'Is your brother a teacher too, Mr Price?'

'No, Mrs Peverell, he's an accountant — very good with figures.'

We kept silent. We had no wish to spoil this slight glorification of Uncle Jim's status, he was Chief Wages Clerk at the colliery. We noticed too, the exclusion of Uncle John from my father's reminiscences.

Mollie was pressing for more information. 'I know your sister was at Margrave Hall. But your other sister — the little girl's granny — was she in service as well?'

'Not in that way. Harriet was a nurse.'

'And did she marry a doctor — as in the best romances?' Mollie was positively sunny.

My father laughed. 'Nothing so grand; she married a local government officer — now sadly dead. Of course she never worked after she was married.'

This time my mother and I did exchange glances. My father seemed to have no objection to his own wife working. But of course he was aiming to please Mollie, bless him!

She certainly seemed to be enjoying the conversation, as she went on to say, 'If you had a stream, you must have lived in the country.'

'Yes, in a very secluded place. We had to walk three miles to school.'

'How interesting! You know I always thought that Aulis had an urban background.'

'No not really, and of course when Aulis was younger, she spent a lot of time at Margrave Hall, so she knows what a country house is like.'

Mollie turned to me, unable to resist a little dart of malice. 'What were the servants' quarters like, Aulis?'

I answered simply. 'The kitchen was lovely — huge, warm and welcoming. But I spent a lot of time in the library. Lord Margrave used to show me books and maps, then I would go down to tea with Lady Margrave.'

I could feel my stock rising as Mollie spoke, 'Well this is all very interesting, it explains some of your finer qualities, Aulis. And on that subject, Mr Price, I do want to say how very much Peter and I appreciate your understanding and sacrifice in allowing Aulis to be married here. I'm sure that you would like the wedding to be from your own home but I'm afraid that farmers do have to put their animals first. We are so impressed with

Aulis for understanding the situation. It shows that she really is going to fit in beautifully at Abbotshall.'

I held my breath as my father answered, 'Thank you Mrs Peverell. Of course we were a little disappointed, but we understand perfectly. We have tried to bring Aulis up to be aware of other peoples' needs and problems and we are glad that she is appearing to do that.'

My mother and I could scarcely look at each other. After all his shouting and sulking, how could he be so two-faced! Was he making a huge self-sacrifice for me? Not entirely. I realized that Mollie's charm had completely disarmed him, as it so often did me, while she had also been softened by him. In his presence, she had even taken the trouble to say my name properly.

My parents left soon after tea. I went outside to see them off and then went in again to collect my belongings before leaving myself. Once again, I caught some of Mollie's conversation. This time she was on the phone, presumably talking to Di. 'Not too bad, darling. The father is quite reasonable — country-bred apparently. The mother's a dreadful little person. I could almost feel sorry for the girl, having a mother like that. Oops — here she comes, I'll ring you back, darling.'

I felt the usual mix of emotions which Mollie constantly provoked. There was fierce loyalty to my mother and annoyance at Mollie's attitude to her, while acknowledging to myself that my mother had brought some of it on herself by her behaviour today. There was renewed gratitude to my father for saving the family honour. Above all there was a spark of hope. If Mollie was sorry for me, could that be the beginning of some warmer feeling — could pity lead to love?

As I tried to get closer to Mollie my parents seemed to be distancing themselves from me. After the visit to Abbotshall they made little attempt to interfere or even take part in my wedding plans. I found their acquiescence quite disturbing.

'Whatever you think, dear. It's your wedding,' my mother would say.

'As long as Mrs Peverell approves, that's all that matters. That's been made very clear,' added my father.

Considering the way he had caved in to Mollie at their meeting, I thought his sarcastic tone uncalled for. But what did it matter? Fond as I was of my family their importance was fading in my mind. The Peverells were my future. So I would smile cheerfully at my father and say, 'I knew you'd understand.'

The weeks sped by. Presents were pouring in; excitement was rising. A few days before the wedding Mollie arranged a party for what she called the "Staff". This was for my benefit, as she explained. 'Aulish, I want you to meet everyone who works here. You see we are so important to them. They expect a lot from Abbotshall and they will expect a lot from you. This will be an important evening.'

I arrived early, full of goodwill. Mollie seemed in a surprisingly good mood.

'I'm so glad to see you dear; perhaps you could take this tray through for me.'

But as I obediently made my way to the lounge, she called me sharply, 'Aulish where are you going? We shall be in the sitting-room.'

'I thought it would be the front room for guests.'
'They are not quite guests, dear. They are the workers.'

My second shock was the age of the group of people who were soon sitting passively in the sagging armchairs.

Mollie, clasping my hand, led me up to an ancient gnome of a man, with a pronounced hump on one shoulder. Her voice was warm with regard. 'This is our longest serving worker, Matthew-Henry. He's been at Abbotshall over sixty years. Now, Matthew-Henry, you must learn to call this lady Mrs Martin.'

The name obviously meant more to him than it did to me. He answered wheezily, but with a touching smile. 'Ee! Mrs Peverell, I remember larnin to call you Mrs Peter. I'm glad to meet you, Miss. Master Martin be a grand young chap. We rang the church bells when he were born, just like we did for the Prince of Wales. I can't do so much these days with my rheumatiz, but Master's that good to me, 'e fetches me every day and takes me'whome. And this be my lovely wife, Daisy.' The old woman beside him was nodding and smiling like a cheerful Buddha.

Mollie continued our royal progress to the tractor driver, Jack, a serious, bespectacled old man, with a very jolly wife. Her words were as warm as her bright red coat.

'I 'ope you'll be very 'appy love. We've given you some really good sheets. Don't you be wrecking them too soon.'

Mollie hurried away from these vulgar comments. Her voice warmed up as we approached the next old man. 'And this is Mr Stoate, our other tractor driver.'

'Pleased to meet you,' he grunted, as I realized, unbelievably, that he looked exactly like a weasel with clothes on. I wondered why he was "Mr", unlike the others. This was my first experience of Mollie's unaccountable liking for this rather unsavoury man.

Mollie was obviously less comfortable with the final introduction. 'This is Sam, our cowman, the baby of the family, and his little wife.'

Sam's wife, well-dressed and well-spoken, took the lead. 'I'm Brenda. Welcome to Monks Leigh. I hope that you will be very happy.'

Once we were alone, busy clearing-up, Mollie made her feelings clear. 'That wife of Sam's is a jumped-up little piece. She works in some sort of dress-shop and thinks that that entitles her to give herself airs. "Welcome to Monks Leigh" indeed! Who does she think she is? You were far too pleasant to her. Don't lower yourself by getting friendly with her, whatever you do!'

I avoided a direct reply. 'She was certainly more pleasant than Mr Stoate. Do you know, he pinched my bottom.'

If I had hoped to shock Mollie, I was disappointed. She laughed heartily. 'Dear old Bert! He just can't keep his hands off anything in a skirt. He does it to me all the time.'

'But don't you mind? It's rather rude.'

'Oh, Aulish, don't be so prissy. He's just a workman — and a good one. He's the sort we want at Abbotshall, loyal and experienced, not college boys with new-fangled ideas, like that Sam.'

Martin, who had played little part in the evening, arrived to drive me to my hotel. He seemed mildly amused as he asked, teasingly, 'How did you enjoy being the young squire's lady, Mrs Martin?'

'Oh, Martin I thought that it was such a lovely idea, and then it was rather horrid.'

'Don't tell me it was too feudal even for you. And there was I thinking Mother had a convert.'

'I'm so confused, Martin. Why are they all so old? Your father told me that Matthew-Henry and Jack worked for your grandfather? I realise that I know very little about farming, but how can men of that age possibly run a modern farm?'

Martin was calm and judicious. 'Sam's not old. He's full of initiative and modern ideas. Jack has moved with the times and is still a skilful tractor driver. Believe it or not, Matthew-Henry, who's only part-time now, is a genius with calves. The only real passenger is Mother's favourite, Bert Stoate.'

I broke in, 'Why does she like him so much?'

Martin was dismissive. 'She has her reasons.' He moved on swiftly. 'I'm trying to change things, Aulis, and I believe that you can help me, with your brains and through your love and trust in me. If I'm strong Dad will back me up — perhaps the three of us can bring Mother round to a slightly more modern point of view.'

I was puzzled. 'But Martin, what has Mollie to do with the farm?'

His answer was enigmatic. 'We must always try to please her, Aulis. It makes life easier.'

I was dubious about this but exhilarated to know that Martin had such faith in me and had not dismissed my criticism. Yet as he drove away after our tender good-nights my uncertainty returned. Had tonight been a warning — to flee from a situation which I might not be able to handle, however strong our love might be? All the arrangements for the wedding were in place; invitations received and accepted, church and reception booked. Could or should all that be unravelled, or was I merely suffering from pre-wedding nerves?

Chapter Seven
The Wedding

'You've had some lovely presents, Aulis,' commented my mother. 'Just think, if you'd suddenly changed your mind, they would all have had to be sent back, with a note to explain why.'

Was she giving me a chance, even then, to escape? No, my mother wasn't so subtle, and she was very keen on my marriage! Anyway, I had stayed firm. Here we were, the night before my wedding, gathered for dinner at The Talbot Arms, Manley's one large hotel, where tomorrow's reception was to be held. Not for me the wild excesses of a modern hen-night. It was just me and "my people" as Mollie called them — my parents, Hector and Norma and Marie.

'I think it'll be all right here, won't it? At least it'll be warm and cosy.' My mother looked round approvingly at the oak panelling and open fires. 'It was very kind of Mrs Peverell, offering to have a marquee on her lawn, but it would have been a bit cold in this weather, wouldn't it?'

No one replied to her well-meant prattle. Few would have guessed that we were preparing for a joyous event. The atmosphere was thick with anxiety, resentment and sheer nervousness. The anxiety came mainly from Norma and Marie, worrying about their children, left with their respective maternal grandmothers.

'At least your three have their daddy with them, as Ken's not coming till tomorrow.' Norma spoke with heavy emphasis.

Marie was not reassured. 'Yes, but it's Jonathan I'm worried about. Will he take a bottle — he's never had one before? At least it'll be full of my own milk.'

'How do you manage that? Not that I really like breast-feeding.' My mother, curious despite herself about this curious procedure.

'I have a little breast pump. You hold it like this...'

As her clear voice carried across the room and my father's lips tightened in disapproval Norma hastily intervened. 'OK, we get the picture, and that's one worry I don't have. I think Edward will be fine — that's the joy of bottle feeding. It's Helen I'm more worried about. She was so upset when we told her she couldn't come to Aunt Aulis' wedding.'

Hector, stiff with resentment, voiced his grievance. 'I see no reason why she shouldn't be here. She and Marie's Katie would have made a perfect pair of flower girls. They should all be here. I've never heard of children being excluded from a wedding — it's not a funeral. I notice his niece and nephew are not excluded, nor that silly little Gillian.'

My father spoke sharply to him. 'That's unfair, Hector. Gillian is representing our family.'

Then my mother rushed in to protect me as she had tried to do throughout these disagreements. 'You see, Hector, Gillian is eight and so is little Lucy. We just felt... I mean Aulis thought... everyone said... children under five can be a bit difficult in church and that.'

Norma found this too hard to take, especially from my mother. 'Come on, Mum, you know that you think children under five are perfect. What you mean is that Mrs God Almighty Peverell decided they shouldn't be there. And as Aulis would jump off a pier if that woman told her to, we all had to agree, whatever the inconvenience or distress.'

On our visit to Abbotshall to view the presents Mollie had immediately alienated Norma by a comment on that very subject of Edward's feeding. 'Your baby won't miss you much, will he? I gather you're not feeding him yourself.'

Her reception of Marie had been very different. 'Oh, darling, I hope you're not dreadfully sore without baby. If only Aulish had reminded me earlier I'd have made some arrangement for you to bring him. We all adored Jonathan when you came before. You're such a good little mother.'

Now a moment of nervous silence followed Norma's outburst. Then my mother and Marie both started to speak, Marie indignant in my defence, my mother trying to calm things down. They were brought to a halt by my father, speaking quietly but firmly, every inch the headmaster that he had never been.' Aulis is to be married tomorrow. Whatever our personal views about this or anyone connected with it, could we please try to keep this last evening pleasant for her?'

My mother lightened the tone. 'Goodness, Bill, you're off on your Assembly talk again. "Last evening" indeed! You make it sound as if she's going to be sacrificed.'

'Iphigenia at the altar' suggested Hector, pedantic as ever.

Amid the general laughter Marie asked, 'Is it true, Mrs Price, as Aulis told us at school, that but for you she would have been called Iphigenia?'

My mother was indignant. 'Yes, can you imagine! I wasn't having a daughter called Iffy. It was bad enough when the old aunts would call her Owl, or even worse, Little Owl. It made her sound like something out of Enid Blyton! I tried to call her Mary but then she went all classical like her dad and decided that she liked Aulis.'

Everyone enjoyed this and my mother's common sense seemed to change the spirit of the evening which became reasonably jolly. Dad called us to order quite early. 'Come on now, beauty sleep for everyone.'

I was sharing a room with Marie, whose first concern was to express milk, pouring it carefully into little bottles. She sighed with satisfaction. 'There, that's a nice lot. Now if Jonathan can go through the night so can I. Just think, Aulis, you could be doing this in less than a year. I do hope you conceive quickly!'

'So do I! It could be tomorrow night, Marie. I so want it to be! I can't wait to hear my own baby crying for my breast. I can't wait to be married.' And as I fell asleep my loins yearned for Martin.

Saturday dawned crisp and clear. 'A perfect day for an autumn wedding,' declared my mother.

The morning flew by. Hairdresser, make-up, sandwiches. Marie worked on me while Norma took charge of my mother's preparations. Hector dashed about collecting flowers, delivering buttonholes and bouquets to Abbotshall, where Lucy and Gillian were to dress. My father read Cicero. I was glad to see him enjoying himself but just hoped that he wasn't preparing a Ciceronian speech, casting Mollie as Catiline, the arch-villain. Anyway, he was Dad and would do what he wanted.

Finally, Marie, blooming in her own forest-green gown, slipped the dress of shining cream brocade over my head, fastened the train around my waist and anchored Mollie's veil to my head with a small hidden comb. She stood back to survey her handiwork. 'Aulis, you look wonderful. Your hair, piled up in coils like that gives the veil height and shape, so that it hangs in stiff, graceful folds, a shimmering sheet of lace. A fussy head-dress would have ruined it. Just look at yourself!'

As I gazed in wonder at my own reflection exclamations of admiration announced the arrival of my family. Norma laid a restraining hand on my mother. 'No, Mum, you mustn't hug Aulis, you'll both get crumpled.'

'Mrs Price, you look amazing.'

Marie's comment was well-deserved. My mother was unusually well turned out. She wore a mid-blue grosgrain dress with a matching coat which swung out to flatter her figure. A hat of lavender coloured petals and long lavender silk gloves completed her ensemble. I had a happy thought. 'Mum, you look just like the Queen Mother.'

'It's all thanks to Norma,' laughed my mother, pleased and flattered. 'She's spent more time on me than on herself.'

'Let's face it, it would have been labour in vain with me,' said Norma cheerfully. 'I'm still lumpy from the baby. This horrible oatmeal tweed suit is my mother's and this dreary brown hat is the only one that would match it. I look like a typical don's wife. Never mind, that's perfectly respectable.'

We all laughed with her as she was swept off by a fussing Hector, anxious to be at the church in good time for his duties. 'Come on, Norma, Aunt Sarah can't be ushed without an usher.'

Next came the car for my mother and Marie, which was also to call at Abbotshall for the two little girls.

There was no escape now. I was alone with my father. He gave me a long questioning look as he used to when I had some schoolgirl fault to confess. He spoke, seriously but kindly. 'Now, Aulis, can I remind you that it's still not too late to get out of this marriage — I will handle everything if that's what you want to do.'

For a passing moment I had a wild desire to say, 'Yes, Dad — take me back to the Loeb editions and the Cicero quotes — to the black kettle on the fire and the warm, uncomplicated loving that you gave me.' Instead, I said, 'Don't be silly, Dad. I can't wait to marry Martin. And Mum would be so disappointed!'

He remained serious. 'Are you sure it's not just the grandeur, or what you perceive as grandeur, that you want? I know that, like me, you've never been quite satisfied with the workaday world, but in reality, you'll find that Martin's world is very workaday.'

'I know that, Dad. I do love the grandeur, as you call it, it's that ambience that has shaped Martin himself, but I would love Martin without that. Abbotshall is a bonus for me — but it's Martin who matters.'

My father seemed satisfied, taking refuge in a droll comment. 'I blame our Sarah, all those visits to Margrave when you were a little girl, she spoiled you for life with the likes of us.'

Then, even as he picked up his top-hat to go, another thought struck him. 'Good heavens, Aulis, you're not marrying him to get away from teaching, are you? Now that I could understand.'

Temporarily diverted from my own concerns, I was surprised. 'But Dad, I thought that you loved teaching.'

He laughed ruefully. 'All I knew was that it was certainly better than the alternative — going down the pit with your Uncle John. But it's different for you, you have a good degree, you could do anything.'

'Dad, all I want to do is to marry Martin, and I'd like to do that today.'

He suddenly noticed the time. 'Goodness, Aulis, you're right. The car must be waiting.'

Our driver obliged by putting his foot down and we were soon at the church. The bridesmaids were at the door, the little girls, in cream dresses that matched mine, dancing with excitement, Marie, tall and serious, behind them. The vicar, in his cream and gold cope (another "nonsense" to Mollie) led us up the aisle.

Through my mist of nervous happiness, I saw the scene set out like a great panoramic tapestry. Certain images stood out, to stay forever in my memory. First, of course, Mollie, resplendent in turquoise, with a wonderful hat swathed in velvet. Peter, slim and elegant in his tails, his white hair shining. Diana's dreary olive-green was redeemed by a smart fur hat. Aunt Emily was a little witch in a hideous steel-grey cloak. Then there was the reassuring sight of "my side". The broad shoulders of Uncle Jim, the aunts, Sarah and Harriet, in almost identical Harella tweeds, "quality without ostentation" they would say. Looking across the pews I glimpsed the bright red coat of Mrs Jack Tractor-Driver and, twinkling from the back row, the sweet smile of Matthew-Henry.

Then I saw Martin, shining with happiness, looking as if he'd been polished. All else paled as he turned to welcome me, his hand outstretched. After that I saw nothing but the love in his eyes. I walked towards it like a ship going into harbour.

We passed through the ceremony in a glorious haze, shivering with joy as the priestly stole bound our hands together.

In the vestry the first shadow fell on the ceremony. As we lined up for our triumphal march down the aisle, my father courteously offered his arm to Mollie. To everyone's surprise she hesitated, speaking in her sweetest accents. 'Oh dear, Mr Price, do we have to follow this vulgar custom? It's really only for village people, don't you think?'

There was a breathless silence, as we waited to see if my father would succumb to the charm, as before, or have an explosion. Neither proved necessary. Before he could make any reply, Peter Peverell had seized my mother's arm and was cheerfully leading her forward.

Mollie and my father were forced to follow them.

My spirits lifted again with Purcell's glorious Airs, as Martin beamed his way out, clasping my hand until the bones ached. Everyone was smiling at us, some with tears in their eyes, obviously touched by the radiance we exuded.

As we formed up in the receiving line at the reception, I was acutely aware of the curled lip of contempt with which Mollie prepared to meet my relations. One of the first was Aunt Sarah. I managed to catch their exchange. Mollie began smoothly. 'I believe that you knew the Margraves?'

'Yes, they were my dearest friends,' Aunt Sarah replied proudly.

Now Mollie thought that she would put the knife in. 'I assume that you worked for them.'

Aunt Sarah's tone was even prouder as she saw the implied insult. 'Yes, I had that honour. I started in the scullery and ended up running their household. Don't worry, Mrs Peverell, Aulis comes of good strong stock, physically and mentally. There are no skeletons in our cupboard.'

I'm sure that Aunt Sarah was just making conversation. So why did Mollie go parchment white, mutter some pleasantry and move hastily to greet the next person, in much friendlier vein?

I put the mystery aside as the reception flew by. I could hear my mother talking away to cover my father's taciturnity. Marie flew about, looking after Lucy and Gillian and chatting to everyone in her cheerful way. Telegrams were read, cake cut, speeches delivered. Martin's contained several references to "my wife", bringing cheers, or at least smiles, from everyone except Mollie. Dad's was masterly, short and to the point, the Ciceronian phrases adding polish. Geraint Llewellyn was a perfectly adequate best man. Then Marie tapped me on the shoulder. It was time to change for "going away".

As we moved towards the stairs, Mollie, accompanied by Aunt Emily, detained me. My heart lifted as, clasping my hand, she spoke in her most charming tone. 'Emily and I just wanted you to know that we thought that your veil and dress were lovely.'

Marie, always quicker than me, seeing the sting in the remark, tried to draw it with her reply, 'You're so right, Mrs Peverell. Didn't Aulis look splendid — really beautiful — I heard people say.'

Mollie was not to be defeated, the deprecating little laugh again. 'Well, it's a pity she didn't tell us that she had no tiara or suitable head-dress. I'm sure we could have lent her something. But I'm sure that her people thought that she looked very nice. The clothes do make the man, or woman, don't they?'

My lips were trembling as Marie hustled me away. She was soon slipping me into my pale blue dress and jacket of fine boucle wool. I had a navy-blue straw boater, with navy blue shoes, handbag and gloves, all in soft leather. Martin was waiting downstairs in his new grey suit. Geraint, who was to drive us to catch our plane, was honking impatiently on the drive. Everyone crowded round, hugging and kissing us. My parents, Peter Peverell, Norma and Hector, Di, Lucy and Gillian, unknown cousins of Martin's, Uncle Jim, Aunts Sarah and Harriet, even Aunt Emily.

I searched the crowd for Mollie. Then across the sea of faces I found myself looking straight at her. Wearing her fox's mask face, she raised her right hand in a slight gesture of farewell. Rejected, I could barely see through my tears as Martin pushed me into the car. In his hurry he caught his cufflinks in the door and took a few minutes to untangle himself, long enough for me to hear Norma's voice, loud and clear, her Northam accent exaggerated by anger.

'You unmitigated bitch. You must know that she adores you, though God knows why. How could you treat her like that on her wedding day!'

Chapter Eight
The Honeymoon

'Oh, Martin, isn't it super? Look at the flowers and the champagne. And what a big bed! Everything's just like they promised in *Brides' Monthly*.

We had arrived in Majorca at three a.m., and I was rejoicing over my coup — the honeymoon I had found and booked.

Martin, busy undressing, came over to hug me. 'Oh, Aulis, you are an adorable baby — you're like a friendly golden puppy. But hurry up, I want to use this magnificent bed, and I don't mean for sleeping!'

'Goodness, whatever else have you in mind?' I joked to cover the fear and nervousness which accompanied my excitement.

Mine was almost the last generation to whom marriage would happen without previous cohabitation. Of course this was the 1960s and sexual mores were far more liberal than they had been, though not as liberal as today's commentators claim. Martin and I had done the "heavy petting" which was generally acceptable. We had lain naked in each other's arms, stroking and fondling, but nothing more. My mother's advice had been unusually firm. 'You look after yourself. We don't want any little bundles here. Make sure that you never go the whole way before you're safely married, or no decent man will look at you again!'

I hated her vulgarity but shared the sentiment. So I had guarded the jewel of my virginity, small wonder that yielding it up seemed a massive step in my life.

I had bought a most delectable nightdress for the occasion, a white silk shift overlaid with chiffon frills bordered the low cleavage and pink satin ribbons nestled at its heart.

As I came out of the bathroom, I paused for dramatic effect to allow Martin to admire this creation. His compliment was swift. 'It's lovely, Aulis, but I can't wait to get it off you. Put that light out, and come here!'

In two minutes, I was on the bed, naked, and Martin was kissing my breasts and belly.

Then he was on top of me, his thighs straddling mine. He was panting. 'Oh, Aulis, I can't wait — I've been waiting all damned day. I'm desperate for you.'

'And I for you,' I gasped, as I pressed myself towards him. I just caught a glimpse of his penis, huge and red, as he entered me. Then I screamed as it tore my hymen. The thrusting and pumping went on, but not for long. I felt the gush of semen as his body relaxed against mine. He withdrew, as quickly as he had entered. Then he saw the blood on his penis and the tears on my cheeks.

He was instantly contrite. 'Oh, my darling, what have I done? Have I hurt you? I wanted you so much, and I didn't realise. I've never had a virgin before.'

Not quite registering the final sentence I clung to him, sobbing like the baby to whom he'd compared me.

'I'm sorry — it was just the shock. I know I'll come to like it, but it did hurt.'

'Well, it's not going to hurt like that again, is it? And we're well and truly married now.'

I revived a little. 'Yes, I suppose it can't be annulled now can it — you know, like Katherine of Aragon?'

Martin laughed. 'That's my Aulis; crying with pain, yet still able to produce a historical allusion. Your dad would be proud of you! Now let me rock and cuddle you to sleep and we'll have some more fun in the morning. You know, I think it's like riding a horse, you fall off and then get up and mount again!'

I sniffed. 'I've never ridden a horse either.'

Martin seemed to find this very funny. 'You poor little deprived thing. But I'm sure you've ridden a bike — same principle. By the way, Aulis, do you want a baby?'

'You know that I do, more than anything.'

'Well unless we give you A I like the cows I'm afraid this is the only way of getting one.'

I thought that was funny and Martin finally managed to soothe me to rest and quietness. He was soon fast asleep but I lay sleepless, my inside desperately sore. No Victorian maiden could have spent a more miserable wedding night. I had felt none of the anticipated pleasure in our union. Was I frigid — was it always going to be like this? Martin knew that I was a virgin, why did he seem so surprised. Who were these non-virgins whom he had "had"? Once again, the age-difference between us became apparent. Common sense should have told me that a man of his age might be presumed to have had some sexual experience, but I was still shocked by the casual way he'd referred to it. I heard my mother again. 'You see it's different for a man, he doesn't have anything to unlock.'

Then a more cheering idea dawned. Perhaps the mess had produced our honeymoon baby.

Another legend prevalent at the time was that you were more likely to get a baby if you didn't enjoy the process of its production. With that comforting thought I finally fell asleep.

I slept long and sound, waking to the delicious smell of coffee and hot croissants. Martin was arranging everything at a table for two, close to the patio doors, which were open, so that we could enjoy the glorious sunshine.

He greeted me warmly. 'Come on, darling. This is the life, isn't it? Let's have a long leisurely breakfast. I've given them a large tip so that they won't be worrying about servicing the room. They're used to honeymooners.'

I put on a warm bath-robe against the slight Mediterranean chill and settled at the table. I was hungry and the fragrant foreign cheese and slivers of Parma ham looked delicious. Martin encouraged me. 'Now eat your breakfast like a good girl — surely you haven't got morning sickness yet?'

We both giggled. Martin's tone changed. 'But don't take too long. God, Aulis, you're beautiful — I want you so much. It's even better than I imagined. Let's go back to bed after breakfast.'

I was still apprehensive so I used my first excuse. 'Are you sure they won't want to service the room?'

Martin sighed. 'I've told you I've fixed all that up! We're not in some B & B at Blackpool you know.'

'I wouldn't know! I've never been to Blackpool nor to a B & B.'

'Don't be so touchy! Your hormones can't have started going funny yet.'

I hated this bickering, so I told him the truth. 'Martin, I'm still sore.'

'Oh, that'll soon pass off. Mother said that might happen if you were still a virgin. But it'll be better this time. I was so eager last night that I was careless. But remember the bike and the horse!'

The resentment I felt at the reference to his mother was dispelled by Martin's silly little jokes and his obvious desire for me.

It was better this time. Martin prepared me so well that I was crying out for him. Yet my muscles still contracted with fear as he entered. Conscious of my resistance, when he had climaxed and withdrawn, he asked wistfully, 'Do you think that you'll get to like it, because I want to do it again and again with you?'

I was so glad that I was giving him pleasure that I determined to control my apprehension. 'Yes of course I will — it's the bedrock of marriage, isn't it? But, you know, it's all linked up with us really getting to know each other. We got engaged so quickly and since then it's just been one long argument about wedding arrangements. Martin, I'm not just scared of sex, I'm scared of being married — it's just you and me now, isn't it?'

Martin immediately picked up my thought. 'Yes, that's what's so great. We have so much to learn about each other. Let's use this precious time to do that.'

So we did — we laughed and talked and walked and kissed. We discovered that we found the same things funny, liked and disliked the same foods and shared prejudices which we could never have revealed to anyone else. Martin was a wonderful mimic and reduced me to helpless giggles by conducting an imaginary conversation between Aunt Emily and Hector on the bad manners of the younger generation.

We found great pleasure in going over all the details of our wedding. Identifying the guests for each other, what they had said, what they had worn. I was delighted to find that, unlike most men, my father for example, Martin took a real interest in clothes. He commented, 'Your mother looked lovely, Aulis, the colours and style she chose were just right for her.'

Although I was pleased, I felt that credit must be paid where it was due. 'I expect Norma helped her choose. I don't think my mother has much sense of style.'

Martin was mildly indignant. 'I don't know why you're so disparaging about your mother. I really like her. She's lively and she's fun.'

'He's just like Marie,' I thought. 'Why does everyone, except me, like my mother?'

Martin was continuing, 'I'll tell you one thing I did notice, Aulis, your mother seems to have no relations of her own, there were none at the wedding.'

I felt slightly guilty. 'She only has one old aunt — her father's sister, Elsie. She lives in South Wales, it was a long way for her to come.'

Martin seemed satisfied. 'Your dad's got plenty of family though. Was the broad-shouldered man with your Aunt Sarah the accountant uncle?'

'Yes, Uncle Jim, but Dad was exaggerating when he called him an accountant — he was really Chief Wages Clerk at the Colliery.'

Martin found this very amusing. 'I knew your dad was clever. When talking to my mother always make a wages clerk into an accountant. Then we'll all die happier! And I suppose the miner uncle wasn't there at all.'

I was defensive. 'We did ask them, but they're old, they don't drive, and they would have found it difficult to come.'

Martin laughed. 'What you mean is they wouldn't have been particularly welcome. You are a snob, Aulis, but you seem to have got the measure of my mother — another reason why you and I will get on fine.'

It was my turn now. 'Well, what about your family? Those cousins of your father's were rather odd.'

Martin laughed again. 'Almost the last Peverells left standing, or at least willing to encounter Mother. Their father was Dad's first cousin. They've always been strange — pots of money though.'

I remembered another oddity. 'And who was that vast woman in a beautiful striped silk dress? There must have been yards of material in it.'

'Oh, that was Ida Ripley — her husband Tom, now his grandmother was a Peverell — more than that I don't know. Ida's all right, though Mother's not too keen on her.'

Resisting the temptation to ask if Mollie actually liked anyone, I continued, 'You don't have many relations do you, Martin, not close ones anyway?'

'No, not nearly as many as you.' Martin mused. 'Dad was an only child and there's just Mother and Aunt Emily.'

I decided to take advantage of this thoughtful conversation and Martin's apparent willingness to make critical comments about his mother. I asked him the question that was beginning to worry me. 'Martin, tell me about Abbotshall?'

He took the question at its face value. 'All right: it's a too-large farmhouse, somewhere in Staffordshire, with a farm which my father's family have farmed for the last 200 years, getting poorer and smaller all the time.'

'What do you mean? Your father's not particularly short, nor are you.'

'I didn't mean that, silly! I meant the families are getting smaller, as we've just noticed.'

I pondered for a moment. 'Yes, that's interesting. Your mother's so fond of children, why didn't she have more?'

He was suddenly sober. 'My dear Aulis, I don't advise you to ask her. If you've got the guts to do so I certainly haven't. My concern is to expand the family — right now!'

In two minutes, we were locked together again, I as willing as he was, and that was the end of our conversation about Abbotshall.

Our lovemaking got better and better. About halfway through our stay I had my first orgasm — crying out with genuine pleasure. Martin was pleased too, but sounded a note of caution. 'That's lovely, darling, but don't get too excited — it might not be good for the baby. He's just getting settled in.'

Both of us were convinced that we had conceived our first beloved child. We saw him in the stars shining over the deep blue sea and felt him in the gentle breeze of morning. Then, ten days into our honeymoon, our idyll came to an abrupt end. Martin found me crying into my pillow.

'Sweetheart, what's wrong?'

'I've got the curse.'

'What — I don't understand.'

Misery made me sharp. 'My period's come.'

My disappointment was as nothing compared with Martin's disbelief and indignation. He stormed up and down the room. 'I told you to take care! I won't be able to spend all this time on you at home, you know. Mother only agreed to the two weeks so that you could get pregnant — and now you haven't!'

I was dumbfounded by Martin's attitude. But I was determined to hurt him too, flinging his words back at him. 'So you don't want me at all! I'm just the vessel for the Abbotshall line and your mother's obsession. I'm good enough for that, am I, despite my lowly origins? You may find that nobody uses me as a dumping ground. Now I want to mourn my baby.'

Martin was immediately on his knees, cradling me. 'Oh, Aulis, I didn't mean it like that. It's just Mother, as you say, but it's you I care about. Let's grieve together for our baby!'

So we did, lying in each other's arms and restoring our love. I was to get used to these mood-swings of Martin's and the terrible power which Mollie exerted over him. I also knew what he meant — I was going home a failure. If I couldn't conceive here, what chance would there be at Abbotshall. I was already afraid of Abbotshall

— the one subject that we had never really discussed. It lay between us like a great boulder.

Mollie met us at Stafford Station on a freezing November Sunday afternoon, the rain falling like pellets of ice. She was as unruffled and elegant as ever. She explained Peter's absence. 'Pa wanted to come but he'd fallen asleep by the fire and I hadn't the heart to wake the dear old chap. These last two weeks have exhausted him; he's too old to be milking at six o'clock every morning. Never mind, the job's done now.'

I wasn't sure whether she was referring to Peter's efforts or my presumed pregnancy. I must have imagined her surreptitious glances at my waist — not even Mollie could think that I would show anything yet. But the subject was certainly on her mind as she turned to greet me. 'Well, Aulish, you've certainly lost your looks. Still, I'm sure it's in a good cause. Not being sick yet, are you?'

Martin shot in to my defence. 'Really, Ma, you sound like some village witch.'

I smiled to myself. Martin knew how to hit where it hurt. The vulgar title always annoyed her and the reference to Mollie's hated "village" customs dealt her a double blow. For the rest of the journey, she drove in an offended silence.

It was better when we reached Abbotshall Cottage and the delicious tea she had prepared.

Peter, refreshed by his sleep, chatted away cheerfully and even seemed mildly interested in hearing about Majorca. As the evening wore on, I caught Martin's eye, with a hint that we might go home to Abbotshall. Mollie pressed us to stay. 'Why not spend the night here? Then you can start fresh in the morning.'

Martin looked inclined to agree but I stepped in swiftly. 'No thank you. We must begin as we mean to go on, and not put on you.'

Mollie was amused. 'Listen to Miss Independence — we'll see how long that lasts. Well, if you must go, everything's ready for you. I've made up the Aga and put a bottle in your bed. So off with you — see you in the morning.'

The cottage door closed on warmth and light. Abbotshall loomed ahead of us, its sharp gables etched against the sky, its windows blank and dark, like witless eyes. We humped our cases up the drive and as Martin pushed open the side door, the dank chill of a largely unheated, empty house soaked into our bones. I felt a brief regret for the cosiness of the cottage.

'Come on,' Martin was busy in the kitchen. 'Look, you lift the lids of the Aga, hang over the hotplates and you'll get warm.'

I followed his example and the warmth flooded over us. Martin was looking around like an excited child. 'Look, here's a tray — tea-things and a plate of digestive biscuits — my favourite. Mother really is a brick! You make the tea while I run upstairs to get the bottle out of the bed, then we can refill it to go up. We'll undress in front of the Aga so that we don't lose heat. You'll need something warm on in bed though — have you got anything?'

'Yes, I brought all my clothes over before the wedding so there are plenty of thick jumpers in the drawers upstairs. They're not very romantic though.'

'Ah well there'll be no time for romance tonight, with my six o'clock start, but don't worry, we'll soon be at it again — we still need that baby, don't we?'

Kissing me quickly on the cheek he clattered cheerfully up the back stairs for the bottle.

As I filled the heavy Aga kettle I dissected his words, why did he say need the baby, not want it? Could we not be complete without it, or was it to be some sort of offering to this house and to his mother? I cursed my linguistic education and busied myself arranging cups and plates.

Tea and biscuits duly consumed, we were soon undressed, hurrying upstairs and into a reasonably warm bed. Through all this Martin barely spoke, leave alone touched me. I thought longingly of Majorca, where he couldn't keep his hands off me. Once in bed he softened a little, taking me in his arms for a cuddle, but as I moved against him, he detached himself, gently but firmly. 'No, Aulis, I've told you, I have to be up at six. I'm back at work now. I told you there wouldn't be so much time once we got home. Now you get to sleep like a good girl, so that you're strong and rested, ready to make babies.'

I was hurt and angry and somewhat repelled by his last phrase. I didn't mind not making love, what I did

112

mind was Martin's coldness and distance. I knew that he was talking nonsense, very few people became pregnant so quickly, loads of men with tiring, exacting jobs had sex frequently. But I also knew that I was no longer living in the logical world, but in a self-governing state where myth and prejudice ruled. Abbotshall.

Yet I had chosen this life — there was no turning back. Jobless, childless, what on earth was I meant to do now that my honeymoon was over?

Chapter Nine
The First Year

When I woke next morning, I had no problem answering that question. Gloom had gone, and I had an exciting if awe-inspiring task — to run the house and look after Martin.

Shocked by the bone-coldness of Abbotshall I had a tingling hot bath, dressed in several layers and rushed down to the ever-comforting Aga. The first ritual of the day was to stoke it — a horrible job which involved carrying a shovelful of hot ashes outside, which the wind then blew back in one's face. Would I have to do this for the next fifty years? Did that matter if I was doing it for Martin?

My happiness increased when Martin came in, for he was his old, sweet self; ready to enjoy his breakfast, which was sizzling merrily on the hotplate. 'Goodness, Aulis, how good that looks — bacon, sausages and eggs — I can see you're going to spoil me. And Oh, Aulis, how good you look, I could eat you!'

I laughed with joy. 'Martin, you really must be in love. These are my old ski-pants and I bet I've got Aga dust in my eyebrows.'

'Yes, you have and it's utterly sweet.' He took me in his arms and I felt his manhood hard against me.

I hastened to move the frying pan. 'Be careful — we mustn't let the food burn.'

Reluctantly he released me. 'Aulis, do you think we could do it quickly — after breakfast?'

I was amused to see that his firmness of last night hadn't lasted, as I reminded him. 'No, Martin! Remember, you're back at work now. And your mother or anyone might walk in.'

'I suppose you're right. But isn't it wonderful to want each other so much?'

I agreed fervently, snuggling up to him, and then we returned to bacon and eggs and reality.

Once Martin had gone out again, I washed up, tidied and then sat by the table, wondering what to do next. All my life up to now had been dictated by timetables, at school and university, as pupil and teacher, I had always known what I was to do and when. I would now have to organise my own time and prepared to do so with the help of a shiny new exercise book which I'd pinched from school.

But even as I gazed at its pristine pages I heard Mollie's rounded vowels. I leapt up, rushing to busy myself at the sink and was vaguely waving a washing-up mop as my mother-in-law walked in, apologising as she came. 'I'm so sorry, Mrs Martin. It was so lovely to see you again yesterday that I quite forgot to tell you that Barbara was coming this morning.'

I realized at once, from the use of my new title, that Barbara was, in Mollie's parlance, a servant. Then I saw, peeping round Mollie's shoulder, the most vivid little woman. Dark eyes twinkled beneath well-marked brows; thick black hair framed her face with springy curls, while her cheeks shone like rosy apples. With her head slightly cocked on one side, she was like a plump, friendly robin.

Mollie, at her most gracious, hastened to introduce us. 'Mrs Martin, this is Barbara. She's going to help you, three mornings a week, we thought. Barbara has been a good friend to the family ever since she married Tom, who also used to work for us.

"Barbara, this is Mrs Martin, our new little daughter-in-law. She's not very experienced in the house so I'm sure you'll help her as much as you can. Now I'm going to leave you two so that you can get on.'

And with her deprecating little laugh, Mollie was off.

Once we had heard the back door close, Barbara visibly relaxed, taking off her coat and speaking cheerfully. 'Now the old lady's gone, let's have a cup of tea and you can tell me what you want me to do. You sit down, love, and I'll make the tea. You've just come back from your honeymoon and if your Martin's anything like my Tom, ever likely you're tired out.'

Enjoying the description of Mollie, which put her in a box like an ordinary person, I bore cheerfully with the innuendo, and my cheerfulness increased as Barbara planned the cleaning. She outlined all the necessary jobs and suggested that I could make a list and a timetable in my lovely exercise book, while she washed the kitchen floor.' 'I'll guarantee you,' Barbara nodded sagely, 'First thing the old lady'll look at, is this floor — once she's seen it's been done, she'll go no further, and you'll have made a good impression.'

The morning flashed by, to good effect. Furniture shone, tiles gleamed and a happy atmosphere prevailed. Barbara chatted as hard and fast as she worked. By noon I knew that she had married at seventeen and been a mother within the year. She had four sons. All had had dramatic births, vividly described by Barbara. The last one, Benedict, had been particularly difficult, as Barbara explained. 'I had to go in the ambulance to Burton with him half hanging out. I often wonder if that's why he's... you know... queer... I mean... he has boyfriends. I don't mean he's handicapped or anything — thank God all my children are perfectly normal... not like some poor folks. You can have money and all that, but if your children's not right it doesn't help.'

I didn't attach any significance to Barbara's comments at the time but much later I remembered them. For the moment I just enjoyed the chat and looked forward to Wednesday when the fascinating saga could be resumed and expanded.

Mollie was pleased when she came to inspect. The kitchen floor won her immediate approval, as Barbara had predicted. Being Mollie, she had to sound a word of warning. 'You must be careful what you say to Barbara, you know. Never forget that she is a servant. There's always the danger that with your background you might not know how to treat these people.'

The contemptuous tone riled me as I thought of Aunt Sarah, but I answered blandly, careful to curb any enthusiasm I might have shown for Barbara. 'Of course; she's just here to do the work. I'm hardly likely to look to her for a deep personal relationship.'

Mollie seemed satisfied, if a trifle baffled. 'You are amusing, darling, but I can see that you know what I mean. Well done!'

I basked in the rosy glow of her approval.

Nevertheless, Barbara's visits became high spots in my week, breaking the loneliness of my days. In the afternoons, when she had gone home, isolation would strike. On one of these days, a few weeks into my marriage, I decided to explore the second floor at Abbotshall, where I had never yet been.

At the top of the front stairs was a small square landing, with rooms either side. The one on the right was carpeted and furnished with a large double bed and an immense mahogany dower chest. Tiptoeing in, though I didn't quite know why, I cautiously lifted its lid. I was mildly disappointed to find that it contained nothing but clothes and linen. Here were old-fashioned heavy white sheets, gleaming damask tablecloths — surely, we could use these. Then I saw that they were all embroidered with initials, E.P. or E. Potts or just Emily. Potts was Mollie's rather undistinguished maiden name. Had I stumbled upon Aunt Emily's bottom drawer? If so, why was it here, like this? I felt ashamed and embarrassed, as if I had unwittingly done something rather grubby. Moving hastily out of the room I saw that there were bolts on the inside of the door. Who would Aunt Emily need to shut out?

I went into the room on the left, also carpeted and furnished with a single bed and small table. I remembered that Lucy slept here when she stayed at Abbotshall. I saw that there were bolts on the inside of this door too and an amusing message fixed to the outside. This room belongs to Lucy Diana Llewellyn. Please note that she bolts the door when she goes to bed. They all seemed very security conscious, against what or whom were they bolting their doors?

I continued along the long corridor that ran the length of the house. The two big front attics were full of junk and dead birds had fallen down the chimneys. But I was more interested in the plaster fallen from the ceiling, exposing some broken joists and revealing patches of blue sky So this was one of Abbotshall's secrets, the grandeur downstairs and this above. A painted face diverting attention from a crumbling body. I remembered how Mollie had avoided showing the attics to my mother. Just as well, I thought, or my parents would have been even more worried about my future,

The first back attic contained hundreds of apples, lying on slatted wooden shelves, their fragrance greeting me as I opened the door. The second remained unyielding as I turned its brass knob. It was locked!

Mad thoughts of *Jane Eyre* flashed through my mind and I screamed as a hand fell on my shoulder. Mollie's voice had never sounded sweeter. 'Were you looking for something?'

Fear and relief made me bold. 'Just getting to know my new home, and wondering why it has a locked door.'

Her tone was remarkably mild, probably as apologetic as she could get. 'Yes, I suppose I should have brought you up here and explained everything. You need to know about the apples — Martin loves a baked apple.'

I persisted. 'But what's in this room?'

'Certain private things — I'm quite happy to show you.' Inserting a large old-fashioned key in the lock she flung open the door. The room was filled with trunks and boxes. a lacrosse stick was propped in a corner. On the floor were stacks of girls' books, of the Angela Brazil type. The most attractive object was a baby's crib. Decorated with blue organdie hangings it looked like an illustration from a fairy tale, a bed for an infant prince. I assumed that it had been Martin's. I softened as I saw Mollie move as if to protect it and her hand caress it as she talked, still apologetic. 'You see if the room is kept locked nothing can be removed and we won't have any unpleasantness.'

'You mean you don't trust me.'

'Oh, Aulish, don't be so dramatic. It just keeps things in order. I must remember to tell you when I'm coming up for something though. That was thoughtless of me. Now let's go down and have a nice cup of tea. It's freezing up here.'

The arm around my shoulder, the warmth of her tone, cheered and mollified me. But the locked room was still a sore point — another suggestion that I didn't belong.

Mollie seemed unusually aware of my feelings. As we enjoyed our tea, she pressed my hand. 'It's mostly old things of Di's up there, and mementoes of their childhood. You'll soon understand when you have your own babies.'

I smiled weakly, aware of the blood even now pouring out of me. Yet again I was going to disappoint them all.

Mollie was continuing, her tone sharper now. 'You're very nervous, aren't you, Aulish. The way you jumped and screamed up there. Whoever did you think it was?'

She seemed to be putting me in the wrong, most unfairly, I thought. So I answered robustly. 'I didn't know — it could have been an intruder. You don't expect to find people wandering round your house.'

Mollie laughed. 'Oh, my dear! How fanciful you are, it's all those books you read. We don't have intruders at Abbotshall. And I'm not people and this is hardly your house. I suppose your people are used to locking doors and peeping through lace curtains. This is the country, Aulish.'

121

She had done one of her swift changes of mood again and also been rather offensive. Much as I wanted to adopt Mollie's ways, I hated her slurs on my family. I couldn't let them go over my head, as Martin advised, so I had to answer, 'We don't have lace curtains, and I was frightened.'

Mollie sighed. 'It's all about you, isn't it, Aulish — how you feel? Try to think a little more about others, dear. You'll have to do that when the babies come — whenever that may be.'

And off she trotted.

That day saw the end of my interest in the attics. I decided to fill my lonely afternoons with reading to increase my knowledge of English literature. But it was no good. Every novel I tried — Dickens, Hardy, George Eliot — all involved childbirth.

So did meeting Martin's friends. Our first guests were to be a couple he'd been very close to in Young Farmers. Sandwiches, cakes and coffee would be fine, said Martin.

Mavis and Leo duly arrived. Leo was obviously ill-at-ease and Mavis was rather giggly, exclaiming at everything at Abbotshall, which she'd never entered before. She explained why. 'I wasn't really good enough for Mrs Peverell. She didn't mind Leo, because his parents are old farming folk, but mine are only tenants. You're lucky she's taken to you. She's never liked any of Martin's girlfriends before.'

Leo joined in. 'It wasn't just girlfriends. I was allowed in, but Martin's mother would spend the whole time making put-me-down remarks. One was that my manners suggested that my father had married beneath him.'

I gasped, and Martin laughed uneasily. To cover the confusion, I started busying myself about the food. Disaster really struck when I brought in the coffee, filling the room with its fragrance.

'Ooh, dear,' gasped Mavis. 'Where's the cloakroom? I'm going to be sick. I can't bear the smell of coffee just now.'

She got there in time and we sat in an embarrassed silence, listening to her retching. When she returned, pale but composed, I had replaced the offending coffee with a large pot of tea.

'Oh, thank you,' Mavis gushed. 'I'm so sorry, I expect you can guess what's wrong with me.' She patted her stomach with a grotesque coyness.

Martin was effusive in his congratulations and the taciturn Leo brightened up. 'Yes, we were getting a bit worried. We've been married nearly a year. We didn't want you two overtaking us.'

Mavis was a kind person, anxious to share her joy. 'Do hurry up and have your baby, Aulis, then they can be little together.'

Just what Marie had said to me. Why couldn't they all mind their own bloody business? Foolishly, I was stung into response. 'We're in no hurry. There's more to life than reproduction, isn't it something rabbits do?'

The three of them stared at me as if I were crazy. Then Leo, who had never seemed comfortable with us, exploded. 'Perhaps you should explain to your lady wife, Martin that her livelihood, like ours, depends on the process of reproduction — no wonder she gets on with your mother — too grand for good honest work. Come on, Mav, the old lady's right, this is no place for us, we're not clever enough. See you at market, Martin.' And they were off.

Martin was less angry than I had feared. 'Leo needed knocking off his perch — he's an arrogant so-and-so. But I'm sorry you upset Mavis, I've always been fond of her. Of course, Mother never thought her good enough.'

For what, I thought. Was Mavis perhaps one of those girls that Martin had "had"? Perhaps it was just as well that I'd offended those two.

Later on, when we were in bed, Martin mentioned the incident again. 'You know, Aulis, I didn't mind your upsetting Leo and Mavis, but I hope you're not going to be like that with all my friends. They will generally be farming folk, you know, and you really can't go rubbishing their livelihood — and ours.'

I was contrite. 'I didn't mean it like that Martin. It's just this obsession with babies.'

He held me close. 'I know — but try not to let it show. It's all most of the women have to talk about, their farms and their children. They've never read Cicero or even Jane Austen, most of them. You must have had some idea of what it would be like before you married me.'

'I didn't think, Martin. I just wanted you, and to be fair your mother does have other interests, her china, for example.'

'Yes, well Mother's never really fitted in either — but it's meant a lonely life for Pa. I don't want us to be quite as isolated as they are.'

Then with a swift change of mood he turned towards me. 'Come on, let's get this baby.' I melted in the ecstasy of his love.

We were soon in the winter season of balls, which Martin adored and I too began to enjoy myself, spending my savings recklessly on evening dresses and hair-dos. Mollie would often find some excuse to be around as we left and, for once, had no criticism to offer. 'Oh yes!' she would positively purr. 'The Peverells of Abbotshall — a very handsome couple. You look your best in a dinner-jacket, Martin, and Aulish is so smart. Well done you!' The little phrase was Mollie's highest accolade.

Like many large people Martin was a wonderful dancer and led by him I became quite proficient. We loved dancing together. When Martin danced with an old friend, I found sitting out with the farmers' wives more of a challenge. They regarded me with a mixture of emotions, curiosity and envy, about Abbotshall, suspicion of my education and career, pity, because I had no children and wasn't even pregnant.

Mavis, despite her increasing bulk, was always at these events. Still determined to be friendly, she leapt to my defence at any appearance of criticism, especially about my continuing childlessness.

'Aulis doesn't care about having babies. She thinks it's something rabbits do.'

In the shocked silence which followed, another kindly soul rushed into the breach. 'Never mind, dear, at least you don't have to go out to work now. You can keep busy caring for that beautiful house.'

Martin loved making me laugh about these encounters afterwards. He explained his good humour as we drove home one night. 'I wouldn't have missed this winter for anything. Every time I see poor lumpy Mavis, I think what fun it's been to launch you on the county looking so wonderful at all the balls. It won't matter you being pregnant next season, you've made the initial impression.'

Oh God, let me conceive, I prayed. Let this happiness last. For Martin no longer sulked over the absence of the honeymoon baby but now seemed convinced that it was his duty to have unlimited sex until a child was conceived, however early he had to get up. He had decided to enjoy these few carefree months, both in and out of bed.

I was enjoying our sex-life too, but always with the knowledge of how much depended on it — that elusive heir for Abbotshall. For me it was like doing an exam every night, for which there were no text-books, at least none that I knew of. Worst of all, my constant failure conflicted with the maxim on which I had been reared, which had always served me so well. "If you try hard, you will succeed".

Heavens, I tried. I found and bought the books; I scattered a revolting substance called Bemax over my breakfast cereal; I browsed through catalogues and discovered a curious little instrument which told me when I ovulated. I spent uncomfortable nights with my legs raised on pillows. I had snatched phone conversations with the fruitful Marie. I had to listen to my mother going on about the pregnancies of my school friends.

It was all hopeless. Month after monotonous month came the curse. When it was a day or two late, hope would spring, to drown again in the flood of blood. Martin would see my whey pale face as I shook my head miserably. He would kiss me, shrug his shoulders and go whistling back to work, less and less cheerfully as the months went by. I prayed even for a miscarriage. That would at least prove that I could conceive.

My body remained stubbornly empty. Spring came but brought no swelling of my breasts. Summer passed but I did not bloom. Mavis bore a son, fat and red-faced, and I coveted him. Would my husband ever have anything to hold except his barren wife?

Chapter Ten
An Autumn Day

It was a few days before our first wedding anniversary and nothing had changed. I had been married a year and had nothing to show for it. And now I was awakened by the familiar sharp pain. I hardly needed the spots of blood on the sheet to confirm that yet again I had failed. Eleven months of marriage, so eleven failures. And this wasn't A Level Latin — it should be such an easy thing to do.

I remembered my mother's dramatic explanation of what she called the "Facts of Life". 'If a girl lets one drop of liquid from a boy's penis get inside her, she'll get into trouble.'

Of course I had learned since that this was an over-simplification of the production of a baby. But I still had the general idea that what is now called "unprotected sex" usually led to pregnancy. Well not with me it didn't. The silly schoolgirl word fitted me perfectly. I was indeed cursed. So I wept, as I did every month, for the emptiness of my womb and my life. 'Pull yourself together and stop this self-indulgent nonsense. You are intelligent, well-educated and trained for an interesting and useful profession. Get on with your life.'

The thoughts and the tone were my father's, as clear as if he had been in the room with me.

But I was no longer in the world of logic and common-sense, so I answered him in silent dialogue. 'Dad, those things are worthless. They don't matter. Mollie says so and even Martin thinks so, deep down. I can't do the only thing that does matter in a wife, have a child!'

For, despite some reservations, Martin and I still subscribed to the Abbotshall creed.' 'Mollie knows best and she's always right.' From that first meeting in the kitchen, I had been an eager, though not uncritical convert, delighting Peter and Martin, my fellow-worshippers. I longed for the close, warm relationship that Mollie seemed to have with Di, the kind of relationship that had always eluded me with my own mother.

Thinking of Mollie reminded me of the exciting action-packed day that lay ahead. Once Martin and his father had gone to market Mollie and I were off to the Mothers' Union coffee morning and Bring and Buy sale. The afternoon would be spent deadheading roses.

So at 10.20 I sounded my horn at Mollie's gate. She came hurrying out, carrying a basket covered with a snowy white cloth, just like Red Riding Hood off to Grandma's. Her plain navy blue "shopping coat" swung from her shoulders with that air of quality which marked all her clothes. Her grey hair shone and her eyes were twinkling. 'A good day,' I thought, with relief.

Leaning over to put her basket on the back seat, Mollie saw my offering for the sale. 'Oh, darling, not books! Whatever will people think? I know that your people can't be expected to understand noblesse oblige, but you could at least have brought some eggs.'

'I need the eggs.' Then I added, less defiantly. 'Lots of people like murders and light crime. It helps them relax.'

'No time for relaxing in the country, dear. Anyway, it can't be helped now, we mustn't be late.'

At the church hall, Mollie was greeted warmly. As she was absorbed into the "doers" she whispered urgently to me, 'Do buy Mrs Barton's tomato chutney, dear. Notice from Abbotshall means a lot to them.'

As I barely recognised chutney, leave alone Mrs Barton, this was a tall order. As I stood hesitating by the door, the village schoolmaster's wife clapped me on the back with horrid familiarity. 'What are you doing here? Don't tell me you're wearing L-plates at last!'

Her harsh voice penetrated the room, so that people turned to look. A flush of shame enveloped me. Of course, this was the *Mothers'* Union. How could I have been so stupid, but Mollie had told me to come.

The odious Mrs Cain (yes really!) misinterpreting my blushes, went off laughing. 'Well, well, watch this space!'

Desperate for obscurity, I saw a hand beckoning. The woman was sitting at one of the little tables. A small head, crowned with pretty, curling, sandy hair, sat oddly on top of a mountainous bulk. Her brown tweed coat, fastened at the neck with one large button, flowed like an army tent over a large bosom and even larger hips. I suddenly remembered her at our wedding, wearing yards of flowered silk. This must be the woman Martin and I had talked about in Majorca. She had friendly brown eyes and smiled warmly from among her many chins as she patted the seat beside her. I sat down gratefully.

My new friend launched into speech, scarcely pausing for breath. 'I'll go and buy your books in a minute, dear. I enjoy a good murder. By the way, I'm Ida Ripley. I don't suppose you remember me, but I was at your wedding. How are you enjoying married life?'

'It's fine, thank you.'

'Not finding Lady Peverell a bit hard to cope with?'

The slight sarcasm roused me to Mollie's defence. 'Martin's mother is very kind and helpful.'

'Oh yes, the nicest woman on earth unless you're related to her. We're distantly connected — only distantly thank God, or we'd suffer too. Believe me, everyone's sorry for you.'

Pride made me abrupt. 'I don't need pity.'

Mrs Ripley remained equable. 'Well perhaps Mollie does then. It must be hard, both your children marrying out.'

The term fascinated me. 'What do you mean — the Peverells aren't Jews.'

'No, but until this generation they've always married within their own family — you know — like the Royals.

And now first Diana marries that solicitor from Wales with the unpronounceable name and then Martin marries you.'

I smiled. 'Also from Wales, and with an unpronounceable name. But — how weird — marrying each other.'

'Oh, they've been doing it for decades, centuries probably. Mollie and Peter are third cousins, I think, and I know that Peter's parents were first cousins.'

'But hasn't it caused problems — I mean inbreeding — having children?'

'Doesn't affect the Royals, does it, well not much anyway? I suppose there's the odd stumble in every family. But every Peverell bride has had a child within the year, until now, that is.'

'Martin and I are in no hurry to start a family.' I felt guilty as I spoke, not only because I was lying in my teeth, but because I knew that Mollie would have hated the bourgeois phrase.

Ida swept on. 'Take my advice, dear, get on with it. Get yourself insured against Mollie's plots. She can be a dangerous woman and she fair idolises those Welsh grandchildren of hers, especially the boy. I suppose she's had her troubles like the rest of us. Well, I must buy the books and be off. Pop over and see me if it all gets too much. You can walk to us through your back fields you know, you don't have to have the police check at the bottom of your drive.' She sailed off, chuckling.

Uncomfortable, I knew what she meant. Mollie had a perfect view of our drive from her picture window. Did she really monitor my movements? Ida Ripley was probably just another rural mischief maker.

On the way home Mollie seemed to confirm this. 'I saw you talking to Ida Ripley — they're some relation of Peter's — good enough people, but not quite, you know. Don't get too close to her, dear.'

Mollie patted my knee in friendly fashion. She was in high good humour after the morning's flattery. Even I was in favour for by some miracle I had acquired Mrs Barton's chutney. Mollie referred to this as we drove home. 'I am glad that you pleased Mrs Barton. She was so distressed about her little granddaughter.'

Wondering if the child was ill or in trouble at school I was surprised as Mollie continued, 'The poor child has just miscarried her first baby — she's only been married six months. Still, as I said to Mrs Barton there was probably something wrong with it, and she'll soon conceive again. After all she's done it once!'

I willed myself not to see anything personal in Mollie's remarks — some reflection of my own inadequacy, my failure to conceive. Mollie had certainly made no direct reference to it but I was beginning to know her little ways. However, she still seemed full of goodwill. Kissing my cheek as she got out of the car, she said, 'Now run off and have your boiled egg like a good girl. We'll meet in the rose garden at two o'clock sharp. Wear gloves and bring secateurs.'

I was more than punctual, waiting with that mixture of dread and delight which being with Mollie always produced. It was a beautiful October day of gentle sunshine with that little nip in the air which accompanies a golden autumn. The garden was like a woman, gracious and ample in her maturity. Under Mollie's direction I could manage this basic job. We snipped in companionable silence for a while, then she began to point out the different varieties of rose. We came to some variegated pink and white blooms, less furled than most roses. Mollie caressed them gently, saying, 'Aren't these little old-fashioned roses sweet? Martin's grandmother planted them when she was a bride. You see, dear, that's what we do at Abbotshall. Each generation makes its own contribution to build one great whole.' She gave me a smile of pure sweetness.

At last, I was being drawn into her plans. I was going to belong. Trying to catch her mood, I said dreamily, 'I wonder what Martin and I will give?'

Immediately the moment was lost. Her mood changed and the fox's mask came down. It was the familiar cold tone. 'Nothing, unless you hurry up; if Martin doesn't have a son Abbotshall will go to Charlie Llewellyn.'

I wasn't defeated yet. 'What if Martin has six daughters?'

'I'm afraid they won't count.'

'Why not, this is the twentieth century?'

'And this is Abbotshall.'

'Then we shouldn't have a queen.'

'That's different. That isn't a farm. She only has to look nice.'

'And be Head of State for a large portion of the world.'

As usual, when cornered, Mollie took refuge in dismissing anything which she didn't understand. 'It's a pity your head is filled with all these silly ideas. I blame your parents. Your job is to have babies and you're not being very good at that. Why, even that silly little Mavis has managed it. Poor Martin, he'll lose everything, and it'll be all your fault.

"Well, dear, we've done a good afternoon's work. I must get Peter's tea and I expect you need to get Martin's.'

Off she went, grace and dignity in every step, sailing away, as always, from any possibility of unpleasant encounter. I could never get used to her trick of turning, sometimes in the same sentence, from vitriolic comment to normal everyday language.

I understood now why Martin had said that we *needed* a baby. He must know that his inheritance, everything he'd worked for, would go to Charlie Llewellyn, and it would all be my fault!

Shaking with the impact of her words and suddenly conscious of the pain that I had almost forgotten, I heard the usual afternoon sounds. The farm van clattered up the drive. My father-in-law banged the door and called a goodbye. I heard Martin calling my name as he went into the farmhouse. A few minutes later he came out and I knew that he was changed and going over to the milking parlour.

I just wanted to be alone, but not inside Abbotshall, where solitude became loneliness. There was a little hut, on the orchard side of the house, used for storing garden tools and supplies. I stumbled into it and sat down on a bundle of old sacks, making a sort of nest for myself. Cuddling my aching stomach, I brooded on Mollie's words. Underneath some of her ridiculous statements there was a core of undeniable truth. I was without purpose. They sent a barren cow to market for slaughter because it couldn't fulfil its role in life. Well neither could I. How could they put me out of my misery?

Yet I knew that some of Mollie's talk was arrant nonsense. Martin already owned half the farm and obviously could leave his half to whomever he chose, there was no reason for Charlie Llewellyn to get the lot. But why was I even thinking like this, we'd only been married a year. Why did Mollie influence me so much? I knew the answers quite clearly. My great admiration for her made me give far too much credence to everything she said. And because my horizons were now so limited these details of daily life assumed a huge importance. I must remember that there was a world beyond Abbotshall. I tried hard to think whether people spoke as rudely or obsessively as Mollie in that outside world, and found it difficult to find examples. Perhaps I had just been lucky in the people I had known. Finally, worn out with worry and emotion, I must have fallen asleep.

The murmur of voices, clear in the evening air, woke me. I stood up, stiff, sore and very cold. Cautiously I opened the door. Just around the corner of the house Martin was speaking, in what I called his "hopeless" tone. 'What did you say to upset her, Mother? I can't find her anywhere I've looked in all the outbuildings, the milking-parlour, the hay-barn, everywhere.'

Mollie, slightly defensive but still in command. 'I've told you. We had a perfectly happy day... She talked to Ida Ripley, but she was all right after that. Then we did the roses.

Martin burst in. 'It was something about children, wasn't it? Why can't you leave her alone? We've only been married a year. She's gentle and sensitive, and you, you can have a wicked tongue.'

So he knew, I thought, knew, and most of the time, just let it happen.

My father-in-law intervened. 'Now, now, don't speak to your mother like that. We're all getting too excited. Are you sure she's not asleep in bed?'

'Not in our bed, and I can't see why she should be in any other.'

Mollie again, sounding slightly disgusted. 'I think she has her period. She had that whey-faced look this morning. Those kind of people always make such a fuss about these things. Perhaps she's gone to sleep in the spare room. Look, it's ridiculous for us all to be out here.

Peter, you go home and keep warm. Ring Ida Ripley in case she's gone running there. No, on second thoughts, don't, it'll get round everywhere if you do. Martin, go and check the spare rooms. I'll wander round the outside again. She's only playing up. She'll be around somewhere. After all (with the deprecating little laugh) she's nowhere else to go.'

They moved off. I got up, slowly and carefully, shaking myself like a dog. Stung by Mollie's last remark I considered running away, driving home or to Marie's. If I struggled down the back fields to Ida Ripley's they would soon find me and I might make trouble for the Ripleys. And what could I say to any of these people. The whole thing would seem unutterably trivial to anyone outside Abbotshall. In any case the car keys and what little money I had were in the farmhouse.

Then there was Martin. He was worried and he did love me, although he seemed powerless against his mother. I crept around the house, through the back-door and into the kitchen, where I hung gratefully over the Aga. I could hear Martin stomping and calling far above me. Did he think I was cowering in an attic?

Ostentatiously banging the kitchen door, I went to the bottom of the stairs and called. He came rushing down, relief turning to anger and amazement at my bedraggled appearance. He spoke roughly, 'Where the hell have you been? We're all frantic. Mother's still out looking for you.'

He made it sound as if she were struggling through the snow with her Saint Bernard. This hardened me for the easy lie. 'I went for a walk down the back fields and fell over. It took me a while to get my breath back. And I was so cold.'

'Into the kitchen with you then.'

Martin bustled about, filling the kettle, while I removed my anorak and boots, all suitably dirty from the tool-shed. The side-door clicked and Mollie came in. Her greeting was characteristic. 'Oh, you're back then. I said you would be. I suppose you couldn't find anywhere else to go?'

Martin, supportive now that his mother was present, said firmly, 'Aulis went for a walk down the back fields and fell over — got herself in a right state.'

She was gently sympathetic. 'Darling, poor you.' I saw her taking in the anorak and boots, doubtless noting that the dirt on them was soil, not mud. Then, to Martin, 'Go and ring Pa, darling, you know what an old worrier he is.'

Obedient as ever, Martin trotted off to the phone in the sitting room. This was Mollie's chance. She moved swiftly. 'Let's close the door to keep the heat in.' She suited the action to the words, then turned swiftly to me. It was pure poison now. 'You little rotter. Martin may be fooled, but I'm not. Where have you been, whining to the Ripleys?'

Weary and worn as I was, I still refused to go under. 'I haven't seen Mrs Ripley since this morning.'

'Well, you've not been with another man, at any rate. No one would look at you. God knows how you've bewitched my poor boy. But you'll stay with him and you'll stay here, useless as you are. Is that clear?'

Martin's return spared me from answering and Mollie did another of her amazing voltes-faces. 'Poor Aulish, she's had quite a shock. Some nice hot tea will set her up, a bath and change, then you must both come down and share our shepherd's pie. The poor girl won't want to cook after all this.'

We breathed dutiful thank-yous. Martin, looking at her with the old dog-like devotion, added, 'What would we do without you, Mother?' laughing, and putting his arm around her.

I was warmer now, but inside I was cold and sick with disappointment. Loss of faith is a terrible experience. My idol had shown her feet of clay in no uncertain way today. And what would be the consequences for me?

Chapter Eleven
The Doldrums

No repercussions followed from my afternoon in the shed. It was forgotten in the advent of a major catastrophe. At the very time when Mollie and I were peacefully deadheading roses, a cow at Oswestry market was found to have foot-and-mouth disease. Within a week a major outbreak was raging.

We four Peverells sat round the dining-room table at Abbotshall while Martin outlined what we must do. 'Ministry rules say no movement of animals, daily disinfecting of all farm entrances and exits, and no unnecessary visitors.'

Peter was anxious to cooperate, Mollie reluctant. 'What about the staff?' she asked. 'You and Pa can't run the farm on your own.'

Martin had thought it through. 'No, I must keep Sam, he can virtually run the dairy, freeing me for the field-work.'

Mollie opposed this in her characteristically cunning way. 'But what about that silly little wife of his in that wretched dress-shop, people going in and out all the time, spreading infection?'

Martin played an unexpected trump card. 'Oh, didn't you know?' he asked blandly, 'Brenda's given up work. She's about six months pregnant.'

Even in the midst of this important discussion I had time to think. Another one! Everyone can do it except me! And why didn't Martin tell me? I suppose he thought I'd have a gloom, for my moods of depression were becoming more frequent.

Martin carried on, well into his stride now. 'So we keep Sam. The tractor-drivers must go, we'll keep Jack on a retainer, and get rid of Bert Stoate. He's self-employed anyway, and pretty surplus to requirements.'

Mollie's attempt to protest was quelled by an unexpectedly stern glance from Peter. Martin continued, 'Matthew-Henry lives well away from the village so Pa can fetch him every day to do the calves and Aulis can take him home.'

Mollie had decided to cooperate. 'Yes and she can go to Stafford to get our groceries and other necessities — we can't have deliveries now.'

My questions were probably superfluous but I felt slight resentment at the way in which they, especially Mollie, were rearranging my life. 'Why Stafford, and why me?'

Mollie was quick to answer. 'Stafford is less likely than the little market towns to have people from farms there. And you are less likely to meet and mix with infectious people, because you know nobody. And of course you'll have to do all your own housework.

Barbara must go. She gallivants far too much and even her bicycle could become infected.'

Peter had another bright idea, joining in to plan my life. 'Aulis can help Matthew-Henry with the calves as well.'

I reflected on my job-list. I would miss Barbara's cheerful presence but in other ways I was gaining. My comings and goings were now increasingly monitored by Mollie and I was convinced that someone was emptying my petrol tank. Under this new regime I would be visiting Stafford regularly, with permission, and they would never know if I strayed into bookshops. I doubted if Mollie's spy-network extended as far as Stafford. Even if it did it was unlikely to cover bookshops, doubtless regarded by the farming fraternity as a wicked waste of time. I wouldn't have had such freedom since my marriage. So I accepted all Mollie's decrees in a suitably meek manner, rewarded by her approving smile.

On the Sunday after the outbreak began, we had to tell my parents that our three-weekly visits to them must stop. My mother, suspecting an ulterior motive, was puzzled and slightly aggrieved. 'Why can't you come here? We haven't got any animals and we don't go to farms. I think it's ridiculous!'

My father spoke with less than his usual tolerance. 'Good God, woman, don't you know any geography? Not only are we less than twenty miles from Oswestry but Martin and Aulis have practically to cross the Cheshire Plain, full of dairy farms, to get here.'

I could have kissed him for being so understanding, especially as I knew that he would miss seeing me far more than she would.

My mother shrugged her shoulders. 'I never was any good at Geography. Well, I daresay we'll miss you of course, but you've never got any news. We'll get news from Australia before we get any from you.'

I knew exactly what news she was expecting, from both places. My brother Jason's wife had recently written (from Australia) to tell my mother that they were "trying for a baby". A use of language which had caused my father to mutter, 'Yes, very trying! Poor baby!'

So the ban on these visits was quite a relief to me. I felt that I couldn't bear one more Sunday devoted to my mother's hints, veiled questions and catalogues of the children born to my schoolfellows.

Abbotshall became a fortress and the long watch began. Every morning when Martin went out to milk, every evening when he went to look up the cows, he walked with fear; fear that the dread disease had struck. Once he knew that we were momentarily safe he would start looking for "smoke signals" as he called them. The great grey clouds with their acrid smell, rising from yet another heap of burning cattle carcases, smoke which darkened the sky for days after the fires had died out. Looking from the attic windows Martin could judge roughly from where the smoke was coming. He would sigh with relief. 'Nothing from the Ripleys yet. Once they go, we've had it, our land is so close.'

Our stress was compounded by the lack of social life. No more balls, no more trips to market — all the markets were closed. Going to Stafford was like visiting a ghost town. All the little shoots of acquaintanceship I had sown were withered before they could grow. Even Mollie was told very firmly that Di and family could not come for Christmas, as they usually did. When Sam's daughter was born, in the middle of the outbreak, the normally obligatory visit to welcome the new baby was ruled out (much to my relief). For weeks it seemed, and in the event for nearly nine months, the four of us, Mollie and Peter, Martin and I, were almost totally dependent on one another for conversation, reassurance and even entertainment. We rarely watched television because both news and programmes focused so much on the epidemic. There was a horrible map on which they illustrated the new cases every day. There seemed to be more and more.

Finally, Mollie got out all the old games — Monopoly, Cluedo, Snakes and Ladders, Ludo — anything she could find. We took it in turns to play host and provide refreshments. Surprisingly, it was great fun. I learned all kinds of Peverell family traditions. Why was I not surprised that they gave Mollie Mayfair and Park Lane at the start of every game of Monopoly? Mollie was at her best on these evenings, increasingly warm and kind. I began to feel as if I might become one of the family.

Not that the barbs were entirely absent. She insisted on early nights. 'So that we're all ready to face whatever the morning may bring.' A commendable sentiment, followed by what my mother would have called a "little dig". 'Perhaps it's not too much to hope that an early night might serve some other purpose too.'

I thought this even less likely than usual. Martin was increasingly tense and irritable. He deeply resented the compulsory visits of the Ministry vets. It took the united efforts of me and his father to stop him standing at the gate with a loaded gun to keep them out. When Mollie remarked casually one day that a neighbouring farmer who had lost his herd had used the compensation money for a foreign holiday, showing that every cloud has a silver lining, Martin was speechless with anger. He often spent half the night standing at the window, staring towards the cowsheds. Naturally all this affected his lovemaking It was fitful and frequently unsuccessful, then on rare occasions it was almost brutally powerful. Perhaps that was why nothing was achieved except an attack of cystitis — a new and unpleasant experience for me.

Mollie was amused. 'The young bride's complaint. Perhaps we're finally getting somewhere.' However, she agreed that a trip to the doctor's was necessary travel.

Only extreme pain would have driven me there. I found the Peverells' doctor, Ronald Arthur, singularly unimpressive. Small, balding and fussy, he always smelled powerfully of whisky. Having inherited the practice from an uncle, "The real Dr Arthur" as old people called him, the younger one had always been known as "Dr Ronald", a familiarity which I found embarrassing. His surgery was a curious set-up where two old sisters, the doctor's cousins, ran their own dispensary.

Dr Ronald was sympathetic about the cystitis and wrote out a prescription. I watched, fascinated, as he tapped a panel in the wall. It slid open and he pushed the paper through, for it to be seized by a wrinkled hand, brown with age spots. He sat back and smiled. 'Now m'dear, (Ugh!) is there anything else troubling you?'

Here was my chance — so I took it. 'Yes, I don't understand why I'm failing to conceive. I wonder if I should have some tests to see if there's anything wrong with me?'

The doctor was obviously embarrassed by my direct approach. He tried to cover this by being mildly dismissive, prefacing his answer with a little laugh. 'Good gracious, you haven't been married for two minutes!'

'Nearly two years,' I replied flatly.

'Is it as long as that? Even so, come back on your fifth wedding anniversary, that might be the time to get worried. Then there would be various tests, for you and your husband.'

He must have been amazed at the grateful look I gave him. 'You mean... It might not be me... it could be Martin?'

'There's probably nothing wrong with either of you. I'm sure it's just a matter of time. If you're really worried come back when the cystitis has cleared up and I'll take a preliminary look at you. But a full-scale investigation would involve your husband as well. It's very old-fashioned to assume that the problems are always with the wife. Now I expect your prescription will be ready.'

Impressed in spite of myself I shook his hand and thanked him. He smiled again. 'My pleasure, m'dear. We're not all dunces in the country you know.'

Feeling as if I had been what Mollie called "ticked orf" I collected my medicine from the sister still called "Young Miss Arthur", despite her grey hair and wrinkles. She gave me a cheery smile. 'Here you are — instructions on the label. Please bring the bottle back.' Behind her I could see the elder Miss Arthur, small and hump-backed, her bloodshot, rheumy eyes glaring at me with a look of pure malevolence. As I opened the door to leave, I saw her claw-like hand pick up the phone.

I drove home, still in pain but considerably reassured about my larger problem. I bounced into the kitchen, to find Mollie waiting for me. Never had I seen her so angry. Blue eyes sparkling like pebbles of ice, she sat bolt upright, her whole frame shaking. I gasped at her. 'Whatever have I done?'

Her words were the more effective because she spoke quietly. Her low controlled tone was heavy with anger and dislike. 'How dare you spread rumours about my son — bleating to the doctor like the little ill-bred milksop that you are. Your family may enjoy discussing their private lives with all and sundry, we don't. If there's a failure here it's you. Let the village laugh at you, not at this poor boy of mine.'

Then, before I could consider this curious reference to Martin, Mollie burst into a storm of tears. Although I rushed into apology, I was extremely puzzled about what I had done wrong, and determined to say so. 'Mollie, I'm very sorry that you are upset, but what is so terrible about asking a doctor for advice about what may be a medical problem? In the world I come from it's a normal and sensible thing to do. It would be regarded as behaving responsibly.'

Her tears did not diminish her anger. 'Your world indeed! So why didn't you stay there, not force your way into our world, where you don't belong, and where you cause continual trouble. We were managing nicely, just the family, private and secure, until you broke in, with your fancy ideas and your complete ignorance of correct behaviour!'

Any sympathy I had for her distress was rapidly being replaced by anger and annoyance of my own, so I answered sharply. 'In my world it's not considered correct behaviour to reveal professional secrets — as someone has presumably done — or you wouldn't know of my conversation with the doctor.'

This argument didn't impress Mollie. 'There you go again, not a clue how the world works. Of course people tell each other things, that's why you never tell anyone

149

anything about this family, or they know and mock. Don't you understand?'

No, I didn't — but before I could ask Mollie whatever she meant she had swept out, leaving me shocked and baffled. Surely the doctor would not have told Mollie of our conversation. Then I remembered the panel in the surgery and saw the elder Miss Arthur's face as she picked up the phone, obviously ringing Mollie! I was disgusted — and sad. All the weeks which Mollie and I had spent together, building up our relationship as I thought, had they been destroyed in one afternoon by an evil old woman? How could Mollie, with her love of beauty and perfection, be friends with such a strange creature? Perhaps Mollie was right, perhaps I didn't understand anything about human relationships? I wanted to put my head down on the kitchen table and howl.

No time for that at Abbotshall. A gentle tap on the side-door announced Matthew-Henry's arrival for his daily lift home.

One of my unexpected benefits from the foot-and-mouth outbreak had been getting to know this old man. He had no time for "hasty modern ways" yet worked with a precision which would have delighted my father. Helping him to feed and bed the beautiful little calves, taking pride in my efforts, I knew a peace which I rarely felt at Abbotshall.

We generally spoke little as I drove him home, so Matthew-Henry would find nothing unusual about my silence today. But he must have noticed my red eyes, because he suddenly said, 'Don't 'ee fret, little lass. Maister Martin will come good, just like his feyther. I remember Missus, along with Miss Emily, when she were but a lass like 'ee. She weren't so grand and proud then, but happen she's had her troubles too.'

This was the longest speech I'd ever heard from him. We soon arrived at his cottage. As I helped him out of the car I felt a reassuring warmth in the pressure of his fingers. This was a huge gesture from Matthew-Henry, and he turned to wave as I drove away — another first.

I mulled over the old man's words as I drove home. What troubles had Mollie had? What had made her so "grand and proud" — an excellent description? I remembered her reference, long ago in the kitchen, to her "great sorrow", but no one had ever mentioned it — leave alone explained it — to me. Was it to do with children, with that strange crib in the attic? Perhaps Mollie was right, I didn't belong in their world, but how could I when she was making such a determined effort to keep me out of it?

I dreaded what the evening might bring. We were due to go down to the cottage for one of our usual games' nights. Would Mollie cancel, or even worse, would she turn on me again, in front of Martin and Peter?

None of this happened. We went down after tea. Apart from a slight air of constraint everything was as usual. I realised that Martin and Peter were to know nothing of my indiscretion. I assumed that Mollie

151

considered it "women's business", just as my mother would have done. Perhaps the two women were not so different as Mollie would have liked them to be.

Then, suddenly, as quickly as it had come, the foot-and-mouth was gone, petering out in a few isolated outbreaks. And there had never been "Anything from the Ripleys". They remained, like us, with herds intact, a small patch of health in the midst of desolation. We had escaped.

Slowly everything was returning to normal. There were markets again, meetings, dances. Over the long incarceration I had decided that when liberation came, I would take my life in hand. So what was I going to do next?

Chapter Twelve
The Row

The first essential was to build bridges with my parents. I had dutifully phoned them regularly throughout the outbreak, but they had seemed very distant. On my call when all was clear again, my mother applied her usual lack of logic. 'You see you didn't get it. You could have kept on coming, I think you thought it a good excuse, Aulis! Getting too grand for the likes of us, aren't you? Oh, you're coming next Sunday — good — we're really looking forward to seeing you. We've got such exciting news! Wait till you hear!'

'I expect the Australian's having twins,' I commented tartly to Martin, for we now knew that Jason's wife, Melanie, was pregnant.

I was getting used to Martin's reproving look. 'Don't be so mean, Aulis. I know that every pregnancy is like a personal insult to you, but your attitude doesn't help!'

'Sorree,' I trilled, another irritating habit I'd developed.

So our first available Sunday saw us taking the familiar roads through the beauty of the Cheshire Plain. I drove so that Martin could study the farming landscape. There was still quietness about the land, an absence of mature cattle, although there were signs of re-stocking. We glimpsed the occasional bare patch where a bonfire had been. We realised again how fortunate we had been to escape disaster. so we were in a slightly sombre mood when we arrived at my parents.

This was soon dispelled as it became clear that my mother's comment about news had, for once, been an understatement. I was immediately aware of change in the atmosphere. The house was not merely tidy— none of the usual clutter — but almost bare. When a glimpse into Dad's study revealed rows of empty shelves, I was really worried. 'Whatever's going on? Are you moving?'

My parents smiled at each other like a pair of mischievous schoolchildren. My father began, 'Not exactly…'

My mother burst in, 'We're going to Australia.'

I was almost incoherent. 'When — how — why?'

My mother's words tumbled out in her eagerness. 'We're going in November, when the baby's due. You know Mel's mother's dead, so I'm going to help her through the early days. We've let the house for a year — it could be longer — so we've put things like most of your dad's books in store. We always meant to do something exciting when Dad retired, and this is it!'

I was still incredulous. 'But are you going to live with Jason for a year?' I felt some sympathy for the unknown Melanie.

Dad took over. 'No, once Melanie and the baby are settled, after Christmas, we're going to travel —

hopefully all over Australia. We're hiring a camper-van, and then we might go to New Zealand.'

He sounded as if he were planning a day trip to Rhyl. I tried to recall them to their responsibilities. 'What about Hector and Norma and the children? Won't you miss them?'

'Oh, don't worry,' breezed my mother. 'They're coming out for a holiday at Christmas, so we'll all be together.'

My father forestalled my next comment. 'We're sorry, Aulis. We'd love you and Martin to come out too, but we assumed that it's not possible with the farm, is it?'

'No, Mr Price,' Martin answered briefly. I was almost deprived of speech and he wasn't much better.

The rest of the visit was spent discussing the trip. My father, always the more sensitive of the two, managed to divert my mother from too many references to Mel's pregnancy. He and Martin pored over atlases and discussed sheep-farming. Martin even remembered some distant Peverell cousins whom my parents might visit. The whole thing seemed totally unreal to me. They might as well be going to Mars.

We left, with many hugs and kisses — there wouldn't be time to see them again before they flew. We drove home in a stunned silence, until I suddenly caught Martin's eye and saw his lips twitching. He pulled into a lay-by where both of us collapsed into helpless giggles. Between snorts Martin asked, 'Will your father wear his pin-stripe suit?'

I replied hysterically, 'Will my mother wear trousers?'

Whenever we seemed to be calming down, Martin would say, 'A camper-van!' and we were off again.

What fun Martin was, I thought. If only we could disappear to Australia. No, not to Australia and the pregnant Melanie, but to somewhere that wasn't Abbotshall and where there were no small children or pregnant women, or at least, if there were, they were not important.

However, I woke next morning to the cheering thought that one pro-pregnancy nagger — my mother — was largely out of my life — at least temporarily. So now to reduce the importance of the other one — Mollie. Millions of people led perfectly fulfilling lives without children — spinster teachers, dons, high-flying business-women. I would aim to do the same, to make something of my life.

So on my first trip to Manley, I strode purposefully into the Public Library. That's where you went in Northam to find out what was going on — courses, societies, events, were all listed there. And so they were in Manley. I was soon armed with fistfuls of information, as well as a bag full of borrowed books.

I was on the way out when I heard Ida Ripley's familiar voice. 'Hello, Aulis, isn't it good to be able to get about again? Still we both survived. I'm off to Bateman's to have coffee with my usual market-day crowd — good to see them after so long. Why don't you come, get to know more people? Of course Mollie's never had time to join us!

I got the message. I would be showing that I didn't share Mollie's snobbish attitudes.

At the café Ida led the way to a large round table, where about six women were already gathered. They were obviously making up for all the chat that they'd missed. Their heads, clustered together in gossip, rose at our approach, the feathered hats of some making them look like hens at bay. They made room for us as Ida explained, 'I found young Mrs Peverell in the library and thought it would be good if she joined us to meet a few people.'

There was a murmur of agreement and welcome, although I was conscious of a slight air of reserve. A small woman, with a scrawny neck and little pig eyes, was more outspoken. 'I'm sure we're very honoured. But does your mother-in-law know you're out, dear, leave alone mixing with the likes of us?'

I could see that most of them were trying not to smile, but Ida was quick in my defence. 'Leave her alone, Maggie. She can't help having Lady Peverell as a mother-in-law. Now let's have some talk and a little kindness.'

I sat quietly, enjoying the coffee and occasionally contributing to the conversation. The coffee club was obviously not going to transform my life, but it was a start.

I arrived home to find Mollie busy weeding our garden. She claimed to enjoy these "little jobs" but I couldn't dismiss the idea that they were meant to make us feel guilty. Unasked, she followed me into the kitchen. Then she saw my bag of books. 'Oh, Aulish, you haven't been buying books?'

I answered cheerfully, 'No, they're from the library.'

'The Public Library!' her astounded tone sounded like Lady Bracknell saying, "A Handbag!". 'Really, Aulish! those places are for poor people. You never know what infection you might catch from the books. And you're suggesting to people that we do not have books. We don't borrow books — if we have time to read, we buy them.'

I was getting bolder. 'You mean those paper-back romances you have — not quite what I mean by books. Anyway other farmers' wives go to the Library. I met Ida Ripley there, and we went for coffee.'

This seemed even worse news than the books! Mollie spoke now more in sorrow than in anger. 'Aulish, dear! you went with those dreadful women — let me see — apart from Ida, there'd be Nancy Woodford, Madge Perkins, Betty Plant, Dolly Reeves, Iris Hill and a dreadful little person called Maggie Somers. Am I right?'

'Yes, but how did you know?'

'That little gang's been together for years.' She was contemptuous.

But I wasn't giving way. 'What's wrong with them? They're farmers' wives, and they all seemed to know you.'

Mollie found that amusing. 'Well of course they would know who I am, but we're hardly on visiting terms. They're not our sort of farmers, apart from Ida they're mostly tenants on fifty acres — and Maggie Somers is a cowman's daughter. You really can't associate with people like that.'

I was getting angry now, but determined to remember what Martin had told me. 'Just let Mother's nonsense go over your head, we all do.'

So I answered quite mildly. 'Don't worry! I'm not likely to. I found them boring and small-minded — like most people round here.'

Missing the implied insult, Mollie smiled with relief. 'There you are then. You see you are learning. Anyway, you'll forget all this nonsense when the babies come. We'll say no more about it.' And off she trotted, totally unconscious of any annoyance she might have caused.

Infuriated, as always, by the reference to babies but cheered by my small victory, I was ready to confront Martin when he came in, for I had seen a disturbing sight on the way home. 'Martin, why did I see Bert Stoate driving a tractor in one of our fields?'

Martin gave me one of his bear-hugs. 'Because, my love, you have the eyes of a hawk and the body of Venus.'

I shook myself free. 'Be serious, Martin. I thought that we finished with him during the foot-and-mouth.'

Martin was brusque. 'Yes, well, Jack has a bad back and isn't sure about coming back. Bert was available and we needed a tractor driver urgently. Anyway, what's wrong with him?'

I was hot with annoyance. 'He's a sexual predator, and Matthew-Henry says he was sacked from a farm for cruelty to animals.'

Martin was dismissive. 'That was years ago and Matthew-Henry is an old gossip. Anyway, Bert doesn't handle animals here. And he can hardly pinch your bottom when he's sitting on a tractor.'

I was not satisfied, and I went too far. 'I suppose your mother wanted him back. Well, I shall know where to come when my fancy-man needs a job.'

I never forgot the look of deep sorrow that Martin gave me, almost looking through me, as if I didn't exist. I hastened to apologise. 'I'm sorry, Martin. My comment was tasteless and vulgar, but please don't look at me like that. I promise you, I haven't got a fancy-man.'

His voice was quiet, cold and dismissive. 'I didn't think that you had. But please never speak of my mother in that way again. We have to give her little pleasures. It's the least we can do. I'm going down now to see her.'

He turned on his heel as I clung to him. 'Be angry with me, Martin, please be angry with me — don't shut me out like this. Just explain — why do you have to please your mother all the time? If you explain, I'll try to understand.'

Gently but firmly, he freed himself from my grasp. 'I can't explain — it's not my secret. I'll see you later, Aulis. Let this be forgotten between us.'

Left alone, I was distressed and bewildered. At least I knew now that there was a secret but otherwise, I was totally confused. When Martin returned, we carried on as normal and when we went to bed he loved me so beautifully that I sighed and cried with joy. When I would have spoken, he stopped my mouth with a kiss, saying gently, 'Say nothing. None of this is your fault.' But from that day on a new constraint lay upon our relationship, more apparent out of bed than in.

Meanwhile I pressed on with efforts to broaden my horizon. Making little headway in my new world, I thought about my old. If I couldn't actually teach, perhaps I could do some tutoring or exam marking. So I wrote to Miss Browning, the headmistress for whom I had worked before my marriage, to see if she knew of any opportunities, and waited eagerly for her reply.

I was lucky, because the day it arrived, I met the postwoman, toiling up the road on her ancient bicycle. I spoke pleasantly enough. 'Do you have any post for Abbotshall, please?'

She was a sour-faced woman, not anxious to please, and answered sulkily, 'I usually leaves all the post at the cottage, with the proper Mrs Peverell, like.'

I spoke firmly. 'But that's illegal, isn't it? You are paid to deliver post to the correct address. So please give me anything addressed to Abbotshall — to Mr Martin Peverell or to Mrs A. Peverell B.A.'

Her reply showed that dim as she was, she had received Post Office training. 'It's illegal to hand out post in the road — it's supposed to be delivered to the address written on the envelope.'

I was enjoying this. 'So it is, so why don't you do that? I'll tell you what — I won't report you for constantly breaking the law if you give me all our post now.'

Unwillingly she handed me a considerable pile, which made me wonder how much of our post normally disappeared into the cottage. Back at home I sorted the letters — and yes, there was one from Miss Browning. As I read it, I became first puzzled, then angry. The headmistress wrote formally, as was her custom:

Dear Mrs Peverell,

I was delighted to hear from you, to know that you are well and had escaped the ravages of the foot-and-mouth disease. I am sorry to say that I cannot help you with any immediate work. Perhaps later on in the year, after the shock of the Mock Exams (!) there may be a few girls requiring some extra tuition before their 'O Level' Latin Exam. I shall certainly bear you in mind if that should be the case.

So far, so quite expected. But she continued:

It now seems a pity that you were not able to help us last year, when Miss Francis broke her leg and we were rather desperate. I was categorically informed then by your mother-in-law that you would never return to teaching. I was somewhat surprised that you did not get in touch yourself, but when Mrs Peverell senior explained that you were recovering from a serious miscarriage, I endeavoured to understand. The loss of a baby must be a very painful experience. I am so glad that all is well now.

Yours sincerely,
H.A. Browning

Completely astounded, I looked up to see Mollie coming in, sounding querulous. 'Mary says you took all the post. What do you think you're playing at?'

All my good resolutions, all my deference, was forgotten. I pushed Miss Browning's letter across the table. My voice was cold with fury. 'Read that! How dare you steal my post, take decisions on my behalf without consulting me, and tell lies about me. And to Miss Browning, a professional woman to whom I owe much and whom I hold in high esteem. Do you have any explanation?'

I realised that anger was making me articulate and authoritative, like my father. But my words appeared to have little effect on Mollie. She tried to answer in her usual dismissive way. 'Oh, Aulish, you are a drama queen! Miss Browning is nobody in our world. I just saved you the bother of replying. There was no way that my son's wife was going out to work. You know, Aulish, we've tried to be gentle and tactful with you because of your family, but you must face facts. A teacher is only a kind of upper servant. My father always called the village schoolmistress a "sewing wench". So I'm not at all worried about Miss Browning and I'm certainly not having you lowering yourself again. So that's settled.'

As she uttered these incredible words so many pictures flashed through my mind — the tears in Mrs Scott's eyes as she read us Vergil's account of the death of Hector — my father worrying about his 11+ pupils — my mother busily collecting pictures to entertain her precious Reception Class.

Then I answered Mollie, 'No, it is not settled. You have done nothing with your life and are in no position to look down on those who have achieved something. A person of the meanest intelligence wouldn't say the things you have said. I can only be sorry for you because you are as stupid as you are ignorant. I would like you to leave this house now and please do not enter it again except by specific invitation.'

Mollie, although obviously shaken, tried to bluff things out as usual. 'I think you need an early night, Aulish. You appear to have forgotten yourself.'

I answered steadily. 'On the contrary I have remembered myself and who I really am. Now will you please leave?'

For a moment she stared at me in amazement, looking as if the dog had spoken, then turned on her heel and left. I watched her go down the drive, walking tall and proud as ever. For me the enchantment was over, never to return in all its fullness. I sat down; my anger was cooling now and I burst into tears.

When Martin came in, I told him the whole story. He sat with his head in his hands and, slightly to my surprise, made no attempt to defend his mother. He sighed wearily.' 'I've seen this coming. She's gone too far this time. I can only apologise for her. As for you forbidding her the house, she's become much too ready to drop in at all times. Fitter far if she keeps away from that damned attic. I'll still see plenty of her around the farm and you'll have more space without her.'

There was plenty of physical space at Abbotshall. Martin's remark showed his love and understanding for me, but why had he mentioned the attic?

When Martin went to look up the cows, I considered my isolated state. My parents were on the other side of the world, I had cut myself off from my parents-in-law (for I was sure that Peter would support Mollie), Martin was certainly being supportive and loving, especially in bed, but the barrier of the "secret" still lay between us. Would Martin one day have to choose between his wife and his mother? Meanwhile would I be able to manage on my own?

Chapter Thirteen
The Miracle

The answer seemed to be 'Yes.' When Martin asked me a few days later, 'How's it going without Mother?'

My reply was very positive. 'It's extraordinary. I seem to have much more energy. I can think clearly and I get much more done.'

He smiled ruefully. 'Perhaps you can see now the damage she does on the farm by her constant interfering. Anyway, tell me some of the things you're doing.'

Leaving aside my desire to ask (yet again) why they allowed her to interfere, I turned with relief to discuss my plans with Martin. 'To begin with I'm getting real satisfaction from the house. I love doing all the cleaning myself and the cooking is sheer joy. I must have inherited some of Aunt Sarah's domestic skills.'

'Yes, I must say we have had some super meals recently. I suppose it's easier without constant interruption and criticism, but what about your plans for hobbies and interests?'

I felt I was making progress. 'Well I've dug out my Latin books and I'm reading a little every day, so if any teaching opportunity does come up, I won't be rusty.'

Martin looked serious as he took my hand. 'Aulis, could you do something to help me and the farm, which I think you would enjoy?'

I answered eagerly, 'I'd love to. Do you want me to help Matthew-Henry again?'

'No, it's paperwork.' Martin showed me an advert in the *Farmers' Weekly*. 'They're running a course on Farm Accounts at the local Agricultural College. It's just two mornings a week, would you like to do it? I have so little time to spare for the farm paperwork, and it worries me, we don't keep a proper grip on finances.'

I already had my own worries about the finances of Abbotshall. I had been rather amazed to receive a £10 note from Martin at the end of my first week at the farm and to be told that this was my week's housekeeping money. From this I was expected to buy all our food and cleaning materials, to pay Barbara, and to deal with any other incidental expenses — possibly even to buy clothes. Of course we got our milk, eggs and potatoes free, fruits from the garden in their season — like the apples in the attic — but it still seemed cheeseparing to me.

At the time I had remonstrated with Martin in a fairly light-hearted way. 'This is a bit mean, isn't it? Whatever are you going to do with the rest of your wages?'

He had looked at me in genuine surprise. 'I don't have wages, nor does Dad. We just take a certain sum out of the bank every week. Mother takes some for the housekeeping — she's given up this £10 for you — and the rest sits in Dad's desk to be used for various things. This is how farms work. If you wanted to marry a labourer with a wage packet you should have told me so!'

Even then, three weeks married, I couldn't believe that many people — even farmers — lived in such a financially illiterate way. But I was still very unsure about my new life so had meekly accepted Martin's hurtful reproof. That was three years ago. I still received the £10 each week and had become rather proud of what I managed to achieve with it.

Now I had the opportunity to find out more about Abbotshall's finances, to be really involved in the farm, and more nobly, to help Martin. I had only one reservation. 'But what will your parents say? Will they like me knowing the farm's business?'

Martin shrugged his shoulders. 'I've already floated the idea with Dad, who raised no objection. He doesn't mind who does the accounts, as long as he doesn't have to.'

'And your mother?'

Martin spoke firmly, 'Aulis, you have declared your independence. You can do as you like. And Mother really can't object to my wife knowing my business, as I shall tell her, if she complains. There must be some way of breaking her stranglehold on the farm, without hurting her of course.'

The old, inexplicable theme, I thought.

So I enrolled on the course and began to enjoy both the work and the outings to college. The other students were mostly farmers' wives, but younger and with a more modern outlook than the dancing wives or Ida's friends. They seemed to lead much more normal lives than we did, with no hovering in-laws. And although they had the unfortunate habit of becoming pregnant, they didn't go on about it all the time.

Meanwhile I began to grasp the concepts and terminology of accounting and to appreciate some aspect of the situation at Abbotshall. I saw how desperately reliant we were on the monthly milk cheque and the bonuses we got for high levels of butterfat in the milk. I understood now why Martin rated Sam so highly. I soon realised that the sheep were, as Martin called them, hobby-farming and wondered if it would be cheaper for Peter Peverell to play golf. Most shocking to me was the money which Mollie had spent on refurbishing the cottage. I pointed this out to Martin, querying whether all the changes had been really necessary. He was immediately on the defensive. 'Mother always has to have two bathrooms. She likes a separate one for the children.'

I stifled rude questions I might have asked about the children's personal habits to make my main point. 'But isn't this needless luxury, draining the farm?'

I got the usual stiff — and puzzling — reply. 'I've told you before, Aulis. We have to indulge Mother. I've also told you that I can't explain why — it's not my secret.'

So I had to be content, and in general I was finding the work very satisfying. My life was expanding and I had a real role at Abbotshall. Apart from our disagreements over Mollie, Martin seemed pleased with me, and I was far less lonely.

So as the third year of our marriage passed into the fourth, I began to be much happier. I assumed that was why all my senses seemed sharpened. I wanted to caress the smooth grey trunk of the ash tree, to trace the veins of the leaves with my finger and the sight of primroses in the orchard almost moved me to tears. I began to understand Mollie's love for the place and to be glad that I was feeling it too. Then I started being sick. I suddenly realised that I hadn't had a period for ages. I had long given up the desperate monthly checks for blood, the leaping of hope if it was a day late.

I was longing to tell Martin, spilling the news out joyfully as I would have done in the early days, but I was reluctant to raise his hopes falsely — to let him down again. Who could I consult? There was no way now that I would confide in Mollie. My parents were in Australia. Finally, I rang Marie. Her diagnosis was crisp and confident. 'You're pregnant — I'm certain — fantastic. Now go and see your doctor right away.'

I still hesitated. 'Shouldn't I wait until I've missed another period? It would be humiliating if I made a fuss about nothing.'

Marie was firm. 'Go!' Sensing my reluctance, she added, 'He can't tell Mrs Peverell before you do. That

170

would be breaking patient confidentiality.' Marie always knew the correct phrases.

Still, I hesitated, remembering the evil old woman in the dispensary. Then the decision was taken for me. I was normally sick during milking, but one morning I had to rush from the breakfast table. Martin was all concern. 'What's wrong, Aulis? Whatever have you eaten?'

My voice was tremulous, a mixture of weakness and joy. 'It's not that. Oh, Martin, I'm almost sure that I'm pregnant.'

He looked absolutely astounded. Then he was holding me so close that I felt his manhood, hard and firm, flaring up against my tiny bump. There were tears in his eyes as he asked, 'Almost sure — have you seen the doctor?'

'No, not yet — I wasn't sure.'

'So you've said, my darling. Let's go and ask him now.'

'But we haven't got an appointment.'

Martin was beginning to brim over with joy. I was still cautious but he was insistent. 'We can't wait for an appointment. I'll go and ring, and I'm coming with you.'

'But what about the farm, your work, your parents?'

'Hang them all — it's my son we're talking about,' and he hurried to the phone.

I seized his arm. 'Martin, be careful! The elder Miss Arthur has a hotline to your mother.'

He slowed down. 'OK, I'll take care.' The call completed he turned round smiling. 'We're in luck! Of

171

course, it's Thursday, no surgery and no Miss Arthurs. Doctor's opening up just for us. That's how important it is!'

I was dazed. 'Shouldn't we change?'

'No time for that. Let's go.'

As we scrambled into the van, Mollie appeared. Since our "row" she had never entered the house, but we spoke civilly when we met around the farm. Now she asked in surprise, 'Aulish, wherever are you going — and Martin — not in your working clothes, darling?'

Martin was brisk. 'Sorry Mother, can't stop, parts for the tractor needed urgently. Aulis just coming for the ride.' And we were off.

The doctor soon confirmed my diagnosis, and began to fill in the necessary form, explaining as he wrote: 'Expected Date of Confinement — 7th November. That's when your baby's due. Place of confinement: You'll want the birth at home, won't you?'

Martin's reply was firm. 'Yes of course. My son must be born at Abbotshall.'

I intervened. 'But shouldn't a first baby be born in hospital, in case there are complications?'

The doctor was soothing. 'No reason there should be, m'dear. Peverells are always born at Abbotshall. My uncle brought your husband into the world and his si…'

Presumably thinking that it was irrelevant to mention Di, he stopped abruptly. 'Yes, well that's all fixed then. Now you must take the iron tablets I'm going to give you and we'll arrange some appointments with the midwife.

172

This is very good news, but if I were you, I wouldn't publish it just yet. Wait until twelve to fourteen weeks — once the danger period is past.'

Martin was brought up short. 'You mean she might lose it — oh surely not?'

He spoke as if I were a careless child with a toy and miscarriage a voluntary act. What a mixture Martin was, I thought. A man who could love me so deeply and then speak like the spoilt child his mother had brought him up to be.

The doctor was reassuring but sensible. 'Everything seems very stable at the moment but you never know. There's far less stress on a first-time mother if she keeps her secret for a while.' Then to me, 'Now m'dear, lots of fresh air, good food and early nights.'

On the way home we pulled into the inevitable lay-by. Martin was jubilant. 'Oh, Aulis, I'm so excited. We won't have time to talk until tonight. And I'm longing to see your body — to feel my son inside you.

I was happy too, as I tried to calm him. 'You won't be able to feel anything much yet.'

He laughed. 'Oh, I will. I'm a farmer.' Then another thought struck him: 'I suppose we should be careful about making love — remember Majorca. Anyway, I suppose we needn't bother now.'

Seeing my stricken face, he hastened to make amends. 'Joke, joke. I've never wanted you so much!'

Relieved, I said, 'I think we should be cautious though — until the baby's really settled — it's only a few weeks.'

Martin went on, 'I know the doctor said don't tell anyone, but I think we must tell Mother and Pa, he can't have meant them.'

My newfound independence gave me strength. 'No, Martin. Absolutely no one must know — not your parents, not mine. They'll have less time to brood. Then when we do tell them they can be pleased without worrying too much.'

He agreed, somewhat grudgingly. For my part I realised that I didn't want my baby to become public property. Now that I had official confirmation that it was really there, I wanted it to be private and special. It seemed to be even more precious because it had taken so long to come. I didn't want to share it with anyone except Martin, and especially not with Abbotshall. For just a few weeks I thought, it can be entirely ours. I guessed that once the news was out, Mollie would begin to stake her claim in her grandchild.

The next few weeks were very happy. Martin was gentle and affectionate in bed, stroking my stomach, pretending the baby was kicking him. 'Don't be silly,' I said. 'We won't feel it move for ages yet.'

Martin laughed. 'No, I know. But Aulis, your breasts are really exciting. Look how they've filled out.'

I was very pleased. 'Yes, the doctor said they were very active. My nipples have improved too. I used to be so ashamed of those silly little crinkles of pink skin.'

Martin fondled my nipples, gently pulling them out and sucking them, till I cried out with love for him and his baby.

Gradually my sickness calmed down and as I passed the magic fourteen weeks I began to feel and to look very well.

For all this time I had managed to avoid Mollie and Peter. But I was noticeably big now so one evening in early June Martin and I went, solemnly, to tell them.

There was of course no need. Mollie took one look at me and said, with her usual frankness, 'Well, Aulish, I never thought to see you bloom, but I must say, pregnancy suits you.'

We gaped and she laughed, coming forward as she had done at our first meeting in the kitchen. She held me close. 'Oh yes, you're a big girl already. What are you, fourteen to fifteen weeks?'

'Sixteen,' I answered with pride, as much of the old love for her nearly came flooding back.

'And you were very wise not to tell us until the danger period was past, not exciting us with false alarms,' she continued, forestalling Martin's prepared apologies.

I felt huge, but now with happiness. Then, suddenly, as so often with Mollie, the mood was broken. It was Peter, obviously delighted in his quiet way, who spoke the four words that clouded the harmony of the moment. 'An heir for Abbotshall,' he said.

Mollie lost her joyous look. 'Oh! Yes, poor little Charlie, but this baby may be a girl.'

Peter was firm. 'It'll still be a Peverell and an heir for Abbotshall.'

They glared at each other. I hated the idea that my daughter was going to be argued over like a piece of property, another victim of the Abbotshall obsession.

Then I cried out as a sharp knock hit my right side. Mollie was all concern. 'Aulish, what is it? You've gone quite white. Come and sit down dear.' She led me gently to the sofa and sat beside me, holding my hand.

There was a moment of fear-filled silence. Had I let them down, again? Then, delighted, I realised what had happened. 'The baby, it moved.'

They were all about me, laughing and excited. 'It's very early for a first baby,' said Mollie. 'That's a good sign — he must be strong if you can feel him already.'

And I could, no sharp kicks now, but a little gentle fluttering.

Martin took me home and we lay happily in bed, fascinated by the movements of our child. I thought that I should melt with bliss as we fell asleep in each other's arms.

My joy was scarcely diminished by Mollie's appearance at ten o'clock next morning. As I answered her knock at the door she asked, with her sweetest smile,

'Please may Granny come in?' So was the great "row" apparently ended.

Seated once more in the kitchen Mollie produced a notebook and pen. 'Now, dear, I've come to make plans about the baby. The first thing is maternity clothes. You're more than ready for them now, lovely loose floaty things that will give him lots of room to breathe. No polka dots and none of those hideous new jumpsuits. You don't want to spend too much but hopefully you'll be using them again now you've started. Now we mustn't tire you, so I thought we'd have a gentle little trip into Stafford next Monday. I'll drive. We can go to that smart new boutique "Ladies in Waiting".'

This was Mollie in charge again, but in a fairly harmless area, so, burying my prejudice against a shop with such a name, I agreed. 'Yes, you're right. I do need clothes, and it'll be fun. I'm so glad that you say no polka dots. I hate them but I always thought that they were de rigeur for pregnancy. All my friends had them and jumpsuits too, I thought that I might even borrow some from Marie.'

Mollie was horrified. 'Out of the question! My grandson is not going to wear borrowed clothes, not even in the womb. Of course it might be different if Di had anything left, that would be family. As anything I had ever seen Diana wearing had been either muddy brown or pondweed green I didn't pursue the conversation but let Mollie proceed with her plans.

177

She seemed to be, not surprisingly, an expert on the details of pregnancy. 'I suppose you're having iron pills from Doctor Ronald. Now I could collect those for you every month when I go for our tablets.'

I was touched. 'Thank you that's really helpful.'

Mollie dismissed my gratitude. 'My dear child, for better or worse, this baby is a Peverell. We must all do what we can. Now what about your diet? You mustn't eat too much you know. Lower-class people have this silly notion of eating for two — quite unnecessary. A smaller baby means an easier birth, big boys have been known to kill the mother. Eat nourishing food, like milk and eggs, which you can get here, but eat it sparingly.'

I was impressed. 'Yes, Princess Charlotte's dead baby boy was huge, and it killed her.'

Ignoring my historical diversion about some woman of whom she'd never heard, Mollie carried on. 'You'll have the baby here of course?'

'Yes, Martin wants it born at home, but I'm a little scared in case things might go wrong with a first baby.'

'Nonsense! Hospital births are only for people whose homes are inadequate. Peverells must be born at Abbotshall. All my children were born here.'

Puzzled, and ever the linguist, I mentally played with her words. Shouldn't all be both? I had no time to ponder as Mollie rushed on. She was into cots and prams now and even nappies — the best terry towelling, of course.

This was where I put my foot down. My pregnancy had let Mollie back into my life, but she was not going to dominate it again. I spoke firmly. 'No, I want none of those in the house until the baby's safely here.'

The old scornful Mollie reappeared. 'Well, well, where's your precious education now? I didn't think you'd be so superstitious.' Then she smiled again. 'I can't be cross with you, Aulish, when you look so beautiful, carrying my grandson, with your breasts blooming, ready to nourish him.' Holding me close, she kissed me again

The expedition for clothes was a notable success. Chosen with Mollie's impeccable taste they were all in varying shades of blue — obviously not even the clothes must suggest a girl. Mollie insisted on dresses; simple cotton and woollen ones for everyday and two blissful garments, a navy-blue dress in fine ribbed silk, and one in fine wool, where tiny spring flowers rioted on a gentle blue background. Fingering the latter, she said dreamily, 'You can wear this afterwards, in the early days. It has a useful front opening and he'll love to look at the flowers when you're feeding him.' And when I demurred at the price, she was firm. 'Don't be silly, dear. You paid for the cheaper ones, I'll get these for you. Nothing's too good for my grandson and his beautiful mother.'

It wasn't pregnancy but happiness that was making me dizzy. The shop assistants were nodding and smiling. One of them said quietly to me, 'You are lucky. My mother-in-law's a bitch.'

For Mollie was positively sparkling, responding to their deference. 'We have such a good relationship,' she purred, 'And now Baby will bring us even closer.'

179

If only I'd been pregnant sooner, I thought, I might have been spared the last few years of misery.

But pleasure was never unalloyed with Mollie. Obviously, I wasn't reacting with sufficient enthusiasm, so as we left the shop, she felt that a little lecture was necessary. 'You don't know how lucky you are, poor Diana looked dreadful all through her pregnancies. You must enjoy your pregnancy, Aulish, letting Baby know that he's wanted. I hope he is after all this time. One never knows with girls that have been over-educated. I remember that even your mother said, on our first meeting, that you might be difficult about children. It's for your own good. If Baby knows he's wanted — that'll make the birth easier — he'll want to come. And you mustn't fuss about little aches and pains, dear, that's very lower-class.'

I took all this in, even the bits which I thought were unscientific nonsense, and I didn't fuss, though I did begin to feel less well. I was often hungry and fantasised about steak and kidney puddings or plates of fish and chips. But mindful of Mollie's advice I would nibble an egg sandwich, eat an apple or force myself to drink a glass of milk. I wasn't actually sick any more but I felt nauseous and desperately tired. The baby moved a lot at night, making me restless, until eventually Martin said that he couldn't have his sleep continually disturbed and decamped into the spare room. He was still very loving, but the euphoria had rather diminished. I was so lonely at night without Martin and as the baby grew, I began to get frightened. I had moments of seeing this baby inside me as an alien presence that had taken over my body and was coming between me and Martin. I was prey to all sorts of strange thoughts. I'd never been that keen on babies. I thought of Hector's Helen. Was I having this baby just because it was the thing to do, to please Mollie and fulfil my conventional role? I forgot how much Martin and I had loved the dream baby of Majorca and how I had sobbed over the barren months and years. I began to think about the baby itself. To which world would it belong — Mollie's or mine? I suddenly noticed that I thought of it now as "the baby" not "my" or "our" baby. It seemed to be draining all the strength out of me. Was there something wrong with it or was I going to lose it after all?

Chapter Fourteen
Complications

There was no one to calm my fears, to tell me that thoughts and doubts like these were common in pregnancy. I was reluctant to endanger my restored relationship with Mollie by loading her with my emotional burdens. I felt an immense longing for my own mother, a totally new sensation for me. Despite all my previous experience of her I hoped that the promise of the baby would forge some new line of understanding between us. So I cheered up when I saw the airmail letter on the mat, tearing it open eagerly. This would be my parents' reply to mine, in which I had announced my pregnancy. My mother had written:

Dear Aulis,

Dad and I were thrilled to hear your news — at last. We hope you're keeping well and looking after yourself. I'm sure that between them Martin and Mrs Peverell will see to it that you don't do too much —they will want a boy for the farm won't they? I expect they will want it born at Abbotshall, but be careful, a first baby can be a bit awkward. If I were you I'd put my foot down about a hospital birth. Your dad says I'm not to give you any advice because you don't listen to us any more anyway, only to landed families. Just his joke, I expect.

I'm sorry that we won't be home in time for the happy event. We promised Jason and Mel to stay for little Gareth's birthday and his first real Christmas so our tickets are now booked to return in March. So we should be home for the Christening — if you can put that off until we come! We can't wait to see your baby.

Mel and Jason send their congratulations. Incidentally (one of my mother's favourite words) *Mel had a mis before she had Gareth. She was asking me if you'd had any mis at all. I told her that we would be the last to know if you had!*

Little Gareth is lovely — he's into everything now and full of mischief.

And so it went on — about Jason and his family. The travelling they'd been doing - loads of totally irrelevant stuff.

I sighed with disappointment and exasperation. Couldn't wait to see my baby, so wasn't it possible to change their tickets, surely not a difficult operation? The baby would be nearly six months old before they were home. Why was my baby apparently less important than Jason's? The apparent quote from my father I treated with suspicion — it could be a joke — or it could be my mother trying to make mischief — she'd always resented my closeness to Dad. I found very distasteful her sly and vulgar reference to miscarriages. That was my mother, the baby obviously wasn't going to change her.

Looking at the letter again I thought how typical it was of her to talk of a baby being "awkward" a meaningless word, making the baby sound like a recalcitrant teenager and rekindling all my fears about a home birth. Did she really think I could overrule them all? Anyway, I wanted my baby to be born at Abbotshall — like all the ones before him — not in some impersonal hospital with harsh lights and bossy nurses. But, with all her faults, I still wanted my mother to be with me. Although we had never been particularly close, she had always been there. Now I wanted her and she wasn't going to be there.

As if on cue I heard Mollie's characteristic knock at the door. Hastily blowing my nose, I let her in. She seemed full of goodwill. 'Hello, dear! I've brought your next lot of iron pills. They're those white ones again, not the brown ones you had at first. Remember I told you last time the colour had changed.'

Then she looked closely at me. 'Good gracious, Aulish, I hope you're taking these pills. You look absolutely washed out. Your bloom didn't last long. Are you feeling all right?'

I answered cheerfully, 'Yes, fine.' I had no wish to reveal any weakness to Mollie lest I be labelled as a member of the whinging lower classes. She seemed pleased with my answer, commenting brightly, 'I expect it's that big Peverell boy taking all you can give him, dear, as they do.' I assumed that she meant the baby.

Martin was certainly not making any demands on me at the moment.

Then Mollie saw the airmail letter on the table. 'Have you heard from your parents, dear? Are they very excited about the baby? Are they coming home? I'm sure you're longing to see your mother. I know that you've never seemed very close but it's different when there's a baby on the way.'

Mollie's kind enquiries and apparent understanding of how I felt compounded my misery. But I was still determined not to break down in front of her so I answered in as deadpan a fashion as I could. 'Yes, they seem quite excited but they're not coming home until next March — they can't change their arrangements.'

Mollie sniffed, echoing my thoughts. 'Good heavens, the baby will be six months old by then! I must say I would drop everything to be with my daughter for her first — or any — baby. I did for Di. Both hers were born here, you know. I've always thought that you were rather a cold family, but this really shocks me. But don't worry, Aulish, I'll be with you. Now don't forget to take your tablets. I must go.' And, patting my hand kindly, off she went.

The whole morning, my mother's letter, the accuracy of Mollie's remarks about both my looks and my family, and then her real kindness, all made me thoroughly miserable. I knew that I looked dreadful, my complexion waxen pale, my hair, dull with grease, and my figure so thin that my bump stuck out like an unsightly lump of disease, not a happy growth of hope. How could Martin bear to look at me? Yet I was halfway through my pregnancy, when most women look their best. And I felt as dreadful as I looked.

I craved reassurance, from someone of my own age — presently or recently pregnant themselves. Of course, how silly I was — the obvious person was Marie — and I was soon pouring out my symptoms to her down the telephone. 'I've got less and less energy. I can hardly drag myself out of bed in the morning. And I think that the baby's less active. I don't know what's the matter with me, I was feeling great.'

Marie's reaction was totally unexpected. 'For God's sake, Aulis, you're pregnant. That's what it means, aches and pains and misery for nine months. You've always seen it in some romantic, rosy glow, but that's because you've never experienced it. Pregnancy is hell, then you get a red-faced, red-arsed, screaming object that leaks at both ends and keeps you awake all night. Grow up! You're never satisfied. First you whinge for years because you're not pregnant and now you're whinging because you are. No wonder your mother-in-law thinks you're a milksop, perhaps she's right! Well, I'm busy. I have three children — remember!'

The phone was slammed, down, leaving me shaking with bewilderment and hurt. In some fifteen years of friendship Marie had never spoken to me like that. We'd had little rows and spats, like any friends, but her outburst seemed quite unfair. And when had she discussed me with Molllie? Coming on top of my mother's letter, it was as if all the people from my old life were distancing themselves from me.

Much later I learned that when we were speaking Marie had recently miscarried her fourth child. But the rock of our relationship was fissured and never quite mended.

Recovering in the kitchen with the inevitable cup of tea, and cheered by some more energetic activity from the baby, I thought of Ida Ripley. I saw her rarely but whenever we met there was always a cheery smile followed by a few kind words. As I waited for her to answer the phone, I hoped that she at least hadn't undergone a personality change.

I needn't have worried. She listened to me and then, as she replied, the confident reassurance in her voice washed over me like a warm bath. 'It may be nothing, Aulis, but I can understand why you're worried. Look, I'll phone Whisky Galore' — her irreverent but accurate name for Dr Ronald — 'come round to pick you up and take you straight to the surgery.'

'What if Mollie sees you?'

'Don't worry, I'm immune. She doesn't get to me — she leaves me cold, you see. I'm a rare bird. See you in ten minutes. Be ready and bring any pills he's given you.'

Ten minutes later I was climbing gratefully into the big old Humber. Ida looked exactly the same as when I first met her. The little twinkly face and the pretty sandy hair crowned the great haystack that was her body. On this warm July day, the army tent had been exchanged for red and white striped cotton, a tent in a medieval fair.

She looked me over gravely. 'You're right, Aulis, you don't look too well. You're much too thin, and you have no colour. I do hope everything's all right.' Seeing my frightened face, she hastily changed the subject. 'Lovely clothes, Mollie's choice, I suppose?'

'Yes! I've put on my best navy ribbed silk dress in honour of the doctor.'

Ida began to turn the car round. 'And how's His Majesty?'

Puzzled for a moment I realised that she meant the baby.

'He's (God I was slipping into it now) more active today. Sometimes he's very quiet.'

'Well, that's how they go. A baby's movements in the womb are always erratic. But we'd better make sure he's OK. You've waited a long time for him. He's very precious, and so are you.'

The warmth of that friendly "we", so different from Mollie's royal "we", and the concern for me as myself, not just as the carrier of the Peverell Messiah, cheered me still more.

The dapper little doctor, totally sober at eleven o'clock in the morning, came out of the surgery to greet us. 'Ida! How good to see you. Bring young Mrs Peverell in.'

He looked at me searchingly. 'You're looking peaky. Is the young man giving you trouble?'

Halfway to an indignant defence of Martin, I realised that he, too, was referring to the baby. I began to explain. 'I feel terribly tired all the time and seem to have no energy. I'm not sure whether the baby's movements have slowed up.'

He looked puzzled. 'You were in splendid shape the last time I saw you. Let's have a look at you. Take your things off and get on the couch.' The examination completed, he moved away. 'Right, get dressed and we'll have a talk.'

Ida and I gazed earnestly at the little man as he gave his verdict. 'Well, m'dear, your baby seems a little small for dates. And you have lost weight since your last visit. I thought the sickness had stopped. Are you eating properly?'

I described my diet with pride. 'Oh yes, I have lots of milk and eggs and fruit.'

The doctor nodded. 'That's fine. But what about carbohydrates? This baby seems to be draining you and yet it's not big itself. And you're quite young. Your placenta should be working perfectly.'

I gave him my adaptation of Mollie's lecture on eating in pregnancy. 'You see if the baby's not too big the birth will be easier and I won't get gross. And we'll bond better because I'll want him more because he won't have hurt me so much.' Even as I spoke, I felt that the words, so convincing when uttered by Mollie, sounded like unscientific rubbish.

The doctor was almost angry. 'What new-fangled nonsense is this? What book did you get it from?'

Before I could answer Ida ploughed in. 'It'll be Mollie Peverell, Dr Ronald. It's her regular pregnancy advice. Of course, I took no notice. I'm quite happy to be gross. But I expect she used me as a dire warning to Aulis.'

She laughed as I blushed, for she was quite right. Then I saw that the little doctor had regained some of his usual pomposity. He cleared his throat. 'Well of course Mrs Peverell is a very wise woman. And she's so excited about this baby. One can understand that it means a lot to her. I think you must have misunderstood her, m'dear, taken her too literally. But you must eat a more balanced diet. Get Mrs Ripley to give you some of her famous stews.'

'She's coming back home right now to share the oxtail I left in the Aga,' promised Ida.

'Good, good! Now what about your iron pills, taking them, I hope?'

'Yes, she is,' Ida chimed in, 'She's got them with her. Show them to the doctor, Aulis.'

I obeyed, thinking that even Ida was starting to treat me like a six-year-old. But as I handed the bottle to the doctor I began to understand. He unscrewed the top, looked at the small white pills in amazement, and shook a few into his palm. He sniffed them and then put one carefully into his mouth. He was sharp and precise now.

'These aren't iron pills. They're simple sweetening tablets. Where did you get them?'

Considering the label on the bottle I was slightly annoyed: 'From your dispensary.'

'But didn't you notice that they were different from the others? Those were brown for a start.'

'I know, but she said they came in different colours.'

The doctor was curt. 'Who is she, my dispenser?'

'No, my mother-in-law, she picked them up for me.'

Again, the stiffening, the withdrawal. 'There must have been some mistake in the dispensary. These are quite harmless, but hardly nourishing.'

He turned to Ida. 'I think you need some iron tablets, Mrs Ripley. I'll prescribe them for you today and perhaps you can get young Mrs Peverell to take them for you. Then Mrs Peverell can continue to pick up the white ones. I can guess who will have given her those.'

'Of course, Doctor,' Ida replied demurely. 'Least said, soonest mended.'

The doctor smiled. 'Ah good, you get my point.'

I certainly didn't. I looked from one to the other. If Mollie and/or the elder Miss Arthur were involved in this really wicked deception, why couldn't they be challenged? Better still, to avoid a scene, why couldn't I just tell Mollie that I was going to pick up my own tablets? I opened my mouth to protest, but once again Ida forestalled me, saying firmly, 'Thank you, Doctor, that's a perfect solution. I'll collect my first dose on the way out, shall I?'

He handed her the slip to give to the dispenser. Then, to me, 'I'll see you in two weeks' time, Mrs Peverell, for your usual ante-natal appointment with the midwife.'

Nodding, I allowed Ida to shepherd me from the room. Back in the car, I could contain myself no longer. 'Why does everyone tread so gently around Mollie? What's all this nonsense about you having the pills and me taking them? Why is even the doctor afraid of her?'

Ida's reply was calm and straightforward. 'Because Mollie's disapproval is no light thing. It can do people a lot of harm.'

'Oh! Come on, she's not a witch.'

'It depends what you mean by a witch. All right, she doesn't turn the milk sour or stop the hens laying, but a slight word from her can affect a business or a reputation. Take the doctor himself, everyone knows about his drinking, but as long as Mollie continues to go to him, he's seen as respectable, and he can't afford to lose that. I mean look at the butchers.'

'The butchers?' I was totally puzzled now.

Ida continued. 'Yes, you know the two butchers' shops in the village?'

I nodded. 'Yes. I once went into Frank Johnson's. Mollie found out and scolded me, explaining that the Peverells shopped only at Arthur Trimble's. I wasn't particularly bothered.'

Ida laughed. 'Perhaps not, but Frank Johnson was. Mollie used to patronise both butchers until she had some small disagreement with Frank about chops. She's never been in his shop since, and as a result, neither has most of the village. If it weren't for passing trade and people in those new houses up Church Lane, who neither know nor care about Mollie, Frank would have gone under. I told you when we first met that Mollie's a dangerous woman.'

I was dismissive and still perplexed. 'But this isn't chops it's my baby, the Abbotshall heir. Even if Mollie wouldn't care if she hurt me, why would she risk hurting the baby? It's her own flesh and blood and she seems so positive about it. She even seems to have told the doctor that she's pleased. She bought me all these lovely clothes and she has been much warmer and nicer since I've been pregnant.'

Ida was judicious. 'Well to begin with we don't actually know if it's Mollie that's practising the deception. The elder Miss Arthur may be fooling her as well as us.'

I was even more puzzled. 'But why on earth would the elder Miss Arthur want to hurt me or the baby?'

'Oh, she's always been bitter and twisted. They say she's the reason why poor Dr Ronald's never married. She hates anyone young or hopeful. Added to that she adores Mollie, she literally can't bear to see another Mrs Peverell in her place. She would loathe the idea that this baby might make you as good as or even better than Mollie.'

I wasn't entirely convinced of Miss Arthur's guilt. Mollie remained my chief concern. I determined to ask

Ida the question that had been bothering me ever since my disagreement with Martin over Bert Stoate. 'Ida, does Mollie have some sad secret which could explain why she might have an ambivalent attitude to my baby?'

I sensed a stiffening in Ida, although she answered readily enough. 'I'm sure if there were anything you needed to know, Martin, at least, would have told you.'

'No that's the point. Martin said that it wasn't his secret.'

Ida looked relieved. 'Then perhaps he was referring to the business with Emily, though that's ancient history and not exactly a secret.'

I was fascinated. 'Aunt Emily? How does she come into it?'

'I'll tell you the whole story. Emily was engaged to Peter.' Brushing aside my exclamations she went on. 'Those two girls, Mollie and Emily, were always going to look after old and sick relatives, who generally preferred having Emily, because she was kinder than Mollie. So off goes Emily to nurse Uncle Somebody. When she gets back she finds she's just in time to be bridesmaid at Mollie and Peter's wedding!'

I was aghast. 'But why?'

'Why do you think? Mollie had been amusing herself with Peter and reckoned that she was pregnant.'

'Was she?'

Ida was sceptical. 'Who knows? Martin was born almost exactly forty weeks to the wedding night. Mollie had two explanations, either that he was overdue, or the more fantastic one, that she had a miscarriage on her honeymoon and then instantly conceived Martin. All very dubious!'

I thought of the bottom drawer hidden away in the attic. 'Poor Aunt Emily! But Peter adores Mollie.'

Ida agreed. 'Yes, and she's probably been much better for him than Emily would have been. Emily has no drive. I don't know if that's the secret Martin means, but it was certainly quite a scandal at the time. It shows you again what Mollie can do.'

As Ida drove into her yard and stopped the car she spoke seriously. 'Don't go hunting round for secrets, Aulis. The past is over and is best left alone. If the secret isn't Martin's, then it need not be yours either. Leave it in the dead past where it belongs. Don't antagonise Mollie now, Aulis. Think about your baby.'

I replied in equal seriousness. 'I'll take care, I promise. And I won't mention the iron tablets, not even to Martin.'

We went happily into the cheerful, cluttered kitchen. The oxtail was done to a turn and tasted delicious. Ida drove me home. I spent a lovely evening with Martin and went to bed fortified with a genuine iron tablet. Some of my earlier serenity began to return. But before I fell asleep, I thought back to the conversation with Ida. Obviously, she'd told me the story of the butchers to warn me off upsetting Mollie. But why did I feel that Ida had used the Emily story as a red herring to put me off the scent of some more serious secret about Mollie? Why was everyone keeping things from me? And why did I mind so much? Why was I so curious about this secret? Why did I feel that it was something that could hurt my baby?

As if on cue he gave me a tremendous kick. Stroking him gently I drifted off to sleep.

Chapter Fifteen
Further Complications

My accounts course was now finished. I knew about fixed costs and variable costs, capital expenditure and running costs and many more concepts, at least in theory. Martin was pleased with my progress, so one Monday morning he said cheerfully, 'Now I'm going to let you loose on the Abbotshall accounts. I know that you had a quick look at them during the course. Now I want you to go through them thoroughly, applying everything you've learned, and tell me what you think.'

I settled at the big old desk in the back-kitchen, easing my bump comfortably into the kneehole. Books of any sort, even arithmetic books, always made me feel good.

My pleasure didn't last beyond my admiration of Peter's copperplate handwriting. The books might look good but their content was dire. The more I investigated the more detailed study confirmed my earlier impressions. The desk was soon littered with paper, as I did sums over and over again, checking to see if these figures could possibly be right. I was more concerned now because there was the baby to consider.

That evening Martin and I sat down to discuss my findings. I came straight to the point. 'Martin, do you know how bad things are? Expenditure is way above income. Nothing seems to make much money except the milk. There isn't enough investment in new equipment. And should you not have some more profitable enterprises? I looked into some of the older books. When you had pigs, they did really well, why don't you have them now? Oh, and why is the farm mortgaged?'

Martin sat with his head in his hands, the old defeated attitude, as he tried to answer my questions. 'Oh, God, Aulis, you haven't really told me anything I didn't know. I just wanted a fresh, intelligent eye on it all. Where shall I start? Well, the farm's mortgaged because we got married. Mother wanted money to do up the cottage, so that's our fault.'

I didn't want to get angry so early in the conversation, but it was hard not to. 'Don't be ridiculous. You had every right to marry, you were thirty-four! They could have stayed here, and we could have lived in the cottage as it was. There was nothing fundamentally wrong with it. Your mother just enjoyed making it luxurious.'

Ignoring my reference to Mollie, Martin continued, 'The milk does well because Sam runs the dairy in a modern way, but it could do even better if we could shop around more for feed.'

'Why can't you?'

'Mother and Pa like the business to go to old-established firms that they've always dealt with.'

I was getting seriously annoyed. 'Too bad, it should go to the seller offering the best, if not necessarily the cheapest, deal.'

Martin shrugged his shoulders. 'Yes, that's text-book stuff, but real life isn't always like that.'

I was scornful. 'I would never accuse your mother of embracing real life, but let's leave that. What about the pigs?'

Martin looked thoroughly miserable. 'I loved those pigs. But they did need a lot of care. I needed a pig-man of the same calibre as Sam, but Mother said we couldn't afford that, so I got tired of arguing and let the pigs go.'

I was appalled! 'You couldn't afford it! No of course not, not when you're keeping old Jack and Mr Stoate in luxury. Far too much money goes on their wages. And what about the housekeeping? You know I get £10 a week to cover everything, while your mother gets £40! What does she do with it all?'

Martin made a mild protest. 'You know what high standards she has, and she's very generous. Look at those beautiful maternity clothes she's bought you.'

'Yes, I know, Martin, but we can't live off one-off gestures and random generosity. Is she going to feed and clothe our baby? But I know that it's no use berating you. You are somehow placed in an impossible position by some secret that I'm not allowed to share. Meanwhile is this poor little baby going to be born into a bankrupt business?'

Martin sat up straight. 'Aulis, I promise that I will sort things out, secret or no damn secret. Once our son is safely born, we'll have a set-to with Mother and Pa and take some decisions. We've got to preserve our son's inheritance. That's what Mother wants too. She's so excited about the baby. She talks to me about him all the time. She's just not very bright financially and she likes things to be as they always have been. With you to back me up I really believe that we can make significant changes.'

I was dubious but trying to be positive. 'But what if we can't, and it will still need to be done if the baby's a girl.'

Martin was adamant on the second count. 'You're carrying my son, and if we can't get them to change, we'll just have to think of another solution. Now let's have some fun, watch TV or something, my head's aching with all this thinking.'

I agreed, but I realised what a mountain of effort I had to face, a baby and a business. Thank goodness I now felt reasonably happy and secure about the baby, especially as everyone kept telling me how much Mollie wanted it. Was I finally going to be accepted because I was his mother?

Next day reminded me never to feel safe about anything at Abbotshall. As I was pregnant, I had reluctantly given in to Mollie's insistence that I have a cleaner again. Foolishly I had allowed Mollie to import one of her choice, not jolly Barbara, but a tall, massive, taciturn girl called Susan, whose presence created a pool of gloom. I could find no common ground with this girl and frankly loathed having her in my house. I found it hard to imagine how she had any connection with graceful Mollie, to whom appearances were so important, though perhaps Mollie's standards didn't extend to villagers. And even I had to admit that Susan was a good cleaner.

On Tuesday mornings Susan's schedule included cleaning one of Abbotshall's glories, the oak front stairs. Mollie had given me strict instructions about their care. 'We've never carpeted the front stairs, that would quite spoil their beauty, but don't ever polish them. We once had an idiot maid who did and old Auntie Grace fell and broke her hip. She was here for months and I was running up and down with trays. The stairs should just be swept and dusted, otherwise someone could break their neck.'

Seeing the sense of this, contemplating the awful thought of Aunt Emily bed-ridden in my house, I'd made these instructions absolutely clear to Sulky Sue.

We usually used the back stairs but this particular morning, knowing that Susan had finished in the front of the house and anxious, as always, to avoid a direct encounter with her, I decided to use the front ones. My care for my precious bump saved me. I was clutching the banister firmly as I put my foot on the top step, so that as it slid from under me, I just sat down with a jolt, rather than falling from top to bottom. As I got my breath back, I saw that the stairs were gleaming like glass. They had been polished.

I don't know how long I sat there, cradling my stomach. Trembling with shock and anger, I somehow got myself back onto the landing and walked carefully down the back stairs into the kitchen, where Susan was cleaning the windows. I think the cold steel in my voice startled even her, as I said, 'Put your cloth down and look at me. Why did you polish the front stairs?'

Bovine as ever she stared at me, saying nothing. I was adamant. 'I want an answer.'

Then the words gushed out, a stream of pent-up resentment. 'Mrs Peverell, the proper Mrs Peverell, told my mum the other day that this place wasn't as clean as it used to be, especially the stairs. I don't like my work being picked on so I thought I'd make 'em shine. My mum said it's daft not to polish them and you don't know nothin' anyway. Everybody knows you're nobody, just a bit of a schoolteacher. We takes our orders from gentry like Mrs Peverell, not from kids like you that aren't no better than us.'

Although filled with dislike and contempt I remained remarkably calm. 'Goodness, Susan, I didn't think that you knew so many words. It may interest you and your mother to know that the orders about the stairs came from the "proper Mrs Peverell". They were never polished in her time. Now you can stay here while I summon her to deal with you, as you object to my doing so. You may make yourself a cup of whatever it is you drink, venom I should think.'

I phoned Mollie and she was soon in my kitchen, lecturing the defiant girl.

'Susan, you have been a very naughty, a very wicked girl. Your mother will be very disappointed in you.'

With the arrogance bred by ignorance she dared to interrupt. 'But you said...'

'Whatever I said or didn't say, I didn't tell you to polish the stairs, did I Susan?'

'No!' Sulky and reluctant as she was, Susan couldn't disagree

'You could have hurt Mrs Martin or my grandson very badly. You can't work at Abbotshall any longer, Susan.'

With a careless shrug Susan began to collect her things, but Mollie intervened. 'Oh no, you're not going yet, you have one more job to do. You will return the stairs to their original condition, under my supervision. But before you do that you will walk down them.'

I made an involuntary movement of protest, but Mollie stood firm. 'No, Mrs Martin, Susan must learn. She must understand what she might have done to someone else by her foolishness. Go up the back stairs please, Susan, and to the top of the front. We will stand at the bottom to watch you walk down.'

I was amazed that the girl didn't refuse or even argue. Obviously, this was the effect achieved by the "proper Mrs Peverell". With such power why hadn't

Mollie used her talents to do something significant, not merely to exercise this petty tyranny?

The wretched Susan did as she was told. At the top of the front stairs, she put forward one large, coarse foot, felt it slide it beneath her and faltered. She looked piteously at Mollie. 'I can't, Mrs Peverell.'

'Oh, but you must, Susan. You expected Mr and Mrs Martin to walk down there, didn't you, and perhaps even me and Mr Peverell? Come on down now, like a good girl.'

Slowly, clinging desperately to the banister, sliding on her bottom, not without some bravery, the great carthorse of a girl got herself down. White and shaking, speaking with unaccustomed politeness, she faced Mollie. 'I'm ever so sorry, Mrs Peverell; I didn't understand.'

Mollie was unforgiving. 'Well now you do, and your foolishness has lost you your job. Go and get your tools and I'll show you how to get the polish off these stairs.' Turning to me she said. 'You go and make us a nice cup of tea, dear. I'm sure that you and my grandson need it after all this disturbance. I know I do.'

I went, thoughtfully. Mollie's punishment of Susan had struck me as extreme. I'd hated the barely concealed glee with which she'd watched the girl's descent of the stairs. There was a vein of cruelty there that made me shudder.

Susan paid and seen off the premises, Mollie came into the kitchen and flopped into one of the Windsor chairs, saying wearily, 'I really would appreciate that cup of tea now, Aulish. Susan was hard work, wasn't she? I don't know why she's so sullen. Her mother's a nice little woman and her father is of course our own dear Mr Stoate. Not that they were ever married, she's one of Bert's little adventures, but she certainly has none of his charm.'

I was fascinated. I had wondered what the link could be between Mollie and Susan. That awful man again, what was his hold over Martin's mother?

But Mollie was continuing, her tone rather wistful. 'I thought, you know, that with Susan being young, you could have trained her into your ways, but I suppose you have no idea how to keep a house clean, have you? Life must be very different in a little semi-detached, with a mother who goes out to work. Never mind, you are giving us the baby at last. You did quite right to fetch me, you're very precious now you know, carrying this little boy. And now I suppose I must find you a new cleaner.'

Determined to have no more of Mollie's protégés and to exert my authority, I replied firmly, 'No thank you. I'll find my own this time.'

Mollie was perplexed. 'But darling, how can you? You don't know the villagers.'

Resisting the temptation to say, 'Thank God' I said cheerfully, 'I shall put an advert in that new shop at the top of Church Lane and try to get someone from the new bungalows up there, who hopefully will come with a fresh mind.'

Mollie was cynical. 'You mean not influenced by me. Well good luck, dear, it's your problem! I wish you success, I don't suppose people who live in those sorts of houses know anything more about cleaning than you do!' And off she went.

Telling Martin all about it over lunch, I dared to question Mollie's behaviour. First, the connection with Bert Stoate. 'Why did your mother wish on me the daughter of that horrible man?'

Martin was dismissive: 'Oh I don't think Susan sees much of her father. And Mother doesn't think he's horrible.'

I was more convinced than ever that Bert Stoate had something to do with the precious secret. Why had Martin not told me before about Mr Stoate's relationship with Susan? But I was willing to let this go for the moment to deal with the more serious aspect of this morning's events.

'Martin, I know that your mother would never have told Susan to polish the stairs. But was it wise even to mention their cleaning to such dim people?'

Martin's reply showed the shrewdness which I so valued. 'Probably not, but Mother's not like your family. She's quite unaware of people's relative intelligence. Think how she brackets Sam with Jack and Matthew-Henry, when there's no comparison where brains and education are concerned. Basically she sees everyone outside her own small circle as a vague mass called "ordinary people".'

Appreciating his honesty, and half-laughing, I replied, 'You mean that "lower order" from which I might just have escaped by carrying the heir of Abbotshall? But Martin, what's going to happen to the baby?'

Martin was alarmed. 'Whatever do you mean? This morning's little adventure didn't hurt him, did it?'

'No, I didn't mean happen physically, but where will he belong? When I first met your Mother, she said, "Martin should marry a girl who shares our standards." I've always thought that was just a put-down to keep me in my place. But now I see that if you had married a girl of their sort your wife would think, as you all do, that earth can hold nothing finer than to farm Abbotshall. I thought that I would think like that too, I wanted to, but now I find that I can't, and I don't see why my child should. Your mother said today that I was giving the baby to the family. He's not mine to give. He won't belong to anyone except himself.'

Martin looked at me kindly and spoke almost whimsically. 'You know, Aulis, I used to wonder if it was me you wanted to marry or the "Ceremonious House". Now, after four years here, you see the tyranny of these traditions. Don't you think that I feel this conflict myself? There were subjects I enjoyed at school, would have liked to study at university, but I knew that if I got a first at Oxford, or discovered a new planet, I'd only have to come back to run this farm. It needn't be like that for our son. We can make sure that he does what he wants to do, what he's good at. He might even end up a Professor of Classics!'

Impressed as I was by Martin's speech, I still wasn't convinced. 'Then why all this Heir of Abbotshall stuff?'

Martin laughed. 'Partly just fun, it sounds like one of those nineteenth-century novels you love, partly to tease Mother out of her obsession with Charlie Llewellyn, mostly because that's what our son will be, heir to all that this place has been and is, all its virtues, all its faults.'

Silently I thought, and all its secrets. Will he, unlike his mother, be allowed to know them? To Martin I said, 'But our son won't be just Abbotshall, he'll have my genes as well as yours.'

Martin gave his usual hearty laugh. 'Of course he will, thank God! He'll bring all that richness with him to this place and to our lives. I don't give poor old Mother much of a chance if you and he line up against her. I just can't wait for him to be here. Come on, Aulis, it's your hormones making you brood, though I suppose you're bound to be broody now.' He laughed again at his own joke, and then said hastily, 'Goodness, look at the time. If I don't go back to work, he'll be heir to nothing except bankruptcy.' There was a long, lingering, loving kiss and he was gone.

I felt much comforted by our talk, though rather ashamed that I'd never realised that Martin had a vision wider than Abbotshall. But while we had faced some facts about the potential nature of the baby, neither of us had mentioned the unthinkable — what if he was an heiress?

Chapter Sixteen
Passage Perilous

As my pregnancy moved into what the books called the third trimester, the baby became very real. On hot August afternoons I reclined in the walled garden, fancying that the sun was warming him through my thin cotton dresses. I felt him stretching his limbs as if to wallow in the warmth. I would fondle my burgeoning breasts, getting them ready for him to suckle.

The baby made both Martin and me very happy. We had agreed to shelve our concerns about Abbotshall until the birth was safely over, but I had other, more immediate worries. The most pressing was who would support me through the birth. I was very isolated. My new cleaner, Mrs Brown, a quiet, polite woman from the new bungalows, did her work and made no intrusions into my life. She had no links with Abbotshall, no children and seemingly no interest in my pregnancy. While all this was ostensibly a great relief, there were moments when I thought what fun it would be to have Barbara fussing over me, with all kinds of homespun advice.

My mother, of course, remained in Australia. She wrote regularly but her references to my pregnancy were always extremely vague. 'I hope you're keeping well.'

'Are you all right?' I remembered that talk about any aspect of reproduction had always been discouraged at home and generally conveyed in nods and winks. Well, she wasn't here now to nod or wink; 'And she won't be here when I go into labour,' I said sadly to Martin.

He tried to comfort me. 'Don't worry, darling, Mother will be here. She was absolutely marvellous with Di when her two were born. I know that you have your differences but she'll come up trumps for this I promise you.'

I thought how excited I would once have been at the thought of Mollie helping me to have my baby. It would have sealed the loving relationship between us which I had hoped to have. Now I was less confident. Although we seemed to be in harmony about the baby, and Mollie had vaguely promised her support, I didn't entirely trust her. She had shown little interest in the modest preparations I had made for the birth. I didn't feel that our relationship was warm enough for us to go through such a close experience as childbirth. So I muddled on, trusting in the professionals and with the hopeful idea that it would be "all right on the night".

Mollie still collected my iron tablets and I still took the ones prescribed for Ida Ripley. These had a double benefit, enabling me to see Ida at regular intervals, when she brought cheerfulness and some of her mouth-watering pies. I thought of asking Ida to support me at the birth but I didn't want to upset Mollie. And Ida didn't volunteer, I expect for the same reason, not wanting to worsen my relationship with Mollie. How that woman dominated everything!

I saw little of Martin during these harvest months when the men worked until dark. He would come in, have a quick bath, wolf down his food and roll into bed. He loved the feel of my stomach now. With his farming expertise he could find the parts of the baby much better than I could. He would do what he called his nightly check, saying, as he nuzzled my nipples, now crimson and full like great raspberries, 'Oh, Aulis, I love you more than ever. You are so beautiful with our son inside you.'

Only two things threatened my happiness. I still had moments when I wondered if the baby meant more to Martin than I did, if I was loved primarily as its carrier. I would remember how distant and cold he had become before it was conceived. Before I joined the farming circle I had known married couples who seemed quite happy without children, but here they were paramount. I shivered as I remembered Ida's tale of Madge Perkins' nine pregnancies, endured until she got her son. And that was my second worry. Martin's insistence that the baby was a boy, his obsession with having a son. I kept thinking about Henry VIII and Anne Boleyn. My sensible self told me that this was a ludicrous comparison. I was getting as ridiculous as Mollie if I could think of Abbotshall as a kingdom. The only worrying similarity with the great king was Martin's determination that the child should be a boy. I knew that I couldn't survive here without Martin's approval, constantly exposed to the dull ache that was Mollie and the whole Abbotshall situation.

Then the summer was over. The nights drew in and Martin and his father returned to their usual schedule of meetings, NFU, Cattle Breeders, PCC. On these evenings Mollie would come to keep me company. I didn't altogether welcome this; I was afraid of becoming dependent on her, but she brushed aside my protests. 'Nonsense dear, it's no trouble; it's bad for you to be alone. I know what the last few weeks are like. You get all kinds of fears and fancies, especially at Abbotshall, where so many babies have been born, and died, some taking their mothers with them.'

She sounded genuinely sad. I tried to imagine the young Mollie, huge as I was now, frightened as I was, all alone in that great house. But in her time it had been full of servants, as I reminded her.

'Worse than useless, dear, until I'd mastered them. It was easier with each child.'

A query flashed through my mind. "Each child", surely there were only two?

These evenings were a curious mixture. Mollie was knitting for the baby while I had discovered an ability to sew and was turning out delicate embroidered garments. Even in the 1960s we must have looked rather quaint, sitting one each side of the fire, plying our needles.

Sometimes Mollie would tell me cosy stories of Martin's babyhood. I would see her looking at me, with what appeared to be real affection. Then the fox's mask

213

would come down and her eyes return to ice-blue pebbles.

One evening she commented on Martin's absences. 'It's a good thing Pa's with him or we might wonder what he was up to, might we not, dear? Pregnant women are not very attractive to men, you know, especially if they've let themselves go a little. Is he still making love to you? The Peverells are quite insatiable. Pa was having me the night before Di was born. We often think that's why she was a mite early. But don't worry, dear, I'm sure your baby won't be early.'

Mollie's spiteful remarks were understandable. I knew that I looked dreadful. My hair, despite constant washing, was lank and greasy. My face had filled out, the flesh masking the high cheek bones which were my best feature. Dark shadows sat under my eyes. For the last couple of weeks, I had scarcely left the farm for I was monstrous, literally "great with child".

Yet Martin had said, only the night before, 'Why is it that other heavily pregnant women look terrible, while you get more desirable every day?' Then he had loved me, softly and gently.

Then came what was to be the last of these evenings, at the end of October, a week before my baby was due. Mollie and I worked quietly for a while, then she started to talk, in a quiet, sympathetic way, picking up my thoughts, as she often seemed to. 'You know, Aulish, you mustn't worry about looking so awful. It's only because you're carrying a boy. Boys do that to one. I remained

214

quite pretty with Di and not nearly so big and awkward, that's why Peter was having me right to the end. But boys are different, I looked awful then, just like you do now.'

Before I could register the ambiguity of her speech Mollie was continuing, still speaking in a gentle and dreamy voice. 'Martin and Diana were quite ordinary babies; they didn't make me feel very maternal. But then I got the baby I loved, and they said that he was deformed and sick, that he couldn't live.'

In a flash all became clear to me. The "skeleton in the cupboard", the crib in the attic, the references to more than two children, the way Peter and Martin cossetted Mollie. This was the "secret".

Mollie was in her stride now. 'He was lovely, Aulish, just like your baby will be. He wanted me all the time and I never left him. I didn't care about Martin and Diana. Emily took them; she could have kept them for all I cared. I had my Geoffrey for six whole weeks. He never came downstairs. I fed him and rocked him and sang to him. People used to come. Doctor Arthur, no use at all. He even had the effrontery to bring that young pup, Dr Ronald, to stare at my baby. The vicar came to baptise Geoffrey. I gave my boy three lovely old names, Geoffry Roland Arthur. They said, "Why bother when he's not going to live?" but I wanted him to have everything he could. Then he died and they took him from me. Darling Mr Stoate carved a beautiful box for him to lie in and they laid him in the ground. I don't remember much after that. They said that I was ill for a

215

long time. Then we all went back to normal and no one but me remembers him now.'

I was crying with her and put out my hand to clasp hers. There was an instant withdrawal as she continued, more in control now. 'You're carrying your baby very high, aren't you, Aulish? You're going to have a lovely little boy, just like my Geoffrey. You can't see yourself, Aulish, but let me tell you that no one who looks as dreadful as you can be carrying a normal baby.'

Not having made a study of pregnant women I couldn't argue. Mavis had always looked terrible to me yet her children were perfectly normal. I told myself that Mollie was talking nonsense but, as always, I was half-inclined to believe her. I wanted to scream as primitive fear possessed me but I held myself together and answered calmly, 'I'm sure that Geoffrey was lovely in his own way. And I'm sure that my baby will be lovely too and I'm also sure that he or she will be quite normal.'

The warm, cultured voice flowed on, as if I had not spoken. 'I promised Peter that I wouldn't tell you but I think you have a right to know. They said that Geoffrey's condition was genetic. That's why I didn't want Martin to marry. I knew this would happen and now that you're such a sight I know that I'm right. That's why I hoped the baby would die before it was born, it's kinder that way. It will be even worse for you than it was for me. After all you don't belong here, you know that now don't you dear? There will be nothing for you here with a deformed baby. You will just be an embarrassment to everyone, especially Martin, and I think that in your own childish way you do care for Martin.'

I stood up, determined to stand my ground, and spoke, still relatively calm. 'I won't listen! I think that you're very upset, Mollie, so I'm going to leave you and sit in the kitchen until you've calmed down.'

She stood up too, seized my arm and swung me round to face her. Her mouth seemed to be full of spittle and her eyes blazed. She spoke harshly, 'You don't walk out on me, you common little milksop! I want to tell you all about my Geoffrey, all the details. I loved him, but even I could see that he wasn't a pretty sight. His dry, yellow skin, his huge lolling tongue. But he was so good, he rarely cried and he slept all the time, because he was so weak he could hardly feed. That's what you will have, and you'll make my son a laughing-stock.'

My self-control broke. I pulled myself away, searching blindly for the door-knob, desperate to escape from the strange, wild-eyed creature that Mollie had become. I was sure now that she was mad. And I was equally sure that she was right. Neither I nor my baby belonged here. We would be better alone, out in the dark night, away from this dreadful place.

I was in the hall, grabbing Martin's old duffle coat from its hook, flinging it over my shoulders. I had to struggle with the heavy fastenings of the side door.

Mollie was right behind me now, speaking more normally. 'Where are you going? Don't be silly, Aulish!

Going off in this mood you could get lost and die out there, you and your baby.'

Yet she made no attempt to hold me back as I finally wrenched the door open. Was she giving me a rational warning or making a suggestion? I did not stay to question. I fled, terrified beyond reason, but not so swiftly that I didn't hear her final sentence. 'Then you'll both be safe for ever, and so will Abbotshall.'

Heedless of my bulk and the cold evening I ran down the back fields. Catching my foot in a cow-pat I went flying. The fall steadied me and I lay quietly getting my breath back. As I tried to rise, I felt a pain so sharp that I cried out. Oh, God, contractions! Mollie was right. My child and I would die out here. This seemed even more likely when a large shape, presumably a cow, loomed over me. Then came the sweetest sound I ever heard. 'Aulis, whatever are you doing here; and so near your time?'

It was Ida Ripley.

Ida put her strong arms under mine, and hauled me to my feet. A powerful flashlight revealed my sorry state. She gasped. 'What's happened? No, never mind, don't try to talk until we're in the house, our house (as she felt my instinctive recoil) — you're not going back to Abbotshall till I know what's going on.'

It was only a few hundred yards to the Ripleys' farmhouse with its welcoming lights. Ida steadied me as another pain shook me. She soon had me in an armchair by the Aga, sipping hot tea, while she issued instructions.' 'Tom, ring Whisky Galore and tell him to go to Abbotshall with a midwife, Mrs Mayes if she's free. Then you go to Abbotshall in the Humber and get them ready. Tell them it's urgent. That bitch-witch should know that anyway.'

Her husband, silent but swift, made for the phone. Then Ida spoke to her equally silent son. 'Mike, get the Land Rover out and drive me and Aulis to Abbotshall.'

I had listened, passive, but now I screamed, not with pain, but fear. 'No, Ida. I can't go back there... ever... please no... I can't.'

A pain shot through the scream, so that I was sobbing and gasping all at once.

Ida spoke gently but firmly, 'Aulis, calm down. This is not helping your baby. He's going to be born tomorrow if not tonight and he needs to be born in his own home.'

'It's not my home, she said so, so why should it be his?'

'Oh, I knew this was Mollie's doing. I suppose she told you the story of Geoffrey, with dramatic effects added?'

Surprise and a momentary cessation of pain stopped my howling. 'How did you know? I thought it was a secret.'

'It's always her last weapon. She's hinted to a few of Martin's previous girlfriends and they've not been seen for dust. Peter must have been unusually firm with her this time.'

'But... is it true?'

'Yes, basically, but Mollie embroiders it.'

'What was really wrong with Geoffrey?'

'He was a cretin, very complicated and not for you to worry about.'

'But that's what the French teacher used to call us, "Mais vous êtes crétines".'

'Well she shouldn't have done. It's tragic and Geoffrey was tragic. I was just a schoolgirl but my mother went to see him and Mollie and was awfully upset.'

'Mollie said my baby will be just like Geoffrey.'

'Nonsense! Whisky Galore would have warned you if that were any more than a remote possibility. It's a very rare condition and in any case, I think it's curable now.'

Ida looked at me. 'Pains passing off?'

I nodded.

'Not for long, I guess. Come on! I promise you, Mollie or not, I will stay in that house until your baby's safely here. And believe it or not, when the chips are down, Whisky Galore will look after you.'

Mike Ripley sounded the horn and reluctantly I left my harbour. They half-lifted me into the Land Rover, Ida heaving herself after me.

When we arrived at Abbotshall it looked as if a party was going on. The Ripleys' big Humber was outside, with the doctor's sports car, and a tiny runabout which I guessed must be the midwife's. The front door was open, light streaming out and for once Abbotshall looked welcoming. As Ida helped me out of the Land Rover the farm van came speeding up the drive, stopping with a screech of brakes. Martin rushed out. In two minutes I was in his arms, words of love pouring from him. 'My darling, what's happened? I'm here now don't cry. I love you so.'

As we moved into the house Dr Ronald came forward to meet us. But beyond him, in the shadows, I saw Mollie, ready, as ever, to cover her sins.' 'Aulish, where have you been? I do hope you haven't hurt the baby.'

Peter Peverell had followed Martin out of the van. Now he swept past us like the wrath of God. He gave Mollie a look in which infinite sadness mingled with disgust. His voice was cold and quiet. 'You told her didn't you? You told her about Geoffrey, after you promised?'

Mollie clung to him. 'Oh, Peter, I forgot. I felt so close to Aulish, I was just treating her like one of us, sharing family secrets. I wasn't prepared for her hysterical reaction.'

Turning to Dr Ronald she lowered her voice, but I could still hear her sibilant whisper, 'Aulish needs certifying, Doctor. She's seriously disturbed and she could harm the baby, if she hasn't already done so. Perhaps you'll attend to that later, the legal details, asylums etc.'

The little doctor was transformed. Despite his whisky-laden breath he spoke with authority. 'I can only guess what's gone on here tonight, Mrs Peverell. Now my duty is to my patients, Aulis and her baby. Will you let us pass, please?' He had never used my name before.

But it was Martin's reassurance that I craved. Was he going to believe what I was sure, would be Mollie's twisted version of events?

As he lifted me on to the bed, he spoke urgently to Whisky Galore. 'Doctor, if you have to choose, let the baby go. Keep my wife safe for me.'

That was all I needed to know. Martin loved me more than Abbotshall. I wasn't merely the bearer of the heir, as I had feared.

Dr Ronald lowered the emotional temperature. Patting Martin on the shoulder, he said, 'I'll do my best for both of them. Now let us get on, there's a good chap.'

Mollie was harder to dismiss. She tried to resume her normal authoritative tone. 'This baby is assumed to be a Peverell, Doctor. Therefore, I should be present at the birth.'

He spoke gently to me. 'Do you want Mrs Peverell here, Aulis?' I shuddered, shaking my head vigorously.

He spoke firmly, 'Please go, Mrs Peverell. Your presence only adds to Aulis' distress and will not help her baby.'

Mollie stalked off, muttering about feeble girls who couldn't even carry a baby to term and were only interested in making scenes.

I felt like a monstrous child while Ida and the midwife, who was Mrs Mayes, undressed me gently. I saw the doctor's grave look when he took my blood pressure and listened to the baby's heartbeat. That was my last clear memory before I went into a trough of mindless pain.

There were snatches of half-understood conversation. 'Sluggish uterus... mentally and physically exhausted... waters won't break... I'll have to rupture the membranes.'

I felt the gush of fluid but still nothing happened. Then I heard Whisky Galore say to the midwife, 'It's no use. I'll have to give her morphia.'

'But Dr Ronald, the baby.'

'Plenty of morphia babies survive. It'll die anyway if this goes on. It's very distressed.'

'Can't you do a Caesarean?'

'Here, in these conditions?'

'We could get her to hospital.'

'By which time the baby certainly would be dead. No, I'll do the morphia.'

He came to me. 'Aulis, I'm going to give you an injection to help us to get your baby out and make you feel much better.'

I nodded. 'Just take the pain away. The baby's dead anyway.'

No one disagreed with me. I felt a slight prick then I drifted off to a lovely place where nothing mattered and I feasted on happy memories. There was no pain as I watched them take a bloodied object out of the swollen creature on the bed. The thing made no sound so I knew that it was dead.

I heard my own voice, thickened by the drug. 'All over, no heir?'

I glimpsed a tearful Ida, nodding soundlessly, as I sank into sleep.

Chapter Seventeen
First Days

When I woke, it seemed to be mid-morning. Martin's old cot was by my bed. Mollie and I, in a rare moment of harmony, had draped it with blue organza. With my new knowledge it now seemed hideously reminiscent of the crib in the attic. I supposed they had put it there for the baby, but how tactless to leave it when there was no baby. I let my fingers roam over my stomach. It was still swollen but definitely empty. The baby really had been born, and it had died.

I had a sudden, illuminating thought. If there was no baby there was no reason for me to stay at Abbotshall. I could be free again. After all, if Martin really loved me, he would be here at my bedside, so that we could mourn our baby together. Instead, I had been totally abandoned. Tears trickled down my face.

Then Ida was at my side. 'Aulis, you're awake. I'll get Dr Ronald. He came back an hour ago and wanted to be called as soon as you woke.'

To tell me the bad news, I thought.

The little doctor went straight to the cot and lifted something out. I will hold it, I thought. Even if it is dead, I will have held my baby.

225

The doctor was making satisfied clucks. He placed a warm bundle in my arms that stirred slightly as I held it. The doctor explained, 'She's still very sleepy and rather messy. I wouldn't let them touch her to wash her. A baby full of morphia must be left alone and then it will respond if all goes well. This time it has. I wouldn't even let Mrs Ripley baptise her, I was so certain that she would live. Now you must get to know your daughter, m'dear. Well done!'

Incredulous, I was still not convinced that everything was all right. Very gently I pushed back the coverings and kissed the blood-stained little head. Full of fear, I looked for the yellow complexion and lolling tongue that Mollie had described. Instead, I saw tiny, perfect hands, cheeks flushed palely pink and a little rosebud mouth. Suddenly my daughter opened her eyes and seemed to look straight at me. I knew then that this love was for life. The baby gave a great yawn and closed her eyes again. I felt dizzy with joy.

The doctor smiled at me. 'She'll be drowsy for a day or two. Your milk won't have come in yet but you can try putting her to the breast as soon as you like, that is if you want to feed her yourself, Mrs Peverell seemed to think otherwise.'

'Of course I do, Mollie knows that.'

The doctor sat down and took my hand. 'Look, m'dear, this is your baby. You do what you want. I'll be popping in frequently over the next few days and so will Mrs Mayes. As for Mrs Ripley, I believe she's brought her suitcase. But when you're quite well all this must be sorted. You and your baby could have died last night.'

He withdrew his hand and patted mine. 'Now I'll leave you in Mrs Ripley's capable hands. Feed your baby whenever you want to.'

I held her close. She opened her eyes and gave a tiny, mewling cry, the first I'd heard. She turned her head to my breast and nuzzled me. Ida moved to loosen my nightie. 'Here, Aulis, give her your breast and let her feel your skin. She had a terrible entry into the world, poor little soul, and missed her first minutes with her mother. Comfort her and let her know she's wanted.'

I needed no encouragement. Lifting my heavy breast I guided the great raspberry nipple into the tiny mouth. We both seemed to know how to do this. The little hands clutched the breast and she was soon suckling, feebly but firmly, half-asleep as she was.

I needed only one thing to complete my happiness. 'Ida, where's Martin? Has he seen her?'

'Very briefly, just after she was born. Dr Arthur wouldn't allow any of us near her after that. I don't think Martin slept at all last night. After the baby came, he sat holding your hand until I sent him off to milk. I thought work would be good for him. I think Dr Arthur's seen him now and told him he can come up.'

Even as she spoke, we heard Martin pounding up the stairs, then pausing to open the door carefully and tiptoe in. He was swiftly at my side, then he saw the baby at my breast. 'Oh, Aulis, she's alive, and you've come back to me. I thought you were going to die. I couldn't have borne it if I'd lost you.'

'Well you didn't. I'm here and we've got our beautiful baby. She's so lovely, when she opens her eyes she looks just like you.'

The baby had dropped off to sleep. Ida took her from me and with infinite care gave her to Martin, guiding his hand to support the tiny head, then tactfully withdrawing. Obligingly the baby opened her eyes, giving Martin the same direct look that she'd given to me. His eyes were full of tears.

'Oh, Aulis, I so wanted a son, and I thought you would give me one. When it was a girl, I was so disappointed, but now I'm afraid I'm going to fall in love with her, although I know it's probably foolish!'

I was puzzled. 'Why on earth is it foolish to fall in love with your own child, just because she's not a boy?'

'It's not that, it's because she's frail and not likely to live, Mother says so. Mother doesn't think that you should feed her, or that either of us should get too close to her. She says we should hurry up and get a proper baby.'

As he said these ridiculous things Martin was cuddling his baby close to his heart.

Weak and tired as I was, I was absolutely furious. My reaction was sharp. 'If you weren't so tired, Martin, you would know that that's all complete nonsense! The doctor has said that the baby is fine. She's a perfectly "proper" baby. I have to say that after last night I'm not interested in anything that your mother says or does. She's out of my life, and out of our baby's life. Your mother may have had a baby that wasn't "proper" but our baby is perfect. That's what she can't accept.'

Martin looked uncomfortable. 'Yes, I know Mother upset you. She seems to be very sorry. You do what you like about feeding, babies are women's business aren't they? I do really love our baby, Aulis, even though she's a girl.'

The baby was fast asleep in his arms. Ida came and took her from him, laying her gently in the cot. Ida spoke firmly. 'Now, Aulis, I'm going down to get you something to eat and let you two have some time on your own.'

As soon as she had gone, I put my arms around Martin. He held me gently as I drew him close. 'It's all right, Martin, I'm not going to break.'

With care he stroked and kissed my massive breast, still warm from the baby. We whispered words of love, it was as if we were melting into each other. Martin was crying again.

'Aulis, my love, motherhood has made you even more beautiful. I want you more than ever. As soon as you're better we'll get our son.'

Words of endearment flowed from me. Exhausted as I was, I could feel my desire for him already flaring up. Finally, Martin stirred himself, saying cheerily, 'I'd better get back to work. There's another mouth to feed now. By the way, we'd better find a name for her, hadn't we?' With one last lingering kiss and a stroke of the baby's cheek, he was gone.

Ida, returning with a laden tray, was pleased to see my smile. 'All well then?'

'Yes, Martin adores her.'

'You're very lucky. Didn't he make any fuss about her not being a boy?'

'Not after the first few minutes. Of course he still wants a son.'

'Farmers always do, and most men, I think. Some of them are quite brutal about it. I told you about poor Madge Perkins, didn't I? She had to go through nine pregnancies and four miscarriages until they got a son. Martin is very enlightened.'

I mused. 'It's remarkable really, with those parents.'

That reminded me. 'Ida, where's Mollie? It all seems very quiet.'

Ida laughed. 'Yes, Peter and the doctor, between them, have put the fear of God into her. But she and Peter do want to see the baby, and you of course. When you've had this food and a good sleep I'll phone and tell them they can come up.'

I sighed. 'I suppose I must face them though I don't know how I can be even civil to Mollie.'

'It's hard for me to comment, Aulis, because none of us knows exactly what Mollie said to you. And we've been far too busy to worry since then. All I would say is that you must remember that the baby is their grandchild.

230

Now eat up, you'll feel more like visitors after a meal and a good sleep.'

I did as I was told, my bliss somewhat blunted. I hated the thought of Mollie being anywhere near my baby. Yet I knew I must accept it, at least for the present. Once I was up and about, I might have other plans.

I woke refreshed, reasonably ready for my visitors. Peter and Mollie entered, all smiles, and came over to kiss me. Before they sat down Peter said gravely, 'Mother has something to say to you, Aulis.'

Mollie, wearing her fox face, spoke like a schoolgirl repeating a lesson. 'I'm sorry if I upset you, Aulish, I had no intention of doing so. I hope it hasn't hurt the baby.' She continued, her voice trembling. 'And now please may I see my grandchild, as I've been excluded from everything.'

I felt slightly guilty, surely I could share a little of my happiness with Mollie. Unmoved, Ida was on guard by the cot. 'Well, here's the baby, Mollie, fast asleep, a beautiful little girl.'

Mollie was excited. 'Now she must have her first cuddle from Granny.' She bent to pick up the baby.

Ida was firm. 'I'm sorry, Mollie, but better not. Dr Ronald doesn't want her handled too much, after her difficult start.'

This was almost too much for Mollie. 'My goodness, Ida, that wartime stint in the Red Cross certainly went to your head. Is my husband allowed to see his grandchild?'

Before anyone could answer, the baby, roused by all this, awoke, and started her little whiffling cries.

'Bring her to me, Ida,' I said, 'then everyone can have a proper look at her.' I deliberately used the word "proper" because that's what my baby was and I wanted to emphasise that to Mollie. Did I imagine her look of disappointment?

As I held our beautiful daughter, the baby gave Peter one of her long, straight looks. He was delighted. 'Look, Mollie, she's pure Peverell. She actually looks like me, and yet she's really pretty.'

Mollie's smile was thin. As the baby began to nuzzle, searching for my nipple, Mollie spoke sharply. 'I hope you're not planning to feed her yourself, Aulish. It would be most unwise, given your tendency to hysteria. And Martin will want his son now, he'll not get that if you're feeding her. You must remember that he's had a great disappointment.'

Ida spoke up again. 'Mollie, Dr Ronald gave Aulis full permission to feed her baby, indeed told her to. It's her baby, Mollie, not yours or mine. And you shouldn't be upsetting either of them.'

For the baby was making little whimpers and clutching me more firmly. I guessed that my tension was getting through to her.

Peter came to the rescue. 'I think it's time we went to get some tea, Granny. Aulis and Baby probably need to sleep.' He stooped to kiss me. 'Well done, my dear.'

He gazed, fascinated, at the baby. 'A real Peverell, the image of my father!'

He shepherded a very dissatisfied Mollie out of the room.

Ida looked rueful. 'It's the sight of breastfeeding that particularly upsets her. Geoffrey was at her breast when he died. He spent most of his short life there. Seeing a woman breastfeeding always brings it back — although she approves of breastfeeding in principle.'

'Yes, I remember how she gushed over Marie when Marie was feeding Jonathan. Well, she's not going to stop me feeding Baby.'

Ida changed the subject. 'You must give her a name, Aulis, you can't keep calling her Baby. Didn't you and Martin have a name ready?'

'No, only for our son. We're going to choose a name this evening. After the excesses of my family, I want something simple. I would have liked Mary, but I'm not calling her after Mollie, that's her real name, isn't it? So I'm settling for Anne. Would you mind if we had Ida for a second name, she owes her life to you.'

'Aulis, I'd be honoured. But I think it might upset Mollie unnecessarily. My favourite name is my daughter's name, Caroline. I'd be happy if you'd accept that, with my blessing!'

I tried it. 'Anne Caroline Peverell, it's lovely!' When we discussed her name later Martin liked it too, so now we had Anne Caroline to love, with, amazingly, no protests from anyone about her name.

Ida went on to talk practicalities. 'Now, Aulis, I'm going to sleep here for a few days so I can see to you and the baby in the night. Tom's bringing a single bed up for me.'

'But Ida, what about your family?' I protested.

'Don't worry. Caroline's got some leave due from her fancy PA job and she's coming to look after them. She might even break a few of those ridiculous nails! Dr Ronald wants you and Baby to have at least forty-eight hours thorough rest, to get over the considerable stress of the birth, before all the excitement starts.'

I was puzzled. 'What excitement?'

Ida was slightly exasperated. 'Aulis, you've had a baby. Everyone will want to see her. Martin and Mollie have been phoning all over, and Martin's cabled your parents. I know Di and Emily are coming on Sunday, then there'll be your people, and the village of course. It'll be like Christmas!'

'Goodness, I don't remember this with Hector's children, perhaps I just didn't notice.' Guiltily I remembered my own lukewarm reception of my brother's children. 'I wonder if Hector and Norma will come, or Marie. Not my parents, sadly.'

'Well, you get rested so that you're ready for visitors. Don't worry about Baby, Doctor says she'll sleep for a while yet.'

So I slept, deeply and dreamlessly. I woke occasionally to find Martin by my bedside, often with Anne in his arms. Lying happily on Martin's chest, she seemed to need the reassurance she might have missed at birth. Then laying her gently back in the cot, Martin held me and we whispered our love to each other, marvelling that we were really now one flesh.

I finally woke properly on Saturday morning, to find myself in a milk-soaked bed and to hear the most beautiful sound in the world, a hungry baby crying for the breast, with that unmistakeable new-born wail.

Ida was bustling round. 'Can you get up, Aulis? I've got the nursing-chair ready for you by the fire. You certainly seem to have plenty of milk.'

As Anne suckled away, I sighed with contentment. 'I'm so happy, Ida. Why did no one tell me that such happiness existed?'

'It's not something easily explained, Aulis. And if you had known what you were missing you might have been even more unhappy. Now does your happiness mean you're going to stop worrying about Mollie?'

'No, I can't quite promise that. I've got to protect Anne from her now.'

'I think you're a bit hard on Mollie, Aulis. She wants grandchildren, she wants Anne and even you. She's not going to hurt either of you, now that she knows that Anne isn't another Geoffrey. Anne's birth may well have broken that spell for her.'

'I'm sorry, but I can't trust her.'

Ida was non-committal. 'We'll see. Anyway, I'm going down to get the post, the cards and presents are starting to come.'

She soon returned, almost invisible behind a massive bouquet of flowers. 'I think these are from your brother and sister-in-law. I know Martin rang them.'

I took the card, written in Norma's firm, round hand and read it aloud:

We're glad to know that all is well. Hope your baby is as super as our two. Give her a hug from her Price cousins. We thought anything we sent might not meet with approval but that flowers could hardly be criticised.

Ida was not impressed. 'A bit cold, isn't it? I suppose Mollie's upset them too.'

'I'm afraid so, Norma especially, she dislikes Mollie's lordly attitude.'

'Well let's arrange the flowers, then you can open this parcel.'

It was from Marie, full of baby clothes. I seized the card eagerly but exclaimed as I read it. 'Oh, no! Listen to this, Ida.'

Marie had written:

So glad Baby is here and all's well. I'm sorry I can't come to see you, but Ken feels that all the emotional issues around Abbotshal, give me unnecessary stress and that isn't fair to him or the children. Perhaps things will improve now and we'll be able to meet again soon. This time Ida exploded. 'Whatever's wrong with these people? What are these "emotional issues"?'

I was resigned. 'In a word, Mollie. Although she's been quite kind to Marie, Marie gets caught in the crossfire of Mollie's general nastiness and her attitude to me. No one likes to be part of the despised majority, which is where Mollie puts most of us, my parents, for example.'

As if on cue the phone rang. Ida hurried to answer it. 'Quick, Aulis, it's your parents, from Australia.'

My mother was incoherent with joy.

What's her name...?

Thank God it's not classical...

What milk is she on?

I've not heard of Bests... as I shouted Breast

Longing to see her.

My father said, *Congratulations!* with apparently less enthusiasm than he'd shown for my A Levels. Then they were gone.

I felt very depressed after their call, longing for Martin to come. If my mother couldn't wait to see the baby, why couldn't they come back now, they'd been gone for a year. I had only been a mother for about forty-eight hours but I already felt an overwhelming love for Anne, I would do anything for her, did my mother not feel the same about me? It seemed not, she had gone half-way across the world to help her son's wife, whom she had never met, but had left me, her own daughter, when I needed her most. Her casual assumption that Mrs Peverell would look after me, was that prompted by thoughtlessness or jealousy? Then I thought, perhaps it was I who had made my own mother feel unwanted.

Whatever the reason might be she wasn't here and that was that.

Ida gave me little time to mope. 'I'm going down to get your lunch, Aulis, and to give Martin his. Dr Ronald is coming up afterwards. He wants to talk to you both together.'

I was alarmed. 'Why? Is there something wrong with Anne?'

'I wouldn't have thought so, but I honestly don't know what he wants. It's obviously something private, just for you and Martin.'

All my fears came crowding back. I looked at Anne, pink and clean in her new clothes, the picture of a healthy baby. Was my happiness to be so short-lived?'

Chapter Eighteen
Disturbing Developments

Martin and I were waiting impatiently for the doctor when he walked in at exactly two o'clock. I gave the poor man hardly time to sit down before bursting into speech. 'Please tell us quickly, is there something wrong with Anne? Don't keep us in suspense, we'd rather know.'

Martin, seeing the doctor's puzzled expression, hastened to explain. 'That's what we're calling the Baby. She's Anne Caroline.'

Dr Ronald laughed. 'Lovely names! No, she's fine. She'll soon get over her rather unorthodox entry into the world.' Then he continued, speaking gravely. 'I have thought hard about telling you these things because in doing so I am breaking patient confidentiality. However, I have Mr Peter Peverell's permission, and in the circumstances, I don't think that I have any alternative. I want to talk to both of you about Mrs Peverell, about your mother, Martin.'

At last, I thought.

The doctor went on, 'As you know, Martin, the birth of your brother Geoffrey was a great tragedy and your mother was grieved beyond measure. I don't suppose you remember anything about it, you were very young.'

Martin looked straight ahead, stonily, as he replied, 'Oh, no, I remember it clearly. It's one of my earliest memories. I was four. Di and I had been staying with Auntie Emily. One day she brought us back home and we came upstairs. Daddy met us and said, "Go and kiss Mummy, she's very sad because your little brother is dead." So we went into Mummy's room and I went over and kissed her. She said, "Go away, you're not Geoffrey. You must kiss him. Mr Stoate will show you." Bert Stoate was in the corner of the room, with a white box on a table. He was so kind. He sort of shielded me and whispered, "Just kiss the box, Master Martin. Don't look inside!" So I did. Then Mummy wanted Di to do the same, but she kicked and screamed, she was only just two. Finally, Auntie Emily said, "You'll have to leave it, Mollie, or she'll have a convulsion." I remember wondering what a convulsion was and if I could have had one, then they wouldn't have made me do it. Then Auntie Emily took us away and we stayed with her for a lovely long time.'

The doctor and I sat silent for a moment, transfixed by this narrative, the vivid memory emphasised by Martin's use of the baby names, Mummy and Daddy.

Dr Ronald looked at him with concern. 'Good gracious, Martin, I had no idea. Are you all right for me to continue?'

Martin smiled. 'Yes, please do. I feel much better now I've shared that memory, after all these years.'

The doctor nodded. 'Yes, Geoffrey was a very bad case of cretinism and little could be done for him at the time. I was just a medical student then but my uncle had me come home to see Geoffrey, as a text-book example of a cretin.'

I remembered Mollie's reference to Dr Ronald as the "young pup". But what was the point of all this history. The doctor needn't think that he could use it to justify Mollie's behaviour to me.

I moved uncomfortably. 'I know it was awfully sad. Naturally it affected, and still affects, Mollie very deeply. But why need we talk about it now?'

Martin nodded agreement with me, but the doctor was firm. 'Because m'dears,' the story of Geoffrey is not over. His cretinism was almost certainly caused by the thyroid condition which Mrs Peverell had and still has. The pregnancy was difficult and that's when her problems were discovered.'

I was still not satisfied. 'But that was years ago. Surely there's now treatment for her condition?'

'There is indeed, and Mrs Peverell receives it — tablets to ensure that the balance of the thyroid is maintained. Unfortunately, Mrs Peverell frequently forgets, deliberately or otherwise, to take them. That is when she behaves badly, as she did on the night that Anne was born.'

The warm glow that had surrounded me since Anne's birth was rapidly cooling. I was the old termagant again, attacking the doctor's euphemism.

'You mean she has mad fits! Martin! Remember the pills and the stairs! And no one would believe me!'

Martin said, 'Don't Aulis!' but the doctor was imperturbable.

'One could call them disturbances of the mind. You must stay calm, Aulis, remember your milk.'

I pulled myself together. 'I'm sorry. Doctor, Martin. But seriously, can Mrs Peverell not have some psychiatric help?'

Dr Arthur and Martin exchanged sorrowful glances, as the Doctor answered, 'I have suggested that over the years. Neither Mr nor Mrs Peverell will countenance the idea.'

I was insistent. 'But why, it seems common sense to me.'

The doctor smiled ruefully. 'M'dear, you are young, modern, educated. There is still, sadly, a great stigma attached to mental illness, especially in the country. Mrs Peverell would feel that she was bringing shame on the family if it were known that she had such problems.'

Much as I would have liked to argue I restrained myself. At least we now had an explanation for Mollie's behaviour. Martin obviously felt the same and moved to close the conversation. 'Thank you for telling us, Doctor. I didn't know half of this, or what the significance was when Dad used to say, "Your mother's forgotten to take her pills again". Now we shall understand better.'

Dr Ronald made no move. 'I'm sorry. I'm obviously not making myself clear. Between her lapses of memory and the fact that her condition is worsening with age, I must warn you that your mother might be dangerous.'

Milk or no milk, I was almost hysterical. 'You mean she might hurt Anne?'

The doctor was sombre. 'We can't rule out the possibility.'

Martin was indignant. 'With respect, Doctor, that's nonsense. Mother would never hurt a child. She's been wonderful with Di's children, right from their births, which took place here, in Mother's presence.'

Dr Ronald answered quietly, 'Yes, I know, Martin, although neither I nor any of my midwives were in attendance. Mrs Peverell engaged some private practitioners.'

Martin muttered gloomily, 'Yes, we had more money then.'

The doctor continued as though he had not been interrupted. 'However, I have spoken to Mrs Llewellyn, since your daughter's birth.' (How conscientious he is, I thought.) 'She tells me that though the birth of the little girl passed without incident, there was an episode involving the little boy.'

Martin and I spoke in unison, 'But Mother/Mollie adores Charlie!'

The doctor shrugged. 'Apparently Mrs Peverell tried to feed the baby and when he, quite reasonably, protested, she attempted to smother him with a pillow.'

Martin had his head in his hands. I was puzzled. 'But why shouldn't Mollie give Charlie a bottle?'

Martin groaned. The doctor looked slightly embarrassed, as he explained, 'Mrs Peverell put the baby to her breast. When he wouldn't, or couldn't, suckle, there was the phrase you quoted, Martin, "You're not Geoffrey. Go Away!" Then the pillow. Mrs Llewellyn had had a hard labour and was fast asleep. Fortunately, your Aunt Emily came into the room, just in time to avert tragedy.'

He went on, 'I felt it my duty to give you my advice, in the light of everything that has happened. I may be fussing about nothing, I hope I am, but I do not think that your child is completely safe. In addition to Mrs Peverell's medical condition, and her obsession with Geoffrey, she seems to nurture a positive hatred of you Aulis, largely based on jealousy, I believe.'

'But why on earth should Mollie be jealous of me? She thinks I'm nobody from nowhere.'

'Oh, m'dear, you have so much, Martin, Abbotshall, and now, despite her best efforts, a perfect baby. It's hard to lose power.'

Martin wanted to talk about practicalities. 'But what can we do, Doctor? As time goes on, we can't protect Anne day and night. Then, hopefully, there will be other children, and you said that Mother will get worse.'

I immediately saw myself with a child permanently attached to me, carrying a baby on my back like an African woman, or be-shawled around me, like a gypsy. Then I saw myself with a toddler and another baby, a boy, whom she would surely hate even more.

I came out of this nightmare vision to hear the doctor saying sadly, 'I have talked to Mr Peverell and it seems that your parents can't or won't move house, to increase the distance between you and them. If that is the case I have to most seriously advise you that you may have to consider moving away.'

Again, we spoke as one, 'Leave Abbotshall!'

In my most desperate moments I had sometimes thought of leaving Abbotshall, being my own person again. Since the night of Anne's birth, I had wondered if I should take her away, to ensure our safety from Mollie's wiles, though for me it would be almost unbearable to leave Martin. But I had never imagined Martin being able or willing to leave Abbotshall. Now it seemed that Anne must leave, which meant that one of us, at least, must go with her.

Dr Ronald looked at us with compassion. 'I am sorry. I realise that this is a great shock for you, but I think it my duty to tell you these things. Obviously, you'll have a lot to think about. I'll leave you now. I'll see you and the baby — Anne, next week, Aulis. Now don't worry and keep resting.'

When he had gone Martin and I just looked at each other. Finally, Martin spoke, 'I just can't take all this in, Aulis.'

'Nor can I. I had no idea that your mother was really ill.'

Martin was dubious. 'I'm still not sure. I've lived with her all these years.'

'Yes, Martin, but without a wife and child. Remember some of those things she did during my pregnancy.'

'You know, Aulis, I feel ashamed. I thought you were exaggerating. You're right to say that I never quite believed you. I thought that they were either accidents or misunderstandings.'

'And finally, you do believe me?

'Yes, I think I must now, although it's still hard.'

I considered: 'Well, Di and Aunt Emily obviously know the truth, would you mind if I told Ida, just in case Mollie tries anything, like she did with Charlie?'

Martin agreed, reluctantly. 'Yes tell Ida, but no one else, we don't want it to become village gossip.'

The phrase, so reminiscent of Mollie, annoyed me, so that I hit out in that tactless way I sometimes had, instantly regretting it. 'Well, I was just thinking of putting on my dressing-gown to go and proclaim your mother's madness on the village green. Darling, don't look like that, I know this is too shattering for jokes.'

'Oh, Aulis, this is terrible. Despite her peculiar ways she's always just been Mother, not some kind of monster.'

As he shook with sobs I hugged him and spoke gently. 'We'll work something out, you know we will. I'm still sure she could have treatment.'

We clung together, both of us feeling lost and lonely, but lost and lonely together, bound now by our one flesh, the beautiful sleeping baby.

As usual, Martin's need to do the inevitable milking restored some semblance of normality. Ida came in as he left, obviously full of curiosity. 'I don't want to pry, Aulis, but first the doctor looked very serious and now Martin's brushed past me without a word, looking like death. Please tell me there's nothing wrong with Anne.'

I managed to smile. 'No, thank God, she's fine. But it's awful, Ida, it's Mollie.'

I gave her a bald précis of what Dr Ronald had told us, especially the possible danger to Anne.

Stout, sensible Ida was inclined to be dubious. 'I find all this hard to believe. Over-emotional, spiteful, class-ridden, obsessed with Geoffrey, yes, but he's saying that Mollie can be deranged.'

I tried to laugh. 'Well you once told me she might be a witch, Ida. And remember the iron pills,'

'Yes, but one could think of all kinds of excuses for that. I'm more impressed by Dr Ronald taking it all so seriously. He's not given to flights of fancy, and by Di and Emily's evidence, because they're both devoted to Mollie.' Ida pondered for a moment, then said briskly, 'Well as long as I'm here you and I between us can protect Anne, but what you're going to do after that I can't imagine. I still think Dr Ronald's exaggerating and everything will settle down. It's a chance in a million she'd hurt Anne. For one thing she's not a boy, after all they said she left Lucy alone.'

I was unconvinced. 'It's a chance I don't want to take. What do you think about us leaving Abbotshall?'

Ida was adamant. 'Absolute nonsense! What would Martin do, where would you go, what would you live on? There have always been Peverells at Abbotshall. But whatever happens I'm on your side, Aulis. Now I'll go and get tea.'

Left alone, I was in sombre mood. If this was the view of dear Ida, who had done so much for me and really was on my side, what reaction could we expect from the rest of the world? Now completely disillusioned with the "Ceremonious House" I couldn't care less whether there were Peverells at Abbotshall, but I was concerned about practical things. What would we live on? I supposed that I could get a teaching job somewhere, but then what about Anne? And what would Martin do?'

We all had tea together then Martin and I spent a quiet evening, talking little, dozing as we lay close to each other on my bed. He watched lovingly as I fed Anne again and then went to look up the cows.

Ida came up from the kitchen, where she'd been having a cosy read by the Aga. Rested, she was full of authority. 'Well done, Aulis, you've seen to Anne all by yourself. Now I want you in bed asleep, like her. You've got a long day with visitors tomorrow and I expect that you'll be required to provide your first night feed tonight.

I obeyed meekly and was immediately asleep.

I woke to a piercing wail and Ida at my bedside. 'Wake up Aulis, this is it. Baby wants you, and it looks as if you want her.'

Dazed, I saw milk running down my breasts. Ida wiped it away as she brought Anne over, still crying lustily.' 'Be careful, Aulis. Don't drown her!'

As Anne found what she wanted the wails were shut off like magic. For a few minutes peace reigned. Then Martin's tousled head appeared round the door. 'Can I come in, or is it girls only?'

Ida looked at him with mock severity. 'You should be asleep, it'll be milking time in four hours.'

'No one could sleep through that racket.'

The love in his voice took the sting from his words.

Ida relented. 'Come on in, Martin. I'll make myself scarce until Anne's finished.'

Martin sat down, feasting his eyes on the suckling baby. 'She's so strong and clever, Aulis.'

I laughed. 'You're besotted, Martin.'

He looked at me seriously. 'Yes, Aulis, I am, with her and with you. When she came and I thought I was going to lose both of you, at first, I could think only of you, and will you to live for me. Then I took a sneaky look at her in the cot, all bloodied and still, and I felt a great yearning for her to live. During that night nothing mattered except you and her, not Mother nor Father, nor Abbotshall, nor the farm. I was unconsciously saying to God, "I will do anything if You let them live." Now this is what I have to do.'

I waited, awestruck. Martin didn't talk like this, especially in the middle of the night, when he was usually quite grumpy. But he was continuing, 'Anne didn't really wake me up. I wasn't asleep. I was thinking about what the doctor said. We have to go Aulis, to leave here. God knows where or when or how, but go we must. I don't care if Mother is totally sane and it's all nonsense. I don't care if we're destitute. I don't even care if you're willing to take the risk of staying here. For me there is no choice. I must keep you and Anne safe.'

He stopped, laughing to cover his embarrassment. 'God, I don't usually make speeches! We need to think about ways and means, but I've made my decision.'

He fled as Ida came in. She looked at me shrewdly. 'Whatever Martin's said, it looks as if it's good news to you.'

'Yes, Ida, I'll tell you tomorrow. I'm so sleepy.'

'I'm not surprised. Give me the baby, you get to sleep. You must try to control all this emotion you know, until your milk's firmly established.'

I nodded submissively. 'Yes Ida.'

I was just settling down when she spoke again. 'I'm so sorry Aulis, with all the excitement I quite forgot. Your mother rang again, while you and Martin were talking to the doctor, so I didn't think I should disturb you.'

I yawned. 'No, quite right. Did she want anything in particular?'

Ida sounded puzzled. 'It was a very bad line. She said to tell you that your father had taken fright. The line went dead before I could ask her anything more.'

I was equally puzzled. 'What's he scared of, the thought of me with a baby? Well, I can't worry now.'

Ida was laughing, as I dropped off to sleep.

Chapter Nineteen
Visitors: Expected and Unforeseen

After Anne's early morning feed, I slept long on Sunday morning, waking to find Ida there with the breakfast tray, and strict orders. 'Come on now, Aulis, we've a lot to do getting you and Anne ready for today's inspection. And I'm dying to know what Martin said in the night, not deeply personal things of course but about Abbotshall and this daft idea of you leaving. Presumably he knocked that on the head?'

Still incredulous myself about Martin's decision, I told her, 'No Ida. He says he's determined that we should leave. He's no plans yet, obviously, but he's clear that we've got to go. He says that neither no one nor nothing, will change his mind'

Ida was amazed. 'You know, Aulis, Martin's changed since the baby came. He's so decisive, and quite frankly he's always been rather a ditherer, a noisier version of his father. Well, babies do change lives. Though what the three of you are going to do I can't imagine.'

I smiled. 'Neither can I. But I'm so happy that Martin seems to have suddenly become his real self that I don't care. I've been so scared, Ida, that I would have to be the strong one — running and ruling everything — just like Mollie, and in perpetual conflict with her!'

'Well, I don't think that's going to happen if Martin carries on like this. Meanwhile, Aulis, I'm ruling now, let's get ready for the visitors. This will be Miss Anne's first real public appearance.'

Ida explained her plans: 'I don't think you and Anne should go downstairs yet, Aulis. So I'm going to bring a table in here and prepare a buffet tea for you all. Then I'm popping home for a few hours.'

Seeing my anxious look, she hastened to reassure me. 'Now don't worry, you'll all be together, you'll have plenty of protection against Mollie.'

Early afternoon brought Di with Lucy and Aunt Emily. They went into very satisfactory ecstasies over Anne, then Di and Emily sat down to chat.

Di kissed me warmly. 'I'm so glad that you know about Mummy, it means that you're really one of us now.'

I shivered inwardly as I thought what that meant, all their lives this shadow had hung over them. At last, I had become one of the family. I had got what I wanted, but at what a terrible price.

Di was continuing, 'Of course Mummy would never deliberately hurt your little one, she can't help it, you see.'

I didn't see how that would make the end result any better — the child would still be harmed — but Di's next words offered some comfort.

'I thought that we could have Mummy and Daddy for Christmas, and perhaps keep Mummy for a little longer. I know Daddy will want to get back for the sheep. I've got Geraint to agree, that took some doing, he finds Mummy a bit difficult. But it would give you a little break, wouldn't it, to get Anne through her first Christmas?'

I was really grateful. 'Thank you, Di, that would be helpful.'

Aunt Emily took my hand. 'I wish I could help more, dear, but you see I'm tied to Mr Noakes. He's my bread and butter, my livelihood, I have nothing else.'

I had never warmed to Aunt Emily but now I kissed her cheek. Another life ruined by Mollie, I thought, remembering Ida's story and imagining Emily's dreary life.

While we chatted, Lucy had been kneeling by the cot, whispering endearments to Anne. She got up now and came to join us, full of enthusiasm. 'Isn't it exciting! I have a cousin. She's so lovely, Auntie Aulis, I adore her. I've never seen such a tiny baby, Granny said she was very small.'

Aunt Emily broke in, quite angrily. 'Nonsense, she's the same size as most new-born babies, nice ones anyway, I don't like these nine-pounders who don't look new-born at all!'

We laughed, but Lucy wasn't easily squashed. 'Why won't you let Granny see Anne? She wanted to come up with us but Grandpa wouldn't let her, so mean!'

This time it was Diana who spoke, quite sharply. 'Grandpa was quite right. Babies mustn't have too many visitors until they've got used to the world. Anyway, Granny will be coming up for tea. Now I suggest that you and I go to see Uncle Martin and the cows while Auntie Aulis gives Baby Anne her tea and Auntie Emily prepares ours.'

Lucy was still being awkward. 'Can't I stay and watch the baby being fed?'

Aunt Emily was shocked. 'No you can't. Dreadful child!'

As she shooed Lucy out Aunt Emily spoke kindly to me, 'Now, dear, I'm sure you'd like to be alone to feed Baby. I think she's getting restless for you. I'll go downstairs for a little rest then I'll come and put out the tea that Ida Ridley's left. I'm glad she's looking after you, she's a good woman.' And off she went.

Anne was indeed whimpering now. Still not understanding the miracle that made my baby want me just when I needed her, I picked her up, settled comfortably in the nursing chair and gave her the breast. As she suckled, I willed myself to keep calm for her sake; not to think about the approaching tea-party and the presence of Mollie. When Anne had finished, I changed her and dressed her in one of the lovely outfits that Di had brought, talking to her all the time. 'There, my darling, you're all ready for your guests.' Then I tidied myself up and put on my smart purple housecoat.

Aunt Emily began to bring in the trays of food that Ida had prepared. Soon everything was ready. Then the visitors arrived, Di and Lucy coming in at the same time as Peter and Mollie. I was holding a rather sleepy Anne. Peter came straight over to look at her, saying, 'How's this beautiful girl who looks like me?'

I smiled up at him. 'Do you want to hold her? Sit down and I'll give her to you.'

Before we could affect the exchange, Mollie intervened, 'Better not, Peter. You know we were told not to touch her, everyone else can, apparently,' glaring at Aunt Emily, 'but not us, not her grandparents, which I assume we are. In any case you know she's frail. As I have said before, Aulish, you must put her on the bottle. Your milk is obviously not suiting her. She's not coming on at all.'

Di protested. 'Mummy, she's four days old!'

Aunt Emily put in a gentle word. 'Surely the feeding is up to Aulis. If she wants to feed Anne herself that's surely much better for the baby.'

Mollie looked pointedly at Emily's flat chest as she sneered. 'And what would you know about it?'

Just then Martin came in from milking and the reorganisation that this involved saved us all from further embarrassment. I heard Mollie's sharp intake of breath as Martin kissed first me and then Anne, but she stayed quiet.

When we were all enjoying our tea again Lucy remarked brightly, 'Charlie's ever so pleased about the baby, Auntie Aulis.'

I was touched but before I could express my pleasure Martin broke in, 'And why is Master Charlie so pleased?'

Lucy obviously thought this a stupid question. 'Because she's a girl, of course. That means he'll still get Abbotshall. There'll be big sulks if you ever have a boy.'

Peter turned on Lucy. 'You can tell your brother, my dear, that a Peverell gets Abbotshall and that I choose Abbotshall's heir.'

Mollie looked mutinous but said nothing. Martin and I looked at each other across the table, knowing that we shared the same thought, would we be there to get or to give? Might Charlie inherit Abbotshall after all, because we had rejected it.

Soon afterwards the party broke up. Martin was going to help Aunt Emily and Di with the washing-up. I heard Peter talking to them as they went downstairs. But where was Mollie, still lurking around? I heaved a sigh of relief as I heard Ida's firm footsteps on the landing, then she spoke, 'Hello, Mollie, you still here? I've just seen Peter on his way home.'

Mollie was disarmingly meek. 'I just wanted a word with you Ida. I'm worried about the baby, she's not coming on at all, I'm sure that girl isn't feeding her properly, she knows nothing about managing babies.'

Ida laughed. 'And how much did you or I know, Mollie, when we had our first? Aulis is doing fine. If

257

you're genuinely worried the midwife's coming in tomorrow. She'll check if everything's going well. It's a pity that you didn't show such concern the night the little thing was born.'

Mollie's conciliatory tone had soon vanished. She snapped at Ida, 'I left that to you, and that drunken fool of a doctor.'

Ida was roused now. 'Not too drunk to save the child you tried to destroy.'

Mollie was as bitter as ever. 'It would be better dead, a weakling, to be brought up by that useless girl and my idiot of a son.'

Ida had lost all restraint. 'No, Mollie, that one died, and that's what you've never forgiven Martin, that he's not Geoffrey. God forgive you, Mollie, I can't!'

Mollie's voice trembled with rage. 'You bitch, Ida! Tom Ripley picked you out of the gutter and it shows!'

Ida's reply was swift. 'At least I didn't steal him from my sister with a lie. Go home Mollie, where a decent man, that you don't deserve, is waiting for you.'

'I shall, and I shan't be back as long as you're squatting here.'

I heard Mollie's sharp footsteps going downstairs.

I was rather shaken by the whole exchange, wondering what this might do to my milk, but Ida came in unruffled and chuckling. 'That's seen her off for a while. And I've agreed with Tom that I can spend the whole of next week here. After that you'll be fully up and about and able to cope, although I think that you'll need more help, that Mrs Brown doesn't seem much use. But at least I'll be here for the first batch of visitors.'

Ida had advised me to welcome all the locals who wanted to see the baby. 'If you don't, they'll only think there's something wrong with her, especially after the rumours that went round about Geoffrey, and God knows what Mollie might tell them. She seems determined to create the impression of Anne's frailty, maybe she really believes it, or more likely it's wishful thinking. It's up to you, Aulis, to squash any gossip by letting people see the real baby, not leaving them to accept Mollie's picture of her.'

So some of the farmers' wives came. Mavis, heavy in her third pregnancy, sweet and kind as ever. 'Don't worry, Aulis, you'll have a boy next time!' Dear old Mrs Barton, she of the tomato chutney, and dearer still to me, Barbara, with lots of laughs and lovely presents.

Ida was careful to see that I didn't get too tired and affect the precious milk. One afternoon, about halfway through the week, she decreed a doze for me after Anne's feed. I slept blissfully. I was having one of those comfortable dreams where different people, all known to the dreamer but not to one another, are having a happy time together. As I came back to consciousness the crowd resolved itself into two people chatting. One was Ida— who was the other? Reluctant to wake, wanting to prolong the dream, I opened my eyes slowly, wondering why someone was sitting by my bed. Then I was suddenly wide awake and in my father's arms. I clung to

259

him, half-sobbing, half-laughing, while all the lost endearments of childhood flowed from his lips.

Finally able to speak, I gasped out my surprise. 'Dad, I am so glad to see you, but how have you got here — why are you here — and where's Mum?'

My father was as precise as ever. 'Question one — I came by plane, train and car.'

I broke in. 'I see it now, you took a flight, we heard it as fright, which didn't make much sense, but we were confused at the time.'

My father continued, 'Question two; I'm here because I knew when you telephoned that you were in distress, and I was determined to come to you.'

'But I only said that the baby had been born, and we didn't even know the worst then.'

'Yes, your mother said I was over-reacting. To answer Question three, she is still in Australia and my sudden flight, or fright, has doubtless caused considerable problems for her and everyone else. But she loves Australia and Mel and little Gareth, so I'm hoping she'll stay safely there at least until I've let her know what's going on, and that's what I need to know, Aulis. What's "the worst" that you mentioned? Is there something wrong with the baby? I've only had a brief glimpse but she looks all right to me, of course I'm no expert.'

I moved over to the cot, picked up Anne and brought her over to my father. 'Now have a long look and agree that she's beautiful, adorable and thank God, absolutely fine. But everything else is in a real mess.'

I told him everything, the story of Geoffrey and the night of Anne's birth, what the doctor had told us about Mollie, Martin's decision to leave Abbotshall, our fears for Anne as long as we stayed here.

My father listened, in that intense way that he had, letting me tell the whole story without interruption. He didn't rant and rave about Mollie's treatment of me, as I had perhaps secretly hoped. His only comment on her was, 'Poor, tortured soul!'

However, he had an immediate solution for our problem. 'You must come home, Aulis, you and the baby, at the end of this week, when Mrs Ripley goes home. Then if Martin really does leave here, you can join him when he's settled.'

Suddenly he remembered. 'Oh my goodness, of course you can't come home! Our house is let until the end of March. I haven't got anywhere to live!' His face cleared. 'I know, the three of us will stay with Uncle Jim and Aunt Sarah.'

'I can't, Dad!'

'Why not, they've got plenty of room?'

'It's not that. I can't leave Martin, not now, he's willing to give up everything for Anne and me, his home, his job, everything he's been used to. It's a massive sacrifice.'

My father thought for a moment. We didn't discuss emotion in our family. Then he said quietly, 'Isn't that what he ought to do? "A man shall leave father and mother and cleave to his wife". One might argue that Martin should never have brought a wife into this situation. But he did and he's now having the guts to deal with it. I've often wondered if there was more to him than the cheerful insouciance with which he faces the world.'

On cue Martin arrived for his pre-milking cup of tea, carrying in the tray for the three of us. I had always felt that Martin, trained by Mollie to despise schoolteachers, didn't value my father sufficiently. So I was delighted with his warm greeting. 'I'm so glad you're here, Mr Price. I can really do with your advice. Has Aulis told you everything?'

'She has and I want her to come home with me, but she won't leave you.'

Martin took my hand. 'And I don't think I could do without her, not now. I must tell you both that I have some more news.'

I knew from his expression that it wasn't good. He continued, 'I've spent the afternoon with my father, our accountant and our solicitor. In a word, we can't go on, Abbotshall is effectively bankrupt.'

My father gasped, but I couldn't pretend to be surprised.

Martin smiled at me. 'You're quite a good accountant, Aulis. You saw this coming, didn't you, going through the books?'

'I wasn't sure, I saw the losses, and the excessive expenditure, but I didn't think things were this bad. Did you know before today, Martin?'

'I had a good idea, but I didn't want to worry you until the baby was safely here. It certainly solves one problem, we'll have to leave now, so I won't have to fight that battle with Dad.'

My father, while warming to my husband for his concern for me, was puzzled by our coolness. He questioned Martin. 'What will you do, Martin? Will you be declared bankrupt?'

Martin reassured him. 'No, Mr Price, it won't come to that. We can save ourselves by selling Abbotshall. By some miracle we've kept the land in good heart. The farm and the stock should fetch good prices, clear our debts and leave each of us with a little capital. Dad and I each own fifty per cent, you see.'

My father was still concerned. 'How will you live, Martin — I mean you've never done anything else have you? If we could organise the baby Aulis could always teach. That's a thought, Aulis, you'd have to live near us and your mother could look after Anne.'

Oh yes, I thought, my mother who couldn't even be bothered to be here when my baby was born!

But Martin was totally in charge. My heart lifted as he said calmly, 'That won't be necessary, Mr Price. I shall have to get a job, preferably with a house. I've never written a CV! I'd better start practising.'

263

My father brightened up. 'I could certainly help you with that. Why don't I stay here until our house is free again? I could provide some protection for Aulis and the baby and help you with all sorts of things.'

Both Martin and I welcomed this suggestion. My father would not be the kind of visitor who needed looking after. He would be reliable and reassuring, but not obtrusive — always happy to sit quietly, reading Cicero. Martin thanked him heartily. 'Mr Price, that will be wonderful. I shall feel so comfortable about Aulis and Anne, knowing that you're here.'

My father was obviously pleased. 'I'll go back to Jim's tonight, that's where I'm staying, get some books and clothes, and come back on Friday, if that suits you, so that I'm here before Mrs Ripley leaves on Saturday.'

'Lovely!' we chorused.

Martin, looking considerably more cheerful, went off to milk. I gave my father a massive hug. 'Dad, I can't tell you how grateful we are. You will be such a help.'

He smiled. 'I'll do my best. I feel much better about the situation now I've seen how purposeful Martin is. And I've had another bright idea, but I'm not going to share that with you yet, in case it doesn't come off. Now I must go. See you Friday.' We kissed and he was gone.

Reflecting on my father's visit I wondered if his mysterious "bright idea" involved my mother. I realised, with some surprise, that while my father had always been my favourite parent, since Anne's birth I had longed for my mother. And yet I doubted if the person who was my mother could have satisfied that longing. What I wanted was mother-love. I had hoped for it from Mollie, a hope now gone for ever. Perhaps I must be satisfied with Ida's warm affection, or, vain thought, perhaps my mother, changed by some Australian magic, would come home transformed.

My good little baby began to whimper and I realised that it was almost time for her feed. We were soon happily settled. As I relaxed in the rhythmic calm, I thought how people were changing. Mollie, fallen from her pedestal, an object of pity rather than admiration; my father, no longer the hesitant pedant; while Martin, formerly so vacillating, had become strong and firm. This little baby had changed all these lives, perhaps she would even change my mother's! And how far, literally and metaphorically, would these changes take us?

Chapter Twenty
Fortunes Change

Next morning, perhaps influenced by my father's compassionate reaction, I seemed to be totally taken up with my pity for Mollie. I found myself pleading with Martin. 'I just can't imagine how awful it must have been for your mother to lose Geoffrey. What if we were to lose Anne? Martin, we can't leave! We can't abandon her, whatever she's done.'

Martin needed to be firm with me. 'Aulis, you know this is foolish. We have to go, there is no alternative financially, it's not just personal now. Once we've settled, we may be able to help Mother from a safe distance. But now we have to concentrate on our own future.'

I was still tearful. Ida, as usual, was full of common-sense. 'Come on, Aulis, you'll feel better after a good cry. Don't worry, Martin. I've been expecting this. A few days after childbirth a little depression sets in — it's hormones or something — usually nothing to worry about.'

Martin went out and I wiped up my tears. Then I felt guilty. 'Ida, I forgot! This morning Martin and Peter are going to tell Mollie about Abbotshall, that we've got to sell it. How could I have been so thoughtless to bother Martin with my crying?'

'You couldn't help it. Now tidy yourself up, see to your baby and be calm and fresh for Martin when he comes in, he'll likely need you then.'

This good advice taken, I greeted Martin with a cheerful kiss on his return, to his obvious relief, as I asked, 'Well, how did Mollie take it?'

Martin sighed. 'To begin with there was a lot of prophetic Cassandra stuff, how she'd foreseen this. She said some hard things about you which I won't repeat.'

I laughed. 'You may as well tell me or I'll imagine them to be worse than they were.'

'OK, here goes, she knew from the first that you were Abbotshall's doom, you brought disaster with you. You are, and always will be, totally unsuitable. You have made no effort to fit in or help in any way. And you couldn't even have a baby without making a massive fuss, and then producing a puny girl.'

I was sanguine. 'Much as I expected.'

Martin continued, 'But you got off more lightly than I did. She said that Abbotshall had rejected me because I was unworthy. It would be glad to be rid of me. Geoffrey would have been Abbotshall's saviour. The Peverells would have failed long ago but for her, a swipe at poor Dad, of course. Anyway, she would never leave Abbotshall.'

'Well, the bit about Geoffrey was sheer dementia. But is she right about not leaving? Can they keep the cottage?'

'Yes, I'm sure we can keep the cottage and an acre or so out of the sale, much less unsettling and cheaper for Mother and Pa.'

I queried Mollie's reaction. 'But how could she bear to stay here with strangers at Abbotshall? I'm surprised that she wasn't more upset.'

Martin agreed. 'So am I. And I don't like it.'

'What do you mean?'

'The fact that she didn't seem to be upset was itself frightening. Either the enormity of what's happening just didn't sink in or she's plotting something.'

'Oh, Martin!' I looked fearfully at the sweetly sleeping Anne.

Martin gave me a reassuring hug. 'Don't worry! Your dad will be here tomorrow.'

My father was indeed back the next day, with plenty of warm clothes and some of his beloved books. He soon settled in and then proposed his "bright idea". 'Jim and Sarah are coming tomorrow, Aulis, to see the baby. Sarah's bringing a suitcase and, if you want her to, she's happy to stay here for a while to help you with the house and so on.'

Martin was first to respond. 'It sounds like a very generous offer to me.'

I was less sure. I had so hoped that the "idea" would be the return of my mother. What was more I had always regarded Aunt Sarah with some awe, having great respect for her. I realised that I didn't want her to see what a mess I had made of my life. Pride held me back from accepting help from her, that foolish pride which I had not needed to learn from Mollie because I had brought it with me to Abbotshall. So now I chose to find an objection to her coming. 'What about Uncle Jim? How will he manage without her?'

My father brushed this aside. 'Don't worry about him. He's not helpless, and Harriet can keep an eye on him. He's quite agreeable. We all want to help you, Aulis. We're your family.'

My family whom I had held so cheap after the advent of the Peverells...

Ida weighed in with warm approval. 'I'm so glad, Aulis. I was worried about leaving you. I'll feel much more comfortable now. I'll take her through everything tomorrow, the Aga ritual, where things are, all of that.'

Next day, once that was done, Ida prepared to go home. Our embrace was warm and close, then she gently detached herself, with a cheerful farewell. 'Good luck, everyone! You know where I am if you need me.' And swinging her great bulk into the old Humber she was off down the drive with a cheery wave.

Her departure had obviously been observed from the cottage, for Mollie and Peter came up soon afterwards. Mollie seemed to make a real effort to be pleasant. I knew that she preferred my family without my mother. But the harmony couldn't last. We had had tea and Uncle Jim was making moves to leave. Mollie looked curiously at Aunt Sarah. 'Get Miss Price's coat, Martin,' she ordered.

Aunt Sarah, small, wiry, apple-cheeked, a complete contrast to Ida, smiled sweetly

'I'm not leaving, Mrs Peverell. I'm here to take care of my niece and my great-niece'

Mollie tried to sprinkle her jibe with sugar, speaking in her sweetest tones. 'Of course, you were a servant, were you not?'

Aunt Sarah was ready for her. 'Yes, I was housekeeper to a noble family in a great house. I haven't spent my life in a farmhouse kitchen. I know how real gentry behave. But I'm happy to help my niece, who seems to have had a rough ride among less compassionate people who are merely trying to be gentry.'

Mollie was furious. 'Take me home, Peter. First Ida Ripley and now this person! This is no place for us while these people remain here. But they needn't think that her whole ghastly family are taking over. Abbotshall will soon be ours again.'

With this strange phrase she swept out, followed by Peter, looking apologetic and harassed.

Aunt Sarah sighed. 'I knew at your wedding, Aulis, that that woman was a fraud, what Lady Margrave would have called a poseur. How could you have been taken in by her, I suppose your mother was pushing you into marriage?'

Then, realising that she had probably offended both Martin and my father, Aunt Sarah added hastily, 'I'm sorry to speak so frankly. After all, Mrs Peverell is just a sad, silly woman. How unhappy she must be.'

The charity of this last remark, taking some of the sting out of her previous speech, saved us from a rather awkward silence.

Aunt Sarah soon took over the house, leaving me free to concentrate on my precious baby. Like Ida, Aunt Sarah had a low opinion of Mrs Brown. 'That woman is more worried about breaking a nail than getting things clean,' she remarked tartly one day as she ran her fingers along the dusty window ledges. 'Aren't there any proper cleaners around here?'

'I thought I had a really good one, a village woman, called Barbara, but Mollie thought she gossiped too much.'

'I can handle a bit of gossip,' Aunt Sarah chuckled. 'You can often learn a lot from it. Anyway, if Mrs Peverell doesn't like her, she must be all right!'

So Mrs Brown went and, to my joy, Barbara returned. She did chat about the past and the Peverells, helping Aunt Sarah to "place" them, as she called it.

My aunt spoke thoughtfully to me one day. 'You know, Aulis, Mrs Peverell has made even this house a fraud. She's changed it into a cheap imitation of what she imagines to be the real thing. But it isn't a stately home, it's a good yeoman farmer's house, and I reckon that the Peverells have always been good solid yeomen farmers. That's what Peter Peverell was, until someone gave him ideas above his station.'

'You mean Mollie? She's always said that she married beneath her.'

Aunt Sarah was indignant. 'That she certainly did not. Her father was a cattle dealer, not always very respectable people, although they can make a lot of money. That's what he did - and then he determined to marry one of his daughters to their distant Peverell cousin, and so send them up in the world.'

I was dubious. 'You must have got all this from Barbara, it's what Mollie would call village gossip.'

'Embroidered perhaps, but I've no reason to doubt the basic facts. After all, Aulis, anyone can see that Mrs Peverell is ill-bred and ignorant.'

'I couldn't! I thought she was wonderful. I so wanted to be like her.' I suddenly found myself in tears.

Aunt Sarah pulled me down on to the sofa and put her arms around me. 'Well thank goodness you're not. You poor child. You thought it was silver and it turned out to be base metal. We all make mistakes.'

'But not like me,' I wailed. 'Oh, Aunt Sarah, you can see what a mess I've made of my life.'

She was brisk now. 'Nonsense! You're still very young. You have a good man who loves you dearly and a lovely baby. Everything will pick up for you now, you'll see.'

It seemed that her prophecy was being fulfilled when Martin burst in one day, looking more cheerful than he had done for some time.

'Has Abbotshall been spared?' I ventured.'

'No, but we don't have to have an auction. Tom Ripley wants to buy it. He's just been over. It's ideal. Their land adjoins us.'

'But what about this house?'

'The boy's getting married. He and his wife will probably live here.'

'Another blow for your mother, she despises the Ripleys.'

Martin was dismissive. 'We can't worry about that. It's the best news we could hope for. We'll get a professional valuation and agree on a price, he might take some stock too. What a relief!'

We needed some good news. Martin's job-hunting was not going well. My father had helped him draft a CV, exclaiming at his School Certificate results, 'Martin, this is excellent, eight subjects, all with Credits, and Distinctions in Maths and Geography. With results like these, couldn't you train for something, teaching perhaps?'

My dad did tend to think that teaching was the answer to everything.

Martin smiled ruefully. 'Too long ago! All I know about is farming. My only bookwork since school was a one-year course at the County Farm Institute. Of course if I'd been able to take up my place at Harper-Adams...' His voice trailed off.

We were amazed. Both my father and I knew about the prestigious agricultural college in Shropshire. My father said, 'A course at Harper-Adams is practically a degree. You had a place there, why ever didn't you go?'

I could guess, but I let Martin reply. 'Mother thought it was a waste of time and money. She said I couldn't be spared and that such places were only for poor people who didn't have their own farms.'

I was swelling with indignation but my father silenced me with a look. He said quietly to me afterwards, 'I know that you feel strongly and I sympathise, but try not to make things worse for Martin. Aulis. He knows what damage his mother has done, he doesn't need it spelling out. Remember that the woman he was taught to see as infallible, almost as a god, has turned out to be a broken idol. That's a terrible realisation. Be gentle, Aulis. That should come more easily to you now that you're a mother.'

I hugged my father. 'Oh, Dad, thank goodness we've got you here!'

The CV completed, Martin scoured the farming press for opportunities. He didn't seem to fit any of the roles required: "Strong Youth for heavy work" or "College graduate looking for further practical experience".

'I suppose I could do contract milking,' he said doubtfully one evening.

I wasn't keen. 'Isn't that a tough life? And wouldn't you be away from home a lot?'

My father chipped in. 'Martin, won't the money you get from Abbotshall be enough to buy you a small farm?'

Aunt Sarah shook her head at my father's ignorance, but Martin was gentle as he answered, 'No, Mr Price. It won't be enough to buy a viable farm. It could buy us a house and some stock, nothing more.'

Aunt Sarah put a seemingly idle question. 'Martin, would you consider being a tenant farmer?'

Martin answered. 'Certainly, if I had the chance. That's what my grandfather was and my father. It was only when the estate was sold during the Depression in the 1930s that Dad bought Abbotshall.'

I was astounded. 'So this isn't your ancestral home, all that "Peverells always at Abbotshall" nonsense?'

Before an indignant Martin could reply, Aunt Sarah stepped in. 'Of course it's not nonsense, Aulis. A long line of tenancy on a great estate is something to be very proud of.'

I still felt that layers of deceit were being chipped away from Abbotshall but Martin smiled at my aunt. 'I knew you'd understand. I'd love a good tenancy. But they're like gold. They're often inherited, it's hard for a newcomer to break in.'

That was the end of what seemed to me a pointless conversation. After all, as both Mollie and my mother had often said, Aunt Sarah had only been a servant, however one dressed it up. She might talk the language, but there was nothing she could do.

Christmas came and went. Uncle Jim joined us and we had a lovely time, enjoying Aunt Sarah's delicious cooking. As she had promised, Di took Mollie and Peter to Wales. With Mollie's menacing presence removed, we all relaxed. Abbotshall, so soon to be left, suddenly felt like home.

My mother's Christmas letter was full of gushing innuendo: '*I'm dying to see you and the baby when I come home in March. I thought about coming earlier but I'm sure Sarah is looking after you, not that she'll be much good with the baby, being an old maid.*'

This was unkind and unfair. Aunt Sarah was great with Anne. Although she'd never worked in the nursery at Margrave Hall, she had obviously loved Master Harry, the Margraves' only son, the little boy who had never come back from Dunkirk. I could see my mother's jealousy, entirely self-inflicted.

We were very grateful to Aunt Sarah, but we had no idea how grateful we were going to be.

One day, after lunch, my aunt seemed rather excited. Her eyes shone as she handed Martin a letter. 'There's a letter for you here, Martin, enclosed in one to me. You can read them both.'

Puzzled, Martin began to read, while my father and I looked on, equally curious. Then Martin gave a great shout, 'You've got me a tenancy! How on earth...? It's like a miracle. How did you do it?'

Aunt Sarah answered simply, 'I wrote to Lord Margrave.'

I chipped in, 'But he's dead!'

Aunt Sarah was impatient. 'Not my Lord Margrave, of course he's dead. But there's still a Lord Margrave, a nephew, who now owns the estate.'

Annoyed by a situation I didn't understand, I seemed determined to be difficult. 'But I thought Margrave Hall had gone.'

'That doesn't matter. You can have an estate without a hall. Lord Margrave just has a cottage there. He's in the City. It's the agent, Colonel Travers, who does the practical running of the estate.'

I was incredulous and fascinated at the same time. 'But what did you tell Lord Margrave?'

'I just sent him Martin's CV and explained the situation. I never worry about talking to a Margrave.'

Even my father, really comfortable only in his own sphere and far less worldly-wise than his servant sister, was amazed.

Since his initial exclamation Martin had been quietly reading the letters. He gave them to me now, saying, 'It's all here, Aulis. My letter is from the agent, Colonel Travers, he describes the farm and the house and sets out the terms. They'd like the tenancy taken up at Lady-Day, we'll have to get a move on. Oh, Aulis, bless the day I met you and your family!'

Indoctrinated as I had been by Mollie and, to some extent, by my mother, I still didn't understand Aunt Sarah's influence. 'But why should Lord Margrave do this?'

Martin was impatient now. 'Read his letter!'

Obeying, I was awestruck to see the esteem in which my aunt was held. Certain phrases stood out. '*Anyone recommended by you... A small gesture of gratitude for your many years of faithful and loving service to our family.*' I began to cry.

Aunt Sarah brought us down to earth. 'Come on, all of you, there's work to be done and a baby to be fed. I know I can't write CVs like our Bill but at least I can send them off.'

As our laughter released the tension Martin began to think ahead. 'First thing is to tell Dad. He'll be so relieved and glad. So will Di!'

I couldn't help myself. 'And your mother, will she be glad? You'll be a tenant farmer, people she despises, and you'll owe it to my family, and to a servant.'

Martin was philosophical. 'I'm such a disappointment to Mother that I don't think anything could make me worse in her eyes. If she starts, I'll ask her if she would prefer me to be on the dole, or being kept by my wife. I'm so happy I don't care.'

He swamped Anne and me with kisses, lifted little Aunt Sarah off the ground in his embrace and shook hands with my father. Then he was off.

A whole new world now lay ahead. We had to plan for the takeover of the farm, for the stock-sale, for our own move, setting up our new farm and our new house. Out of the deepest misery had come these wonderful opportunities.

All seemed positive. Yet I was always conscious of that presence at the bottom of the drive, the one who couldn't or wouldn't rejoice. I felt that Mollie was unfinished business, not just because of what she might do to us, but what we might do for her. Was there any way of rescuing that relationship, or was she to remain an object of fear and bitterness?

Could we achieve some kind of reconciliation before we left?

Chapter Twenty-One
Farewell to Abbotshall

The weeks sped by, leaving little time for brooding.

Di came up for the stock sale and spent a long day helping her mother clear out. 'Geoffrey's' attic. When they had finished Di came into the kitchen. 'There Aulis, that's all done. We've put several bags out for the bins and your father's been very kind, helping me to load the boxes that are going down to the cottage. Mummy's gone home but I had to come to see my gorgeous niece.' She leaned over to smile at Anne in her pram.

I needed to be sure. 'So the room is totally empty, is it, Di?'

She answered sharply, 'Yes of course.'

But as she spoke, I saw that she was wearing Mollie's foxy look, her eyes not meeting mine, so I didn't quite believe her. All I said was, 'Can I have the key please?'

She was flustered. 'Oh dear, I'm afraid Mummy went off with it. I'm sure she'll remember to give it back to you. I'd better go and see if she's all right, she found it all rather distressing.' She hurried off.

Aunt Sarah sniffed. 'Hm! The one that got away.'

On a cold, wet day in February, Martin, Anne and I set off to see our new farm and house. I had tentatively suggested taking Peter with us, but Martin was adamant.' 'No, this is our great opportunity, for our family. I've no particular quarrel with Dad but I want to start unencumbered by the past. For goodness' sake, Aulis, cheer up.'

Martin himself was euphoric. The agent, Colonel Travers, was there to meet us. He and Martin were to go round the farm, for Martin to see the lie of the land and explain his projected plans for farming it.

Meanwhile, Colonel Travers took me to the house, where Mrs Jennings, the late tenant's widow, gave me a warm welcome, saying, as she clasped my hand. 'Oh, my dear, you're frozen! Come and thaw out by the Rayburn. I'll put the kettle on, then you can have a hot drink and warm up Baby's bottle. Oh, you're feeding her yourself, how lovely, I fed all our three.'

These priorities dealt with Mrs Jennings showed me round the house, extolling its virtues. 'You'll find it roomy but manageable, nothing grand but good sizeable rooms, and a lovely warm kitchen.'

As I measured, planning where to put our furniture, Mollie had said we could have "the Peverell stuff" I tried to sound enthusiastic. 'It'll be such fun coming here. We're so lucky!' Mrs Jennings seemed satisfied, but I realised with sadness that after my experiences at Abbotshall joy would never be undiluted again, embracing happiness was dangerous, especially where a house was concerned.

I needed to say little on the way home, because Martin talked non-stop. 'It's wonderful, Aulis. Good land, well-kept buildings, all suited to what I want. Milking parlour small but adequate, and plenty of room for my pigs! Colonel Travers is likeable and helpful, I don't think he'll interfere. We are so lucky!'

I willed myself to cast no shadow on his joy, just a few more weeks, I said to myself, then we'll be safe.

Meanwhile I and my family ensured that Anne was never left alone. My mother came home in March and was swiftly enrolled into the guarding party, making up for lost time by lavishing affection on Anne. Not that her admiration was undiluted. My baby was constantly being compared with the idolised Gareth in Australia.' 'Now Gareth slept through the night much earlier than this.'

'Gareth was sitting up and taking notice in no time at all.'

The breastfeeding was a constant bone of contention. Studying Anne critically my mother would say, 'You know, Aulis, I think she'd come on a lot faster with a bottle. Would you like me to try her with one? It was lovely to see Gareth taking his bottle. Mel liked me to give it him, to save her, you know.'

Then there were the sly digs at Aunt Sarah. 'A new experience for you, Sarah, holding a baby. Oh, look she's looking for her dinner, she won't find any there, will she? (crude laugh) Better give her to her mother.'

My steadfast little aunt maintained her dignity and good humour, yet gave as good as she got. 'Don't worry, Bron. Anne and I are old friends, she was less than two weeks old when we met. I love to watch her suckling.' Sarah knew that the blunt word would annoy and embarrass my mother. And as I flinched from one of my mother's jibes Aunt Sarah said quietly, 'Don't get upset, Aulis. All this talk about Gareth, you know your mother's always preferred boys. I think that she stayed in Australia because she felt so loved and wanted there. She's closest to Jason because he doesn't look down his long intellectual nose at her like you and Hector.'

I protested laughingly. 'That's not fair, Aunt Sarah! We don't, and my nose isn't long.'

Aunt Sarah laughed back. 'Don't worry, Aulis! We Prices have always been a domineering lot, and your mother's always felt dominated by us. Her nasty little comments are just her way of trying to get her own back. Let them go over your head, my dear.'

I was becoming very close to Aunt Sarah, appreciating her straightforward affection. I realised that with her and Ida I now had two loving relationships with mature women which helped to alleviate my problems with my own mother. I also realised that I had so longed for Mollie to love me partly because of my unsatisfactory relationship with my own mother. Almost physically repelled by my mother's slapdash ways I had seen in Mollie the ideal of domestic felicity. I knew now how wrong I had been, yet against all reason and common sense I still longed for Mollie's affection.

There was certainly no sign of any reciprocal feeling from Mollie. While Peter came up frequently to see the baby, Mollie's visits were rare, and she never came alone. She continued to take little interest in Anne. To the rest of us she was civil but cold. I was saddened by her attitude when I remembered the closeness we had sometimes achieved during my pregnancy and how I'd hoped that she would love me through my child. However, her behaviour now seemed perfectly normal and I still yearned for some kind of reconciliation before we left.

We were preparing in earnest now for our departure, clearing out the rubbish of years and packing carefully all our possessions, my mother and aunt working together quite harmoniously. In the midst of all this activity, looking at our china and silver, I had my bright idea, hastening to sell it to Martin as I gave Anne her ten o'clock feed, our cosiest family time. 'Martin, it's high time Anne was baptized, she's almost six months old. Let's have her done in the church here where we were married, before we leave, with a tea-party in the house afterwards. It'll be a real Peverell family occasion, and the last one to be held here at Abbotshall.'

Martin was dubious at first. 'Is it wise, Aulis? Wouldn't it be better when we've moved, part of our new start? And what about Mother?'

I was slightly impatient. 'I do wonder if we've all been over-reacting a bit, Martin? All this is so sad for Mollie, wouldn't it be good to involve her in a happy family event? And there's enough people to watch her if she does have an episode.'

'Well, it's your decision. Perhaps you're right, and Di and Aunt Emily will be here, it should be all right. Let's do it, but don't drop your guard, my baby is too precious.' As he took Anne, drunk with milk, into his arms, she snuggled up to him, as she loved to do. I kissed him.

'Thank you, Martin, it makes me feel better about being so happy.'

We went ahead with arrangements for the baptism. Di and Ida were to be Anne's godmothers and, at my insistence, Dr Ronald her godfather, though Mollie thought this last, "something that a villager would do". Di brought Lucy; Aunt Emily and Uncle Jim came over. it had all the ingredients of a potentially happy day. The star of the show was of course Anne, enveloped in the billowing lace of the Peverell christening robe, which Mollie had handed over with no hesitation, a good sign, I thought. The service went well, then it was back to Abbotshall for tea.

Everyone seemed happy and busy. Martin bustled about with champagne. Di and Ida were quietly helpful while the aunts, Emily and Sarah, ran a magnificent kitchen. Anne was passed around for cuddles, and then put to rest in her pram, under the nominal charge of Lucy.

The most wonderful thing was Mollie. Beautifully dressed, as always, she was chatting like everyone else. I held my breath as I heard my mother say cheerily, 'The baby's done quite well on breast milk, hasn't she? But it's time Aulis gave that up now, don't you think, Mrs Peverell?'

I waited for a cold, contemptuous reply. But Mollie's tone was gentle, if slightly sad. 'Let her do what she likes, Mrs Price, it doesn't matter. There's no point Martin having a son now. We must all just get on with things.'

Any sting in the words was softened by the lovely, slightly rueful smile she gave me. One of her old, loving smiles.

My heart leapt up. Everything was all right. Mollie had got over her sulks, accepted the situation and had made no attempt to hurt Anne. We could all go forward positively and happily. I relegated all my previous forebodings about Mollie to the back of my mind. I reminded myself that she wasn't a witch with occult powers. She wasn't a psychopath. She was just a sad and lonely old lady who had the lost the person she loved most, however strange that love might seem to others. Loving Anne as I did, I could begin to understand. And after all, despite our concerns, she had made no attempt to hurt Anne. Reassured, I smiled back at Mollie and gave myself up to enjoying the occasion.

The buzz of talk and laughter went on. We were all relaxed and off guard, somehow lulled into a false sense of security. I don't know how long it was before anyone noticed, Mollie was missing and the pram was empty.

Even as we registered these facts, Sam, who had been milking the cows which we had kept to move with us, burst in, shouting, 'Martin, your mother's at an open attic window, holding the baby.'

Martin led the way as everyone, except the two old aunts, pounded up the backstairs, Ida puffing in the rear. We burst into "Geoffrey's attic". The room was bare of everything except his crib with its blue hangings, freshly washed and ironed, and with clean, fresh linen.

Di, white and trembling, couldn't meet my eyes.

We stopped short as Mollie, holding Anne quite firmly, turned round from the window. My frantic fear abated just a little. Mollie was smiling as she had smiled downstairs and seemed to be her sweetest self as she spoke in her usual mellow tones, 'Goodness, what a crowd! Granny is just showing Anne what she and I are losing, the green pastures of Abbotshall. Then Anne is going to have a nice long sleep in her Uncle Geoffrey's cot, after her tiring day.'

Although shivering slightly at this familial reference to Geoffrey I was moved by Mollie's gentleness. I went over to stand by her, slipping my arm round her. Then I saw that she was holding a feeding bottle, almost empty. I saw the milky residue around Anne's lips.

She looked heavy with sleep. I turned on Mollie.'
'What's in the bottle, Mollie? What have you given her?'

Her reply was soothing. 'Nothing but Mother's milk, my dear.'

A small trembling voice came from the back of the room. 'I gave Gran the milk, Auntie Aulis, your expressed milk from one of the bottles in the fridge. I thought you were all so horrid to Gran, keeping her away from Anne.' Lucy ended on a sob.

Mollie laid Anne in the cot. She still spoke gently. 'Look, Aulish, look how peaceful she looks. She really belongs here, doesn't she?'

Everyone seemed to have turned to stone. I felt totally alone with Mollie and my baby.

I remembered the night of Anne's birth. But I so desperately wanted to believe that Mollie meant no harm. I asked her again, 'You're sure you gave Anne nothing but my milk?'

Mollie smiled, the smile I had once loved so much, an almost teasing smile, as she answered slowly, 'Well... Mother's milk plus a little something from Granny to help her to sleep, then perhaps she won't wake up, so she can stay here with Granny, where we both belong. You might join us, Aulish, then you would belong at last. You know that's what you've always wanted...'

She turned to embrace me, as I so loved her to do. But this time I pulled away and bent to snatch the sleeping baby. Even as I saw Martin and my mother rushing towards me as if released from a spell, I felt something warm and wet. Looking down I saw a stream of blood running down my thigh. As if in a dream I saw

Mollie turn to plunge a blood- stained knife into her own chest. I saw Peter wrest the knife from her and throw it through the open window. I heard it clatter on the cobbles below.

***

I woke to full consciousness to find myself lying in a hospital bed, with various tubes attached to me. Ida was sitting beside the bed. To my immense relief, she was holding Anne.

'Oh, Ida, my baby, is she all right?'

Ida seemed equally relieved to see me. 'Aulis, you're really back with us, that's wonderful! Let me just get a nurse to look at you.'

The nurse came, adjusted various things, took my temperature and said, 'All seems fine.

Just take things gently, Mrs Peverell, I'll bring you a cup of tea.'

'Please may I hold my baby?'

'Yes, if you're careful.'

They settled Anne beside me. She snuggled up and made straight for my breast. A dreadful thought struck me. 'Ida, will I have any milk?

'I would think so. We've kept her going with what's in the freezer and I fed her quite recently. We'll soon see if she finds anything.'

Anne got what she was looking for, and I and my baby were comforted. Then the memories came flooding back.

'But Ida, I thought Mollie had killed her.'

Then I felt the heavy dressing on my side. 'And what did she do to me? Oh, God, it's all coming back. How long have I been here? And where's Martin?'

Ida was firm. 'Now keep calm, Aulis, and I'll tell you everything. You've been here since Sunday and today's Wednesday. Martin has been here day and night and so have your parents. You've been in the valley of the shadow, my dear, and given us all a fright. They told us this morning that you were out of danger. Martin and your parents have just popped out for something to eat. Would you like me to tell you everything before they come back, they're still in pieces.?'

'Yes, please, Ida. I promise to keep calm.'

'Right! Do you remember that Mollie said that she had given Anne something, and then she stabbed you?'

'Yes, that's almost the last thing I remember. What happened next?'

'Complete chaos. Your mother snatched Anne and rushed off with her, calling Sarah. The pair of them made the baby vomit, which the doctor said probably saved her life. They analysed the vomit in the hospital. It seemed that Mollie had crushed some of her sleeping tablets into the milk, which could have been fatal for a young baby. Sam drove Anne to the hospital with your mother and Sarah. They washed her stomach out, put her on a drip and she was soon back with us, though rather sorry for herself.'

I hugged Anne. 'Poor baby! But why on earth didn't the doctor go with her to hospital?

Ida was indignant. 'Good gracious, Aulis, he was far too busy saving you. He and I were desperately trying to stem the blood, you were losing so much. Dr Ronald even ripped up his shirt. Then he had to bring you back twice, once in the attic and once in the ambulance.'

'Bring me back… you mean?'

'Yes, artificial respiration. I came in the ambulance too, with Martin, he was frantic.'

I reflected for a moment. 'You know, Ida, that's twice Martin's nearly lost both of us and each time it's been her fault. What happened to her?'

'I was too busy with you to notice much, but when Peter took the knife from her, she attacked him, trying to throw herself out of the window. She fought with manic strength. Then she suddenly collapsed, crying and sobbing.'

I felt little pity. 'I suppose she's queening it now. Does she know I'm not dead?'

Ida looked sober. 'She's not queening it, Aulis. She went straight to a psychiatric hospital. She's in a secure unit, no one knows for how long.'

I was sober too. 'Will she recover?'

'No one knows that either.'

I shivered: 'Ida, will I have to go back there?'

Ida knew what I meant. 'To Abbotshall? No everything's arranged. We're not far off Lady-Day, so Martin must go to take up the tenancy. He's organising all that. Your uncle and aunt are arranging the house-move and going down to fix everything up for you.

Meanwhile your parents and Anne are going to stay with me. You'll need to be in here for a little while yet, but when you're discharged, they're going to take you straight to your new home, where everything will be ready.'

'Goodness, Ida, everyone is good to me.'

Kind Ida did not tell me, as my mother did later, of the ramblings they had heard while I was unconscious, my cries of fear and terror, my pleas with Mollie to be kind to me. She merely said, 'I think you deserve a little help after all you've been through.'

Ida kissed me, took Anne and prepared to leave. Then, not looking at me, she said carefully, 'You were lucky, but they couldn't save the baby.'

I was flabbergasted, looking at the lively Anne. 'What baby?'

'Martin said you didn't know, or you would have told him. You were about ten weeks pregnant.'

I hardly dared ask. 'Was it …?'

Again, Ida knew what I meant. 'It was too young for them to know the sex.' She hurried on. 'Don't be too upset, Aulis, it was very soon after Anne, you might have lost it anyway, what with the upheaval and everything.'

292

I was not consoled. 'It was conceived in the middle of upheaval, wasn't it! So she did kill my baby, just what she wanted. I bet she guessed! What irony, the heir she so much wanted, no Abbotshall, no heir.'

'I told you, Aulis, they couldn't tell.'

I looked at Ida, who was still firmly not looking at me. 'It was a boy, wasn't it, Ida, just tell me the truth.'

Now Ida did look at me and nodded silently, tears rolling down her cheeks.

I suddenly knew what the word "bereft" meant. I had miscarried of hope and joy. Martin's longed-for son, who would have sealed the promise of our future, to die in a flood of blood on the attic floor.

I hated Mollie now, my words reflecting my bitterness. 'May she rot in hell! May she live to wish that she had never been born!'

Ida's tone was gentle as she rebuked me. 'Try to have some pity for her, Aulis, you loved her once. Do you not think that she already lives in her own private hell? I know that you have had a grievous loss, but you still have so much to look forward to. You have Martin and Anne and I'm sure that there will be more babies. Your shadow will lift, she may be permanently in the shadows. You've been so brave, Aulis, now be a big person and spare some pity for Mollie.'

I was not to be easily persuaded. 'I had pity for her, Ida. It was pity that made me arrange that Baptism and brought me to this pass. It was pity that killed our son! After all those months of taking care and despite all the warnings I thought that I knew best. Perhaps I was as responsible for his death as Mollie was. Perhaps I should be locked up!'

Then came a storm of weeping for the whole sorry business, for my own stupid conceit, for this needless loss of our baby, perhaps, even, for Mollie. The nurse came hurrying over to take Anne while Ida held me close and let me cry against her broad bosom. 'There, there, my love, have your cry out. You've needed that for a long time.'

As my sobs finally subsided into hiccups Ida gently detached herself. 'I must go now, Aulis, but I'll try to bring Anne in fairly regularly now for her feeds.'

'Thank you, Ida, thank you for telling me, and for everything.'

We hugged and kissed again, then Ida and Anne were gone.

The nurse came hurrying over, full of concern. 'Are you all right, Mrs Peverell? Mrs Ripley did go on rather long, but perhaps it was better for you to learn everything.'

'Yes, thank you; I think it was. Now I'd like to rest please.'

'Of course.' she tiptoed away.

I lay back in bed, waiting for Martin. My bruised and battered body ached for him, even as my breasts filled up with longing for the dead baby. After the years of waiting for Anne, Martin and I had swiftly made another beautiful child who had been rudely butchered almost before he could begin to live. I must weep for him, but Ida was right, I must be grateful too, for my own life, for Anne's, for this consuming love that Martin and I had for each other. And I must be ready to comfort Martin, who would also be mourning for his boy.

Then, reluctantly, I thought of Mollie. She had left Abbotshall, never to return to the house she had known and loved so much. She had herself killed the male heir she had longed for. She was dead, at least for the moment, to sanity and reality. She could still press her dream-child to her breast, but could never again lay him gently in his cot with the blue hangings, never sing him to sleep and creep quietly down the backstairs, knowing that he was safely locked away from prying eyes.

Her dream house, the Abbotshall she had loved and nurtured until it destroyed her, that was dead too. The ceremonious house was to become a simple farmhouse, happy and wholesome, where there was no place for Mollie Peverell and her dark dreams.

The house was gone and she was gone, but her blood still flowed. It flowed in the veins of Martin and Diana, in those of Lucy and Charlie Llewellyn and in those of Anne Peverell.

Epilogue

It is a beautiful sunny day, one of those days which September steals from June. I am sitting in my favourite place on the front lawn, rejoicing, as always, in the mellow Cotswold stone of our little house and our farm buildings. We have a substantial holding by most people's standards but hardly comparable with Abbotshall. I rarely think of Abbotshall now, although Martin says that I still cry out in my sleep. Today the memories are sharp.

Anne is with me, jumping about on a curious ball with ears, Ida's Christmas present. The new baby sleeps sweetly in the pram at my side. Anne, wearing her best smocked dress, white tights and her now almost permanent frown, jumps along to speak to me. 'I suppose they're coming to see vat baby?'

'She's not "that baby" Anne. She's your little sister.'

'I wanted a bruvver. He would have played with me. We could have had races on our hoppers.'

Squashing the guilty thought that I too had "wanted a bruvver" I answered firmly, 'That's silly, Anne. New-born babies can't play until they've done lots of growing.'

'Well vat baby jumped about in your tummy, so why can't it jump now? Anyway, it's not my fault I was late.'

This non sequitur puzzled me. 'What do you mean, Anne? You didn't come late, a little bit early in fact.' I could never forget the manner of Anne's coming.

'Granny Price said everybody liked vat baby because it came quickly and was no trouble "not like you" she said to me.'

I inwardly cursed my incorrigible mother, whose tact did not mature with the years.

Anne was in full flow now. 'And she said it was rude to watch you feeding it, but Daddy shouted at her and said it wasn't. It isn't rude, is it?'

Hearing a quaver in the little voice I lifted her from her hopper on to my knee. 'Of course not, Darling. I love you to watch Baby feeding.'

Anne scrambled down, she wasn't going to be so easily placated. 'I don't want to watch it anyway. It was my place, and it's got my pram,' giving my beloved Silver Cross a push as she spoke, so that the baby uttered a faint protest.

I was getting tired of this. Some signs of jealousy, like the little speech errors, I had expected and had even thought that, at nearly four, at least Anne would be able to articulate her feelings, but her behaviour was becoming impossible. So I answered sharply. 'It's a family pram, Anne, not just yours. I hope that you're not going to be sulky and difficult like this all day, with our visitors coming.'

Back on her hopper Anne didn't answer me, just said, 'Here's Daddy.'

With a sigh of relief, I saw Martin crossing the yard and opening the little side-gate to join us on the lawn. Four years of intensely hard work had aged him, and the hair at his temples was flecked with grey, but nothing had lessened the upsurge of gladness which I always felt on seeing him. He ruffled Anne's hair, peered in the pram, and sat down beside me, putting his arm round me and kissing my cheek. Martin loved his children dearly but I knew that he would always be mate first and parent second. Today, of all days, I rejoiced in that, as I drew closer to him, saying, 'I'm so glad you came over. I'm getting nervous. It will be strange, to say the least of it, seeing your parents again after all this time.'

Martin smiled. 'Well I couldn't let you greet them without me. And I seem to be just in time, there's a car coming up the drive. Yes, it's Pa driving.'

We stood up as Peter Peverell parked the car and the passengers got out. Martin moved towards the gate to welcome them, while Anne, suddenly shy, clasped my hand and peeped round my skirt. I had a few minutes to study the three visitors: Peter Peverell, wearing a well-cut grey lounge suit and his usual air of distinction, his white hair shining, was little different to the man I remembered. Aunt Emily, dumpy as ever, smiled uncertainly. I saw that her reported prosperity had not reached her wardrobe. She was wearing a maroon woollen two-piece, shapeless and baggy, with a horrible smudgy green viyella blouse. I thought, irreverently, of a beetroot with its leaves on top. Why on earth couldn't Mollie give her some fashion advice, but no, of course Mollie preferred Emily as a foil for her own elegance.

Poor Emily certainly had that role today for Mollie looked amazing! She was wearing a dress of fine wool on which tiny blue flowers rioted across a white background. Its long sleeves and high neck hid any tell-tale signs of age. Such a dress would have looked ridiculous on most elderly people, but it suited Mollie perfectly. Her hair, pure white now, rose in a well-set aureole, highlighting her porcelain complexion and the well-remembered marble-blue eyes. Suddenly she stooped slightly and held out her arms. Anne, dropping my hand and no longer shy or sulky, rushed into them.

With a terrible sense of both déjà vu and foreboding I heard the old phrases, 'Grannie's girl, Grannie's special girl!' I looked across at Peter and Emily but they seemed to find only pleasure in the scene. I comforted myself with the thought that at least Anne's behaviour had covered any embarrassment we might have felt, meeting after nearly four years, and we were all able to exchange cheerful greetings.

Then Anne remembered. Clutching Mollie's hand, she began to lead her to the pram. 'Look at Baby,' she said. 'I know that's why you've come.'

'But I want to see you first. I've come to see you. You are so beautiful. Will you show me your flowers and talk to me? Baby can wait.'

Much to my relief Aunt Emily took Anne's other hand and the little girl, obviously delighted, skipped between them towards our modest flower-beds.

The three of us left all started to speak at once, then Peter took over. 'I don't know which of you to congratulate first, you're looking wonderful, Aulis. Motherhood really suits you.'

I blushed with pleasure, I was still ample from the baby and was feeling fat and awkward.

'Thank you, Peter, this was a much easier pregnancy and birth.'

'I'm sure it was.' He answered gravely as he and I exchanged a long look, remembering without words the vicissitudes of my first pregnancy, Anne's birth and what had followed.

Peter turned to Martin: 'The farm looks splendid, Martin, so well-cared-for. Very different to how it was on my brief visit three years ago.'

Martin was equally pleased. 'It's not been easy, you know farming, a difficult calving or a drop in the milk yield can blow you off course in a minute. But we manage to keep afloat, and I have a good helper.'

Peter looked surprised. 'I didn't know you employed anyone.'

Martin smiled. 'I don't. It's my wonderful wife. She looks after the calves, does the books and a hundred other things, as well as giving me lovely children.'

Slightly embarrassed by this last remark Peter smiled ruefully. 'You were always good at doing the books weren't you, Aulis, even if they sometimes made grim reading?'

Remembering all the misery of the end at Abbotshall I ventured to ask, 'How is Mollie?'

Peter smiled. 'Fine, virtually cured. As you can see, she retains her old magic, and there's no bitterness now. She never mentions him. I was wise to spend some of the Abbotshall money on our world cruise, that's really opened her mind. And having Emily with us is a great blessing. You know old Noakes died and left her everything, no more than she deserved!'

I agreed. 'Yes, we're so glad. And does Aunt Emily live with you now?'

'Yes, she has her own bed-sitting room, so we're not on top of each other. But she's able to keep Mollie up to the mark, make sure she takes her pills, and she's on hand, just in case.'

He left the sentence unfinished, but we understood, "just in case", Mollie lost control again. I said, 'Well there seems no fear of that at the moment. Just now I'm blessing Mollie for making Anne look so much happier. Anne's been feeling a little pushed out by the baby, inevitable I suppose.'

As I spoke Mollie, Emily and Anne completed their garden tour. Mollie sat down on the garden seat and asked Anne if she could see "Her Baby". 'Get Baby out, Mummy.' Anne's tone was peremptory.

Martin looked sternly at her. 'You should say "please" Anne, not speak to Mummy like that.' He lifted the warm, sleeping bundle out of the pram, delighting me by this demonstration of our unity. He handed the baby to Mollie, smiling as he said, 'Here you are, Granny, another one for the family tree.'

Mollie was still her astringent old self as she replied, 'That hardly matters now, another girl, Aulis, bad luck, but then, tenant farmers don't need sons.'

I found myself able to exchange smiles with Martin, rather than rising to the bait as I would have done in the old days.

Baby had opened her eyes now. I held my breath as she turned instinctively towards Mollie's breast but Mollie remained unmoved, observing critically. 'H'm, this one doesn't look much like the Peverells. Oh dear, Aulish, I'm afraid she looks horribly like you, never mind, perhaps she'll grow out of it. She's not at all pretty like Anne, is she? Anne is so definitely one of our family.'

Hiding my hurt at this denigration of my baby and at the hidden implication in Mollie's remark I was concerned to see Anne's smug expression. Peter, Martin and Emily were laughing to cover the moment, Martin exclaiming, 'Oh, Mother, you never change!'

Their laughter disturbed Baby, who began to whimper. Mollie hastened to hand her to me, where she quickly settled down. Mollie regarded me critically. 'Oh dear, Aulish, I hope you're not going to leak. You always had a tendency to do that didn't you?'

Aware of Peter and Emily's embarrassment I answered calmly, 'No I won't leak. I fed her about an hour ago to give us a good long afternoon. She just wants comfort. It's quite tough, being inspected. I remember how Anne used to hate it.'

The others looked uncomfortable, both at the memory and the fear that I was going to be difficult. Anne looked positively offended. But Mollie carried on regardless, 'And what's this little one going to be called? Nothing outlandish, I hope!'

Martin answered, 'Her names are Sarah Jane, and we're going to call her Sally, at least while she's little.'

Mollie digested this. 'H'm, not so pretty as Anne's names. I suppose Sarah is after your auntie, Aulish. I always think of it as a servant's name. But Jane is most appropriate, she's certainly Plain Jane. Oh dear, Aulish, and perhaps she'll have your brains too.' She made that sound like some chronic disease.

Martin broke in hastily, anxious to stem my growing irritation and to move things along. 'Shall we go in and have tea? Then I can show you round the farm, Pa and you can help me with the milking, if you like, while the girls have a cosy chat and Sally has her tea.'

Despite the irony of the "cosy chat" I loved him for using the baby's name, stressing her place in our family. Perhaps Mollie's criticism of the baby had done some good, it had dispelled any last lingering regret about Sarah Jane's sex, she was our little girl and I loved her as unconditionally as I loved Anne.

So in we went. Sarah Jane, safely asleep again, back in her pram which Martin pushed, Peter and I chatting amicably, Anne clutching Mollie and Emily's hands as if she would never let them go.

Exclamations of approval greeted the tea I had prepared as I whipped away its covering cloth to reveal delicate finger sandwiches, tiny sausage rolls, scones accompanied by raspberry jam glowing in its cut-glass dish and clotted cream: there was a Victoria sponge of magnificent proportions and a succulent coffee cake. Our best china and silver graced the table.

'How lovely, Aulis,' purred Aunt Emily. 'Have you done all this yourself?'

Before I could answer Anne piped up, 'Mrs Jennings made the sponge-cake.'

Mollie was on to that in a flash. 'Who's Mrs Jennings?'

'She's a woman who fetches me from play-group.'

'Anne!' I protested, saying to Mollie, 'Mrs Jennings is a very good friend. She lives in the village and she's helped me these last few months by bringing Anne home from playgroup, where she goes on Tuesdays and Thursdays.

Martin added, 'Mrs Jennings is a widow. Her husband was the tenant here before me.'

Mollie was satisfied, if dismissive. 'I see, quite an ordinary person. And what about this playgroup? I suppose it's full of village children?'

'Yes,' said Martin, an edge of exasperation creeping into his voice. 'Yes, Mother, lovely children that Anne is lucky to have as friends. Mrs Jennings has been very kind to us. She babysits when we have an evening out, though that's not often.'

Mollie gave the deprecating little laugh that I remembered so well. 'No, I don't suppose there's anywhere much to go. You won't be anyone around here, will you?'

As I reflected on our apparent lack of personhood Martin answered, in a tone which only Mollie could provoke, 'Oh, I don't know, Mother. Any tenant of Lord Margrave is assumed to be somebody around here.' He turned to talk to his father about milk-yield and market prices.

But Mollie hadn't finished yet. 'By the way, Martin, I thought I smelled pigs outside. Does some neighbouring farmer keep them?'

'No, Mother, I do!'

Before he could add, *Now that you can't stop me* I chipped in 'They're doing awfully well. Martin does some showing and he's been asked to judge the pigs at a local show.'

The murmurs of approval from Peter and Aunt Emily were drowned out by Mollie's, 'Some village event, I suppose?'

Martin soon terminated this painful conversation, saying that it was almost time for milking. He strode out, his father following obediently.

This was the moment I had been dreading, left alone with Mollie and the rather ineffectual Emily. Again, I was saved by Anne, asking eagerly, 'Mummy, can I show Granny and Aunt Emily my room and all my things while you get Baby ready?'

I agreed with enthusiasm. 'What a good idea, Darling. Show them Baby's room too, that Daddy's just decorated, and all the house, not that it's very big!'

Off they went. Almost immediately that special young-baby wail reminded me that Sally really needed me now and I hurried to get her ready for her feed. We were settled in the sitting-room, with the baby suckling energetically, when the three returned. I knew a moment of panic, wondering if the sight would upset Mollie, but she seemed perfectly content, indeed in high good-humour.

'Look, Anne!' she exclaimed. 'There's Mummy doing what she does best. You know the last time that I saw Mummy feeding a baby she was feeding you! Don't Mummy and Baby both look lovely?'

I prayed that Anne wouldn't repeat my mother's comment, but she just gave a thin smile as she settled herself on a humpty, leaning against Mollie's knees as Mollie and Emily sat on the sofa.

Mollie gave me the old lovely smile. 'You are a good mother, Aulish, but I do hope this is the last one. Two children are very right and proper. But no more, you can't afford it, nor have you room for them in a house with only four bedrooms, and Martin is looking very tired.'

Dear old Aunt Emily, perhaps emboldened by her wealth, chose to disagree. 'Now, I think that Martin's looking very well and happy.'

Mollie swiftly slapped her down. 'No one asked your opinion.'

Anne had grasped what the conversation was about and voiced her protest. 'Granny, I want a bruvver.'

Mollie stroked her hair. 'Do you, Darling? But you've got a nice little sister. I never had a brother. Aunt Emily is my little sister and, as you see, we're still great friends even now that we're old ladies. You will be a good little girl for me and love your little sister and help Mummy, won't you?'

Anne looked up at Mollie and nodded. 'I will for you, Granny.'

We all smiled, but my feelings about Mollie were as confused as ever. While I was grateful to her for breaking through Anne's sulkiness about Baby, on the other hand there was my perhaps natural resentment that Anne seemed able to do for Mollie what she couldn't or wouldn't do for me. Added to that was my residual deep-seated fear of Mollie and her manipulative ways. She had tried to take Anne's body long ago in the attic. Was she now trying to take her soul?

I was brought back to reality by the return of Peter and Martin, Peter unusually talkative as he enthused about the farm, with particular compliments to me on the calves.

'Of course, you learned your skills from Matthew-Henry,' he laughed.

I agreed as I remembered that strange foot-and-mouth winter and the dear old man who had been so kind to me.

We continued to chat, in apparent harmony, while Sally, drunkenly cheerful after her feed, submitted to being handed round for cuddles. Aunt Emily came with me into the kitchen to make "a cup of tea for the road" as she described it. She was pleasant and friendly, but, as always, there was no substance to her conversation. Tea drunk, goodbyes were said and they were gone, we four waving them off from the top of the drive, Martin's arm, protectively and symbolically, around my shoulders.

Hurrying in from the chill of the autumn evening I said to Martin, 'It's time these children were in bed. You see to Baby, and I'll do Anne.' He looked slightly surprised, despite considerable experience he was still not too keen on nappies, but I think the set of my jaw warned him not to argue.

As she prepared for bed Anne was chatty and confiding, the child I had always known, not the little misery of the last six weeks. As she snuggled into bed she asked abruptly, 'Mummy, will you teach me to write?'

'Goodness, why this sudden request? I know that you like drawing and colouring but there's no hurry to write is there?'

'Yes, because I want to write to my new granny. She axed me to, Mummy. And she said I can call her G'ma because I have two Granny Ps. Isn't that funny, Mummy?' She laughed happily as she continued, 'But I can only write if I've been good and nice to Baby. G'ma says that it's silly to hate Baby because Baby doesn't matter, she isn't special like me.'

Filled with a plethora of Mollie-provoked emotions, I tried to keep calm, it wasn't the child's fault. I merely asked, 'And why are you so special?'

'Because I was born at Abbotshall, of course, silly Mummy!'

She flung her arms around me, kissed me and lay down to sleep.

I don't know what else I said or how I got out of the room, to flee into the kitchen and Martin's arms. Still occupied with washing-up and tidying he was rather taken aback, but as the tears began to roll down my cheeks he led me into the sitting-room and took me on his knee, as if I were one of the children, as he asked, 'My darling, whatever's the matter? I thought that things went rather well in the circumstances. Pa was really interested in the farm.'

'Blast the farm!' I sobbed. 'Don't you understand? She's got Anne.'

'Who's got Anne? What are you talking about?'

'Your mother of course! We should have seen it coming. First, she flatters the child, telling her how beautiful she is, and then she brings Abbotshall into it. I can't bear it, she's like a bad fairy, this is the price we have to pay for Anne being nice to Baby.'

Martin gently detached himself, went to the sideboard and came back with a glass of brandy. 'Drink this, take a deep breath and then tell me everything.'

So, in a speech peppered with hiccups, I did. 'First of all your mother kept praising Anne's beauty, and you heard her going on about Baby being plain.'

Martin interrupted my flow. 'But wasn't that to cheer Anne up and stop her being jealous of Baby?'

'Yes, on the surface, therefore helpful. But you know how we've never told Anne how pretty she is, in case she falls into the arrogance that comes from "being beautiful overmuch"?'

Martin quickly picked up my allusion. 'That's that damn poem again, that "Ceremonious House" thing. I really thought that all that we've been through had knocked that nonsense out of you, Aulis. Anyway, (more gently) wasn't that some comfort for Anne? For the last six weeks every blessed person that's been here has gone on about the "lovely baby", virtually ignoring Anne. Hasn't Mother just redressed the balance a little?'

'Yes, that's what I thought at first and I was grateful.'

'Well then?'

'It's the mention of Abbotshall that really frightened me. Mollie told Anne that she "was special because she was born at Abbotshall". She wants Anne to write to her, with a special name and all sorts of things.' I ended on a sob.

Martin did not dismiss my fears out of hand but was reasonable and sensible.

'Anne's still a very little girl, Aulis. The novelty will soon wear off. You can easily delay the writing lessons. And Anne isn't going to be seeing much of Mother, is she? I think that our relationship will be civilised but distant. There'll just be this kind of ritual visit every time we have a baby and that's all.'

'That's another thing.' I hiccupped. 'Your mother says we're not to have any more children, we can't afford it.'

Martin was firm. 'We'll be the judge of that. Aulis, I thought that you had stopped doing what Mother told you even before we left Abbotshall. Look, you are worried, quite reasonably, because you remember Mother when she was a very sick woman. That's all over. She's still tactless and critical, that's Mother, but there's nothing sinister about her now.'

I was not entirely convinced. I shivered as I remembered Peter's reference to Mollie's pills. Reluctantly I agreed with Martin. 'You are right, but I still fear her influence on Anne.'

We were interrupted by a thin wail from upstairs.

'There,' said Martin, 'Our lovely baby wants her ten o'clock feed. I'll go and look up while you deal with her. And, Aulis, may I remind you that Sally is six weeks old today. Are you ready for me? Shall we try to see if we can defy Mother immediately?'

My smile gave him my answer. I had been longing for what are stiffly called "marital relations" to be resumed. I hurried up to our baby and my loins melted as I suckled Martin's child. She was so good: well-fed, clean and fresh she snuggled back to sleep. Martin came in and together we said good-night to our children, Anne fast asleep and still smiling. Then we went to bed.

I was ridiculously excited, I remembered how quickly after Anne's birth I had conceived the boy whom Mollie had destroyed. Could I possibly conceive a son tonight, a boy who would be safe from Mollie's malign influence? But even as I lost myself in the tide of Martin's love I had a passing thought of the old woman, back now in Abbotshall Cottage, surely pleased with the spell she had wound round my lovely Anne, happy now in her untroubled sleep.